LAWS IN CONFLICT

LAWS IN CONFLICT

Cora Harrison

This first world edition published 2012
in Great Britain and in the USA by
SEVERN HOUSE PUBLISHERS LTD of
9–15 High Street, Sutton, Surrey, England, SM1 1DF.
Trade paperback edition first published
in Great Britain and the USA 2012 by
SEVERN HOUSE PUBLISHERS LTD.

British Library Cataloguing in Publication Data

Harrison, Cora.
  Laws in conflict.
  1. Mara, Brehon of the Burren (Fictitious character) –
  Fiction. 2. Women judges – Ireland – Burren – Fiction.
  3. Burren (Ireland) – History – 16th century – Fiction.
  4. Detective and mystery stories.
  I. Title
  823.9'2-dc23

ISBN-13: 978-0-7278-8178-6 (cased)
ISBN-13: 978-1-84751-434-9 (trade paper)

All Severn House titles are printed on acid-free paper.

Severn House Publishers support The Forest Stewardship Council [FSC],
the leading international forest certification organisation. All our titles that
are printed on Greenpeace-approved FSC-certified paper carry the FSC logo.

Typeset by Palimpsest Book Production Ltd.,
Falkirk, Stirlingshire, Scotland.
Printed and bound in Great Britain by
MPG Books Ltd., Bodmin, Cornwall.

Prologue

The early part of February 1512 was spent by Mara the Brehon in the alien society of the city of Galway, whose laws were in conflict with the laws which she practised. This resulted from a chance meeting at a horse fair.

Mara had been born into the law. Her earliest memories were of the chant of scholars in her father's law school at Cahermacnaghten on the Atlantic coast of western Ireland. She became a qualified lawyer when she was sixteen, an *ollamh* (professor) of Brehon Law by the time she was eighteen, and a Brehon (judge) at twenty-one. For the last eighteen years she had been in sole charge of the law in the one hundred square miles of the limestone-paved kingdom of the Burren.

If it hadn't been for Fiona, the only girl scholar at the law school of Cahermacnaghten, Mara would not have attended the horse fair at the end of January. The scholars had returned for the Hilary term at the beginning of the year 1512, the third year in the reign of Henry VIII. They had been looking tired and the work, that relentless memorizing of thousands of laws, was dragging. On the day in question, spring had suddenly arrived. On her morning walk between her house and the school enclosure, Mara glimpsed a pale primrose in the hedge and noticed how the leaves had burst through the twisted stems of woodbine above it, while small brown linnets sang melodiously as they bustled about foraging for nesting material among the straw-like remains of last summer's flowers. She was as reluctant as her scholars to shut the school-house door and order work to begin.

Fachtnan, the twenty-year-old trainee teacher, was patiently endeavouring to coach fourteen-year-old Hugh in the decrees of hospitality, the two seventeen-year-olds, Moylan and Aidan, were groaning over a piece of Latin translation and even Fiona herself, with all her brains, was struggling with some of the more obscure

passages of medical law in *Bretha Crólige*. The sound of horse
hoofs on the stone road outside caused every head to rise.

'They're going to the horse fair, Brehon,' said Moylan wistfully.
Though sharp and quick-witted, he was not someone who worked
for the love of his subject.

'Wish we could go,' muttered Aidan under his breath. He glared
at his Latin grammar with an expression of disgust.

'I think we should go,' declared Fiona. 'As Fithail says: "Full
Mind Brings Good Understanding." When we are qualified we
may have to judge a case that took place at a horse fair. If we
haven't attended one we may judge wrongly.'

Aidan looked up from his Latin hopefully and Moylan eyed
his companion with respect. The thousands of sayings of Fithail,
a ninth-century scholar, had been drummed into them from the
age of five onwards and to quote his words always added weight
to an argument.

Mara glanced out at the pale January sunshine, and relented.
She herself loved horses and she was wise enough to know that
little work would be done if the minds of her scholars were
elsewhere.

'Perhaps we should go after all,' she said. It was a great event
in the Burren and the scholars would be disgruntled at missing
such a sociable occasion.

Every year a great horse fair was held at Aonach in the centre
of the Burren. And every year the three fields surrounding the
small lake were crammed to bursting point with people who
came to buy the horses raised in that small kingdom. The Burren
was famous for the quality of its horses as well as for its cattle.
There, amidst the shelter of the encircling mountains, young
horses drank the lime-rich water, ate the lush grass and grew into
magnificent animals. Buyers came not just from the city of Galway,
only thirty miles distant across the hills, but also from the north,
the east and the south of Ireland, and even from England itself.

On that day at the end of January 1512, therefore, it was no
surprise to see many strangers among the familiar faces of the
four clans of the Burren: the O'Lochlainn, the O'Brien, the
MacNamara and the O'Connor. The buyers conversed in a multi-
tude of languages – resorting from time to time to the use of
sign language. There were numerous dialects of Gaelic to be
heard, spoken by men from the five provinces of Ireland, as well

as a few English speakers, and here and there a Spaniard tried to make himself understood.

But this man looked alien among the sea of horse-traders.

Mara had not met Lawyer Bodkin from Galway for two years but she recognized him immediately. He hadn't changed much during those two years, she thought as she looked at him; a tall, thin, distinguished-looking man, dressed in a black lawyer's gown. A clean-shaven face was set off with a small pointed beard tinged with grey and a pair of intelligent pale blue eyes.

'I wonder what he is doing here?' she said half to herself and half to Ardal O'Lochlainn. Ardal was not just the *taoiseach* (chieftain) of the most numerous clans in the kingdom of the Burren, but he was also famous as a breeder of fine horses.

His eyes followed hers and he chuckled. 'You'd be surprised at the number of unlikely people who deal in horses,' he said. 'Of course, living in Galway, with the ships going to and fro to Spain . . .' He stopped then as the lawyer began to make his way across to them. Mara, also, moved forward and met him with a smile.

He had recognized her instantly, his eyes lighting up with pleasure as he extended a well-cared-for slim hand. There was no surprise for him, of course, in the fact that Mara, Brehon, or, in his own language, judge and law giver of the Burren, should be present at this most prestigious horse fair in that stony kingdom on the edge of the Atlantic.

'Brehon,' he exclaimed, 'how well you are looking. I hear you have become a wife and a mother since I saw you last.'

He did not use the word 'king' in his language when enquiring about her husband, she noted with amusement. Galway, of course, though a city state, was ruled under English law, and owed allegiance to the young King Henry VIII. To the inhabitants of that city, King Turlough Donn, Lord of the three kingdoms of Thomond, Corcomroe and Burren, was just an Irish chieftain ruling with an outmoded and alien set of laws.

'Turlough is very well, I hope,' she said now. 'He has deserted me for a couple of weeks. At the moment he is visiting Ulick Burke, Lord of the Clanrickard – you remember Ulick from the time when we met at Newtown Castle? And your sister, Jane, how is she?'

'Jane is very well, also,' he said. 'And before I left she charged me with a message for you. Do you remember when last we met we discussed the workings of the court at Galway. Why not come to visit us for a few days – you and your young scholars? We have a big, empty house – I no longer take pupils so there is plenty of room for your boys. It would be interesting for them as well as for you.' He pulled his beard with a slight smile adding, 'We can argue about the differences and merits of our respective law systems over some good wine during the evening.'

'*Conflictus legum*, in fact,' said Mara, and he laughed.

'You have the advantage over me, my lady judge,' he said. 'That's something that I have forgotten since my days in Lincoln's Inn in London. You know your Roman law as well as your Brehon law. What do you say? Will you come?'

'And what is—?' Mara broke off to turn to her youngest scholar, twelve-year-old Shane, who had approached with a polite bow at Lawyer Bodkin and an appealing look at her.

'Excuse me, Brehon, but the *taoiseach* wants to know whether Hugh and I have permission to ride a couple of his young horses – just to show their paces.'

Mara nodded permission – the word '*taoiseach*' could have been applied to any one of the leaders of the four clans on the Burren, but when used in conjunction with horses, it had to be Ardal O'Lochlainn, near neighbour to the law school at Cahermacnaghten. Her scholars would come to no harm with him. However, never being able to resist a little showing-off about the excellence of her scholars, she detained the boy with a hand on his arm.

'Shane, will you tell Lawyer Bodkin what you understand by "*Conflictus legum*",' she said and watched with amusement as his eyes, though staring ahead at the busy scene of horses trotting up and down the emerald-green swathe of grass, were obviously looking inward, sifting through the accumulated store of facts in his young brain.

'*Conflictus legum* is a set of procedural rules that determines which legal system, and which jurisdiction, applies to a given dispute,' he said promptly, speaking correct and fluent English. Then he added thoughtfully, 'I seem to remember reading some-where that the acts of people, valid in their own country, should be recognized under other jurisdictions unless they are contrary to the morals and the safety of the foreign country.'

'Well done!' exclaimed Lawyer Bodkin as Shane ran back to

the coveted ride on Ardal O'Lochlainn's strawberry mare. 'What a clever boy. How old is he?'

'Not yet thirteen,' said Mara proudly.

'He'd surprise them in Lincoln's Inn in London; he should be sent there when he's a bit older.'

'Remind me,' said Mara coolly, 'who teaches Brehon Law at Lincoln's Inn?'

Lawyer Bodkin laughed quietly, smoothing a hand over his well-kept beard. 'Do say you will come. For the sake of these clever boys of yours. They should see the world, not one tiny kingdom.'

Mara hesitated. She had been about to refuse, but it was true that these boys, growing up in a divided country, would need to know far more about English and Roman law than she could teach them.

'There is another factor that might influence you,' said Lawyer Bodkin. 'The case is coming up in two weeks' time – you could time your visit to be there for the hearing. A fellow countryman of yours, accused of the crime of theft, seems unable to speak English and with no means of defending himself.' He tugged his beard and added so quietly that only her ear heard the words, 'The Mayor of Galway – or *the sovereign* as he is still known as – a man called James Lynch, is very keen to uphold the law against theft. It makes him very popular with the shopkeepers of the town.'

Mara turned the matter over in her mind. There was no reason why she should not go. She had often thought of a visit to Galway with her scholars, but had not liked the idea of housing them in an inn. This offer was a very good one. She made up her mind swiftly.

'Well if you're sure that it won't be a burden to your sister, then we'll come for a few days with pleasure. Just Monday to Wednesday in two weeks' time – you will have had enough of us after that.'

One

Uraicecc Becc
(Small Primer)

There are three grades of judges, or arbitrators. The first is fit only to determine matters relating to craftsmen and has an honour price of seven séts. Above him is the judge who is competent in both traditional law and poetry with an honour price of ten séts. Then above these two is the judge who is known as the judge of three languages. This judge is experienced in traditional law, poetry and canon law and is deemed to have an honour price of fifteen séts.

'A hard, cold man,' said Ardal O'Lochlainn.

Mara looked at him with surprise. They were riding side by side through the rocky mountain pass that had been hewed out of the limestone peak of the Carron Mountain on the north-eastern fringe of the kingdom of the Burren. Ardal had business in Galway and had offered his services as escort to Mara and her scholars on their journey to the city.

Mara was glad of Ardal's company. The scholars were wildly excited at the unexpected break in their routine and wildly excited adolescents capping each other's jokes began to get tiresome after a while. Ardal knew Galway well as many of the horses that he reared on his rich grasslands were exported to England, France and Spain through the port of Galway, and Mara was anxious to get some information about the ruling powers in that stone-built city. She listened with interest to him explaining the government of Galway, the place of the *Gall* or stranger.

'Think of it as a kingdom,' he advised, 'but a kingdom where the king is voted for every year – by the merchants of the town, of course, rather than by the royal family. The mayor is king – he has power over life and death, the power to tax everything that comes into the city – even the prisage, the tax on wine – one tun out of every tun brought in. The revenues from wine alone are enough to make any man rich.'

'But at the end of the year he loses his power and one of the two bailiffs is elected instead,' remarked Mara. She found herself glad that she had accepted this invitation. It would be interesting to go outside the kingdom of the Burren – every yard of its one hundred square miles as well known to her as the palm of her own hand. In the city of Galway she would meet new laws, new customs, would see a world that was run on totally different principles. Her lively mind began to teem with questions.

'Unless the mayor is re-elected, of course,' remarked Ardal quietly. 'The present man, James Lynch, member of one of the powerful merchant families, has been mayor for the last five years.'

'Yes, I remember that Lawyer Bodkin said something about that. A popular man, then.'

Ardal said something in reply to this but his voice was lost as Aidan, in a boisterous mood, was keen to impress sixteen-year-old Fiona by a spectacular display of how the surrounding rocks threw back his voice when he yodelled. Fiona had been teasing him about how small the mountains were compared with her native Scotland, and Aidan and she had been arguing vociferously for the last quarter of an hour.

It was only when the scholars all paused to allow the echo to reply that she heard Ardal's quiet remark – *a hard, cold man.*

So this James Lynch, a man with the power of a sovereign over the city state of Galway, was perhaps a man who might misuse that power. Not an easy man to deal with, she thought, but deal with him she would. There was no way that she would abandon a man from the kingdom of the Burren to his fate without making an attempt to help him. Galway was not under English rule, but it ruled itself by the laws of the king and the emperor – by a mixture of English law and Roman law, and both were equally cruel to those who infringed even minor examples of these laws, she thought, as she turned back to address her scholars.

'You can ride ahead until we reach the coast road,' she said, 'but after that we will be out of our kingdom and you must ride sedately and do credit to Cahermacnaghten law school.'

'Race you to the bottom of the hill, Fiona; Ireland against Scotland,' Aidan said, and in a minute the five youngsters, with Fachtnan in the rear, went galloping past them, the horses' hoofs sending up a cloud of limestone dust from the dry road. Mara was glad to see them go. There were few men that she could rely on as much as Ardal to hold his tongue about subjects she discussed with him.

'I'm not sure that I am doing a wise thing or not, Ardal,' she said, turning impulsively towards him, 'but I'm thinking of interfering in the affairs of another kingdom, or state,' she finished.

He took his time about replying. Very characteristic of Ardal, she thought with amusement. If she had said something like that to her husband he would immediately have exclaimed. A thousand questions, pieces of advice, appeals would have instantly come to his lips. But Ardal just looked at her intently for a moment, his blue eyes thoughtful. He was a good-looking man, she thought, admiring the way he rode his strawberry roan mare with such ease and sat tall and slim, with his long-fingered hands holding the reins loosely. His red-gold hair was burnished by the pale winter sun.

'I think you, yourself, may have doubts about the wisdom of becoming involved, Brehon,' he said eventually. He and Mara were almost the same age and had grown up together, lived near to each other, played with each other – Ardal's sister had been Mara's greatest friend – but his respect for her high office meant that he always addressed her by her formal title. She smiled now at his diplomatic answer.

'You refuse to pass judgement yourself,' she said lightly. 'I suppose you're right,' she said more seriously. 'I wouldn't have asked you if I had been sure that I was doing the right thing. And, of course, I still need to do nothing, but I strongly feel that I should try to appeal on behalf of the man who is held in the gaol – have you seen this gaol, Ardal?'

'From the outside, only, Brehon – an unpleasant, stinking place even from there.' His high-bridged nose wrinkled fastidiously.

That decides matters, thought Mara. A man used to the clean, windy atmosphere of the limestone land of the Burren was languishing in a stinking gaol set among alien people who did not speak his language or live by his laws. If possible she would rescue him; she would appeal to this mayor, or sovereign, of Galway.

'James Lynch,' she said aloud. 'Tell me more of him, Ardal? And why has he been re-elected four times?'

'I suppose you could say, Brehon, that he is in his fifth year of office because he is an honest man. When the English King

– King Richard, the third of that name – granted a charter to Galway, he waived all his own rights to taxes on the goods; the mayor was to have the taxes, supposedly for building walls and paving the town, but . . .'

'But not all mayors used the money for that purpose.'

'Not even a fraction of it,' confirmed Ardal with a slight smile. 'These merchant families of Galway have been swapping the office of mayor around between them for the last thirty years or so and they have become more and more wealthy during that time.'

'But not James Lynch,' put in Mara quickly.

'James Lynch has grown rich, though not outrageously so,' corrected Ardal, 'but he has also seen to it that the increased prosperity of Galway has been shared out amongst the people of the town, that they are protected by high walls, manned by men with guns – even cannon – and that the streets of the city are paved and kept in good repair, and, of course, as I said to you, he governs with a strong hand, so no lawlessness, neither theft nor drunkenness, can affect the trade in the city.'

'Can anyone be a mayor?' Mara turned over in her mind the power that was exercised by this man – a power over life and death.

'The bailiffs are elected every year, but the choice of mayor is then limited to the mayor and his two bailiffs. I suppose in theory anyone can be a mayor, Brehon, but in practice it is restricted to the great trading families of Galway: the Lynches, the Blakes, the Joyces, the Skerretts and the Brownes – there are more but these are the ones that I remember. They tend to be related to each other as they intermarry a lot. For instance, the wife of James Lynch is the sister to Valentine Blake and Valentine Blake is married to the sister of Philip Browne.'

'And Philip Browne is married to the sister of James Lynch,' suggested Mara, interested by the links. In Gaelic Ireland most marriages seemed to take place within the clans.

'Well, no, not so,' said Ardal, tugging at his moustache with his right hand while the left hand slowed the mare to a standstill. The scholars were all waiting obediently at the bottom of the steep hill leading from the Carron Mountains down to sea level and marking the division between kingdoms. 'Philip Browne is married to a Spanish lady, in fact. They have one daughter, a girl called Catarina.'

'Oh, that's exotic! A half-Spanish girl!' Mara was amused to see that her scholars were listening to this piece of gossip with interest. 'Where did Philip Browne meet this Spanish lady?'

'Like your friend, Lawyer Bodkin, he imports horses from Spain,' said Ardal, and then waited while Mara marshalled her scholars so that the very-adult Fachtnan was at the front beside Moylan, the two youngest scholars, Shane and Hugh, were in the centre and Fiona and Aidan were bringing up the rear, where she could keep a strict eye on any silly or noisy behaviour. It was only after they had moved on at a decorous pace that Ardal spoke again, keeping his voice so low that she could barely hear him.

'They are very powerful men, these merchant princes in Galway, Brehon. You know your own business best, of course, but I would say that you should hesitate to interfere too deeply into what they regard as their royal right to govern the city in the way that they choose.'

Two

Charter of Richard III

A new charter was accordingly granted, dated at Westminster, the 15th December, 1484, whereby the king confirmed all former grants, and renewed the powers to levy the tolls and customs, which he directed should be applied towards the murage and pavage of the town; he also granted licence that they might, yearly, forever, choose one mayor and two bailiffs and that the mayor should continue to hold sovereign rights . . . The first mayor and bailiffs were accordingly elected under this charter, on the 1st August, 1485, and were sworn into office on the 29th September following.

Mara had often visited Galway – her daughter, Sorcha, had married a merchant, named Oisín, and they lived there with their three children – but for most of her scholars it was a first visit and they were overawed by the sight of the great stone city surrounded by a high wall and packed with tall houses squeezed together like herrings in a box of salt. A large amount of those houses were tower houses or even small castles and they reared up, their castellated roofs outlined against the sky. The streets were well paved with limestone cobbles – a drain running down the centre of each street and a narrow pavement for pedestrians on either side. It was a city built around a western seaport on the Atlantic Ocean, and despite the crowds of people and numerous houses it was a fresh airy city on this fine, breezy day in early February.

Ardal O'Lochlainn courteously conducted them through the Great Gate, capped with a stone tower, straight down the High Street, past the church of St Nicholas, whose size made the scholars open their eyes widely, and then on towards the sea until they reached Lombard Street, where he instantly found their host's house down a short lane leading from this and took his farewell once the door had been opened to his knock. Mara did not attempt to detain him. Ardal was a mysterious person who went his own way and kept details of his private life very much to himself. For years he had a relationship with a fisherman's daughter somewhere north of Galway – a wife of the fourth degree, as Brehon Law phrased it – but that now seemed to have come to an end. Was his visit to Galway for business or for pleasure? she wondered as she greeted the stately manservant who had opened the door to this large crowd of guests.

Lawyer Bodkin's residence was a tower house – not unlike the one in which Ardal O'Lochlainn lived back in the spaciousness of the Burren kingdom. The legal business must be very prosperous, Mara thought as servants thronged around the doorway, some coming from behind the house and leading the horses and ponies to the stable yard, some taking satchels upstairs and others escorting the guests to their bedrooms high up in the tower.

There was no sign of either Lawyer Bodkin or his sister Jane – it would have been strange behaviour in hospitable, Gaelic Ireland, not to have the hosts at the door, exclaiming 'Come in, come in, you're very welcome . . .' – but there was something to be said for this custom of first allowing guests to refresh themselves and change their clothing first, thought Mara as she tested the softness of the four-poster bed, well screened with curtains, and then strolled to the window to look out. Her beautifully furnished room faced west and she had a clear view of the harbour with the large sailing ships rocking gently at their anchorage points. Fiona had been lodged just across the corridor to her and the five boys were all in a large attic where Lawyer Bodkin had formerly housed his law pupils.

Mara washed her face and hands in the soft, warm water – rainwater, she thought with interest and wondered how they managed to store it in sufficient quantities in order to provide enough for such a large household.

Then she changed her clothes. Her daughter Sorcha had told her to be sure to wear a fine silk gown and a silken hood – had even sent a messenger with a bundle of suitable clothing – but Mara was not minded to try to look like a lady from Galway. She knew that the wives of Gaelic chieftains dressed up whenever they went to town, wearing swathes of linen around their heads and elaborate, fussy gowns, but she did not like that fashion either.

She was Mara, Brehon of the Burren, judge and lawgiver, and she would dress as she always dressed, she thought as she pulled a fresh *léine* over her head – woven from the flax that grew on the mountainside of the Burren, the creamy shade of the linen tunic suited her dark colouring. Over it she wore a gown of soft moss-green with loose sleeves and a laced bodice. The neckline was low and allowed the lace-embroidered *léine* to be seen above it. Next she combed out her long dark hair, plaited it and coiled it at the back of her head while gazing at the dim reflection in the silvered glass that was placed helpfully beside the window. For a thirty-eight-year-old grandmother she looked good, she thought with satisfaction, before going to tap on Fiona's door.

Fiona was also dressed in the Gaelic fashion, wearing the traditional *léine* topped with a blue gown, which matched her blue eyes. She was a tiny girl, but with a perfect figure, perfect features, hair like spun gold, gleaning white teeth. She had been at Cahermacnaghten law school for almost a year now, and the boys had settled down into regarding her as a companion, though when she first came she had caused a lot of excitement. Only Fachtnan, guessed Mara, still hoped to be something more than a friend to her, but Fiona treated him with friendly indifference.

Lawyer Bodkin's sister, Jane, gave Mara's uncovered head a slightly scandalized look, but said nothing. Her brother now addressed his guest by the English word of 'Judge' rather than the Gaelic 'Brehon' and this, Mara thought with an inward smile, probably made her hostess feel that she was entertaining some strange, hybrid creature. She seemed relieved that they all spoke English and smiled kindly on the boys, though their tight, woollen trews, knee-length *léinte* and short sheepskin jackets probably made them look very strange to her eyes.

'What polite, well-mannered young men,' she remarked to Mara. 'When Henry had law pupils here they used to vex the life out of me. Always playing tricks and shouting, and so rude, too. One day one of them even put a frog into my bed. I said to Henry that I couldn't stand it any longer – surely we don't need the little money that they bring, I said to him – and there was all the washing to do with them too. How do you manage about their washing?'

'I shall tell them how you approve of them,' said Mara with a friendly smile, declining to go into housewifely details. Her scholars had been bribed with the prospect of a few hours' liberty to explore the town and port if they behaved well during the meal and she wanted to keep an eye on Aidan. She would have to invent a similar bribe for future meals, she was thinking when Henry Bodkin, who had taken a whispered message from a servant, turned to her with a smile.

'My neighbour, Valentine Blake, has heard of your arrival and has invited us all to supper at his place. It's only around the corner from here and he has sent a message to say that there will be plenty of young people present to entertain your scholars. The Lynch family and the Browne family will be there, and Valentine Blake himself has three daughters by his first marriage – there may even be others.' He beamed at the boys and added consolingly to Fiona, 'And so there will be a few young ladies for you to talk with, my dear.'

'I don't really like other girls; I'm just used to boys – in my father's law school and here.' Fiona ignored the look of horror on Jane Bodkin's face and cross-questioned her host on what these 'youngsters', as he called them, were studying.

'In training to be merchants, I should imagine,' he said with a smile. 'Even the law is not a very popular subject here in Galway.'

'Perhaps they don't have as much power as the merchants,' said Mara thoughtfully. She added some extra milk to her porridge and then controlled an expression of distaste with effort. The milk was slightly sour, something that would never have occurred in her own well-run establishment. Brigid, who had been Mara's nurse and housekeeper to her father before that, would never have served up anything but milk fresh from the cow. Still, she thought charitably, it was probably more difficult in Galway. Her host and his sister had not seemed to notice anything and Mara sent a warning glance around at the younger members of her school, and pushed a jar of honey in the direction of Moylan who would be quick-witted enough to take the hint.

The meal passed peacefully and the scholars, with an eye on Mara, were effusive in their praise and thanks for the many dishes of food. Jane Bodkin openly praised the system of young children beginning their studies early as it seemed to make them so well mannered. 'This young man tells me that he came to the law school at the age of five,' she added, patting Hugh on the arm and causing his freckled face to turn scarlet with embarrassment.

'I was eight, when I came to law school,' said Shane, and added politely, though with a twinkle in his eye, 'but I hope that I managed to learn good manners even at that advanced age.'

'*O tempora, o mores!*' exclaimed Moylan dramatically. Judging by the slight jump that he gave a minute later, Aidan had kicked him quickly on the shin to warn him against showing-off and Mara thought it was time to dismiss her scholars before their behaviour began to deteriorate to its normal level of silly jokes and teasing. While they fetched their outerwear, she rapidly embarked on an explanation to Jane Bodkin about the Irish cloak, which was famous for resisting the continual rainfall due to a secret ingredient that Mara revealed to be honey combed into the tightly curled sheep's wool outer surface of the garment.

'Looks lovely on you, my dear,' said Jane generously to Fiona as she drew the wide hood over her golden curls, and even Lawyer Bodkin smiled with appreciation of the picture that she made.

'Would you like me to send a manservant with them?' he asked Mara in a low voice, his eyes on Fiona. 'The streets of Galway will not be like your quiet lanes in the Burren.'

'I don't think so, but thank you for offering it,' returned Mara quietly. 'I've had a word with Fachtnan and told him to make sure that they all stay together. They are strong, able boys and they won't allow anyone to get the better of them.' Aloud she said to the scholars, 'I've given Fachtnan some silver for you all and the rule is that all six stay together. And please be back here by . . .?' She looked enquiringly at their host who responded immediately by suggesting that they listen for the four o'clock bell from St Nicholas's Church and return when they heard that sound its call for evening prayers.

'Is it possible for me to see this unfortunate man who is lying in your town gaol?' Mara decided to put the question as soon as the scholars had departed. Lawyer Bodkin would, no doubt, be wondering what to do with her this morning and she had no desire to be left to gossip with Jane.

'It would be better not to,' he said a little uncomfortably. He tugged his beard, his shrewd eyes downcast and hooded by his bushy grey eyebrows. Mara waited until he continued. 'I feel that it would be best if you met the mayor in a social setting today – at the Blake supper – this evening – and then perhaps put the question to him as to whether you could attend the trial.'

'Perhaps I could interpret for him,' suggested Mara mildly. 'He speaks no English, is that correct? What actually did he steal?'

Lawyer Bodkin's face looked more cheerful. 'That's a good idea. That might work very well,' he said. 'Of course, the view of the court is that English is the official language so anyone in the city should speak it – by law no one should be in the city without a knowledge of the English language and English customs. In fact, strictly speaking, the man had no right to stay within the city walls when he had lost the employment that brought him here.'

'And his crime?' persisted Mara.

'He stole a meat pie – of over a shilling in value.' The lawyer's voice was heavy with significance and Mara nodded her understanding. The death penalty, under English law, could be exacted for any theft of an article worth more than a shilling.

'Why did he come here?' Mara was curious about this. A young man, adventurous, perhaps looking for work on one of the boats that went from Galway harbour to Spain – but Lawyer Bodkin just shook his head and spread his hands as if denying all knowledge of the culprit.

'Let's go for a walk and I shall show you my chambers,' he said, to her relief. 'Perhaps we'll take a tour of the city first, or would you like to see The Green outside the city walls? I keep my horses stabled there and hardly an hour goes by when you cannot see a fine example of horses being put through their paces at the spot.'

'The Green,' responded Mara promptly. She had no particular interest in Lawyer Bodkin's horses but did not want her scholars to think that she was dogging their footsteps as they explored the city. Perhaps tomorrow afternoon she would get them to show her around. She was prepared to bet that a morning's exploration by six curious and uninhibited young people would result in a thorough knowledge of the whole place.

Lawyer Bodkin took her on a leisurely saunter, naming each street as they walked along it – Lombard Street, North Street, Great Gate Street – and pointing out the stately stone tower houses and their gardens belonging to the great merchant families – D'Arcy, Athy, Browne, Lynch – her mind buzzed with the names and every few yards she stopped to shake hands with expensively dressed gentlemen, in English hose and doublet, who eyed her with curiosity but greeted her with great politeness. There was, she thought, some sort of statute against the wearing of Gaelic clothes in Galway, but in the company of a respected lawyer no one took exception to her *léine* and *brat*. Then she thought of her scholars with a flash of compunction. However, Ardal O'Lochlainn, as well as others from the Burren, often visited Galway and she had never seen him change his clothing in order to do so. They were well dressed and confident, she thought, and would be sensible enough to give Lawyer Bodkin's name if they ran into any trouble. It was never her policy to feather-bed them, but rather to rear sensible, quick-thinking responsible lawyers.

'Perhaps we may be embarrassing you by wearing clothes that appear strange in the city of Galway,' she said to her companion.

'No, no, there is no exception taken to peaceful visitors no matter how they are dressed; it's those that come looking for trouble who find themselves at the wrong side of the law. In any case, you are in my company and no one would question your good status,' he assured her.

Mara smiled politely but inwardly she seethed at the condescension in his words. This very English settlement right in the heart of Gaelic Ireland maintained its position by force. The high stone walls, manned by well-armed soldiers, the cannon perched on the gatehouse above the Great Gate all sent out their message to the surrounding countryside. No doubt, though, she comforted herself, the scholars were safe. Lawyer Bodkin was the perfect host and had left word of their coming at the gate. Also, they had come into the city in the company of Ardal O'Lochlainn who was well known as a trader in fine horses. As they came to the gate now, the man on duty bowed and as they passed out of the city they were saluted respectfully by a troop of parading soldiers, guns in hand.

The Green, placed just outside the northern wall around the city, was a large rectangular piece of grass with a path of fine limestone gravel all the way around it. In the summer months it was probably emerald green but now it was mainly mud. A windmill stood on a small hill to the west side of the park and on the east side a great broad road stretched out for as far as the eye could see. There was another, smaller green there and Mara winced when she saw, set right in the middle of its expanse, a gallows with the dead body of a person, completely covered in black sticky tar, dangling from it. The body swung in the slight breeze but few of the many people that passed even turned to look at it.

'Gallows' Green,' said Lawyer Bodkin following her gaze. 'An unpleasant sight, I grant you,' he said, responding to the expression on her face, 'unpleasant, but a necessary evil, I'm afraid.'

Mara said nothing. She did not trust herself to argue dispassionately while that body swung there in front of her eyes. She murmured something about the number of riders and saw the relief in his eyes that she had changed the subject.

There were several riders on The Green but Mara's eyes immediately went to one horse and its rider. The horse was a rich chestnut with a small, refined, wedge-shaped head, a broad forehead, large eyes and large nostrils. It pranced playfully, displaying an arched neck, and high tail carriage. Something about it reminded Mara of her own horse, Brig, a gift from her now-husband King Turlough Donn.

But the rider of the chestnut matched the horse in beauty. It was a girl, upright as a young larch tree, with a mane of glossy, jet-black hair flowing down her back. Even in the depths of the winter her skin was delicately tanned and as the horse came prancing towards them, Mara could see that a pair of bright brown eyes, slanting at their outer tips, lit up the beautiful face.

'Isn't she gorgeous?' groaned Henry Bodkin.

Mara looked at him, slightly startled, but realized that the lawyer's eyes were fixed, not on the girl, but on the mare that she rode.

'Gorgeous,' she agreed. 'Both of them,' she added, but her host could only think of the horse.

'Good morning, Mistress Browne,' he called. 'I see you have a new steed. Arab breeding, is she not?'

'She's beautiful, isn't she?' said the girl. 'She's my father's present to me for my eighteenth birthday. Yes, she's fully bred Arab. Came from the south of Spain. My cousin brought her over.' She turned to Mara with an inquisitive look and then smiled, displaying a perfect set of brilliantly white teeth inside a pair of red lips.

'You are the lady judge,' she said. 'I thought you would be old and ugly.' And then she laughed charmingly. 'Instead of which you are young and beautiful.'

'This is Mistress Catarina Browne, my lady judge.' Lawyer

Bodkin presented the girl to Mara almost absent-mindedly, his eyes still devouring the horse, examining the large hoofs and running his hand along the withers and stroking the large throat.

A spoilt child, very sure of her own charm, thought Mara, but she could not help responding to the compliment, praising the horse and telling the girl what a lovely pair they made.

'Have you heard that a Spanish cousin of mine is visiting us, sir?' Catarina enquired of Henry Bodkin.

'For a visit?' asked the lawyer, while Mara suppressed a slight smile. This was the second time within the last couple of minutes that Catarina had mentioned this Spanish cousin.

'No, well, yes, originally I believe it was for a visit, but he has determined to stay here permanently. He is going to set up a business importing Spanish mares and breeding from them. He has lots of ideas,' she finished, trying to sound dispassionate but her cheeks flushed to a bright rose colour and a small smile twitched the corners of her mouth. Mara guessed that this Spanish cousin had seen more than a business opportunity to make him decide to remain in Galway.

'What's your cousin's name?' she asked obligingly.

'Carlos.' The girl's voice became more foreign as it lingered lovingly over the two syllables. 'He's just two years older than I am. But you will see him tonight. We are all coming to supper with the Blakes – it's in your honour.' She bestowed another smile on Mara and then trotted off on her Arab steed.

'So that is Philip Browne's daughter,' said Mara remembering Ardal's story. She watched with amusement how the heads of the parading soldiers on the wall turned and gazed in the girl's direction until a sharp command from the sergeant made them swivel back again. She was a tall, strong, well-made girl with a great seat on a horse. 'Ardal O'Lochlainn told me that he had married a Spanish lady,' she added.

'Huge expense,' muttered Lawyer Bodkin, and then when she looked at him with surprise, he added, 'Importing Arab horses, I mean. Anyway, come and see my horses, and afterwards I'll show you the windmill.'

Mara was very fond of horses and admired his. A lot of horses for one man, even if his sister Jane rode, she thought. She counted ten and one mare was obviously near to giving birth. The mares were mostly sturdy Connemara horses, but the stallion looked to have some Spanish blood in him. After a while she ran out of compliments and waited for him to make the next move. I'm bored, she thought. I'm so used to being busy, to packing so much into every minute of the day, to doing three or four tasks even before breakfast. If only Sorcha and the children were here I could go to visit them – she saw little enough of her daughter as during the school holidays she felt a duty to be with her kingly husband as much as possible, and Sorcha herself had three small children and Oisín's business interests kept them tied to Galway. This month, however, by an awkward coincidence, Sorcha had accompanied him on a visit to his family in the kingdom of Thomond.

Henry Bodkin was determined to prove the perfect host and insisted on showing her the windmill. A broad, stone path ran up to it and the grass grew thick and undamaged around it. There was little to see – a dusty ground floor filled with heaped up empty sacks, the huge vertical shaft, the horizontal wheels, the hot grinding stones, nothing was new to her. The lawyer was slightly surprised to hear that they had a windmill also in the Burren – thinking, no doubt, that they were primitives who each ground their own oats with the aid of a couple of stones.

'Could I visit your law chambers, now?' she asked, and then, suddenly inspired, said, 'I would love to have an opportunity for studying any books that you have on law.'

'Dull work for you; I had planned to take you to visit some of the foremost families – the Browne mansion is quite near to here – but if you would prefer . . .' He looked concerned, but she thought she discerned a note of hopefulness in his voice.

'I'll meet them tonight.' Mara made her voice sound quite decisive. The law books would be interesting to her. Perhaps if he had an abundance he might present one to her, but if not perhaps she could commission a copy. Printing, she had heard, had almost replaced handwritten books in England, but possibly in Galway there was still some old-fashioned scribe who would take on the task.

The lawyer's chambers were at quite a distance from the Great Gate – almost down to the inlet from the sea and near to a fish market, she guessed, judging by the pungent smell and the cries of the stallholders.

'This is the courthouse,' said Henry Bodkin with pride, pointing to a stately stone building with matching piers outside the well-cared-for door. 'A couple of hundred years ago this belonged to the De Burgo clan – now known as the Clanrickard and Clanwilliam – but they . . .' He hesitated, and then said, 'Well, they did not keep to the customs and laws of their ancestors . . .'

'Ulick Burke is a friend of my husband's,' said Mara quietly.

'Indeed, I think I did meet him in your company.' He was a little embarrassed and concentrated on explaining the layout of the courthouse to her. Everything seemed shut up.

'Nothing going on there today,' she remarked.

'Nothing official,' he replied. 'The clerks of the court are working, of course, but they go in and out of the back door. They get the papers ready for the cases to be heard by the judges,' he added.

'I see.' Mara was amused. She herself was the only judge in a kingdom two hundred times larger than the city of Galway but she did her own paperwork, pronounced judgements, arranged and supervised the paying of retribution fines, and in addition taught at a school.

'You will find it all rather overwhelming tomorrow,' said Lawyer Bodkin, kindly. 'I remember how you told me that you try cases and pass judgement in a field beside an old dolmen.'

'It will certainly be very different,' said Mara cautiously. 'And your own chambers – you don't occupy the whole building, do you?'

'I have the ground floor and my two colleagues, John D'Arcy and William Joyce, occupy the other two floors – you can see that even the lawyers belong to the great twelve trading families of Galway,' he added with a smile. 'Some people even, jokingly, call them the twelve tribes of Galway: Athy, Blake, Bodkin, Browne, D'Arcy, Deane, Font, Ffrench, Joyce, Kirwan, Lynch, Martyn, Morris and Skerrett.'

'And the prosecuting lawyer, at the trial tomorrow, which one of the lawyers is he?' asked Mara.

'The prosecuting lawyer,' said Henry Bodkin, not meeting her eyes, 'is Thomas Lynch. He has his rooms at the courthouse itself.'

'Lynch?' Mara was startled.

He nodded. 'Yes. Thomas Lynch, the chief lawyer in the city, is a first cousin to James Lynch, the mayor. He sums up, and then the mayor, or sovereign as we call him in court, directs the jury about the verdict, passes judgement, states the penalty – he has that power.' His voice was soft, but it was only after he had escorted her into his chambers, introduced her to his clerk and then taken her into the inner room, that he said with emphasis: 'The power over life or death will lie in the hands of Mayor James Lynch. The two bailiffs, Valentine Blake and a very elderly man called John Skerrett, will be present, but they have no voice. They are there to observe only.'

Henry's chambers were extremely comfortable, well heated – too well heated, thought Mara, by a coal fire. It was the first time that she had experienced coal and though she missed the sweet peaty smell of the turf, the heat was very much greater. She almost drifted off to sleep in the comfort of the well-padded armchair where he insisted that she sit while leafing through his rather meagre collection of books. His practice seemed to be mainly a commercial one, she thought as she eavesdropped shame-lessly on the conversations that he held with his clerk – most of the letters that he dictated were to do with claiming his fee for drawing up bills of sale. Buying and selling, that was what made Galway so prosperous. One man imports one hundred and ten tuns of wine, pays eleven tuns of that as tax to the mayor and then sells the remaining ninety-nine casks to someone like her son-in-law Oisín. The sums involved, even for wine alone, since each cask held over two hundred gallons, were immense. No wonder the city seemed filled with small castles! No wonder, also, that the office of mayor was so lucrative and that there was enough employment for three lawyers within a space of less than half a square mile.

By the time the four o'clock bell chimed from St Nicholas's, Mara was glad to accept Henry's escort back through the crowded streets. Her scholars were just arriving from an opposite direction when they turned into Lombard Street. They seemed pleased to see her and even from a distance she could make out Aidan saying to Fiona, in what he thought was a low voice, 'You tell her.'

But it was only while Mara was getting dressed for the even-ing's entertainment that she remembered the overheard phrase and she was not surprised when a tap came at her door. Quickly she pulled her purple gown over her head, slipped on a light pair of shoes and then went to the door.

'Thank goodness,' said Fiona, coming in, clad only in her *léine*.

'I thought that woman, Jane Bodkin, would be hovering around for ever.'

'Let's hope she wasn't still hovering – she would be rather shocked if she saw you going around the house dressed like that with all the young men upstairs,' pointed out Mara, and then her face grew serious as Fiona said impulsively, 'Brehon, Fachtnan is very worried. The man in the gaol is called Sheedy. Do you know who he is? Sheedy O'Connor?'

'Sheedy O'Connor!' repeated Mara in a shocked whisper. 'So that's what's become of him! Poor Sheedy! Whatever brought him to Galway?'

'That's what Fachtnan said.' Fiona looked troubled. 'He told me that you had announced at judgement day a few years ago that he was to be classified as a *dásachtach*.'

'That's right,' said Mara unhappily. And then she stopped. Heavy footsteps were coming up the stairs. 'Go back into my room,' she hissed, feeling relieved that she herself had already changed. This was the master of the house himself, not a bad fellow, she thought, basically honest, keen to make money, that had been obvious from what she heard today, but not in favour of a death penalty for a poor old man half out of his wits.

'I'm sorry to delay you on your way up to get ready,' she began rapidly, 'but one of my scholars caught a glimpse of the man that you have in custody and he is a man that I have formally declared to be insane.'

'He escaped from a Bedlam hospital or something equivalent; is that the case?' Lawyer Bodkin looked at her enquiringly.

'We don't have hospitals for the insane in our kingdoms,' explained Mara. 'Brehon law stated that an insane man should be held by his nearest relative until he could be questioned at the law court on judgement day. If he were found to be permanently insane then the kin group, that was all of the descendants of the same great-grandfather, would have to care for him, either by drawing lots or by some other arrangement. The usual thing is to pass the insane person around from household to household on a monthly rotation, unless some charitable person could be found to take permanent care of him.'

Lawyer Bodkin raised his eyebrows and looked rather sceptical. It did sound a little haphazard, thought Mara. But mainly speaking it worked. It was just very bad luck that Sheedy had escaped from poor Diarmuid who had been devastated at his failure to keep him safe.

'It usually works very well,' she said defensively. 'Unfortunately the man who was caring for Sheedy when he disappeared, a most compassionate man, has a rather fierce dog – half wolf in origin – and Sheedy took a great dislike to that dog and managed to escape from Diarmuid's custody. The people of the Burren hunted for him, but eventually were forced to believe that he had died in some mountain cave.'

'But he made his way to Galway,' mused Henry. 'I suppose we will never know how, or even when he arrived. There was no mention of the man being insane as far as I can tell; Lawyer Joyce is acting for the shopkeeper, of course, but . . .'

'But no one is acting for the accused man, I suppose,' interrupted Mara. 'And the shopkeeper who brought the charge, who is he?'

'His name,' said Lawyer Bodkin, eyeing her in a troubled fashion, 'is Stephen Lynch. He is a first cousin to the prosecuting lawyer and to the mayor.'

'And the mayor is the judge,' stated Mara.

'And Mayor Lynch is the judge,' he confirmed.

Three

Ⰴⱁ Ⱂⱈⱃⱗⱛⰰⰹⰱ & Ⰻⰵⱃⱆⱛ & Ⰴⱑⱄⰰⱍⱛⰰⰹⰱ

(On Idiots, Insane Persons & Lunatics)

A person who is deemed to be an idiot, insane or a lunatic is not liable for any penalties even if he or she breaks the law. The penalty will be incurred by the guardian or nearest kinsman unless it can be shown that every effort was made to restrain the person. The care of a person who has been deemed by the court to suffer from any of these conditions is the responsibility of the clan and its taoiseach *(chieftain) must make provision for the safety and well-being of such persons.*

The streets were still very crowded when the party from the Bodkins' tower house set out to walk the short distance to Blake's Castle. Jane Bodkin, to Mara's relief, walked between Hugh and Shane. Hugh, though not outstandingly intelligent, was a gentle, sweet-natured boy and Shane, whose father was Brehon to the O'Neill, lord of most of Ulster, had very courtly manners. Both of these could be relied to be polite to their hostess. Fiona had been instructed to keep Henry Bodkin occupied and she slipped her arm into his with such a sweet maidenly expression that he beamed down on her paternally. This left Mara free to walk with Fachtnan.

'Tell me about poor Sheedy,' she said in a low tone.

He looked at her with a troubled expression.

'I've never seen anything so awful – even pigs are much better housed than he is. Filthy straw on the ground – hadn't been changed for a week, by the look of it – no means of relieving himself; the poor fellow is shackled and manacled.'

'How did you discover him?' Mara fought back the anger and distress. Now she had to think clearly and cleverly.

'Well, I was getting Hugh to ask the names of all the streets that we passed through – you know you said that he needed to practise his English – so when we found that we were in Gaol Street we went looking for the prison, and then we saw it. The warder was outside so we went up to him.' Fachtnan glanced down at Mara and said unexpectedly, 'You know, Brehon, Aidan is very clever really. He is just so humorous, so funny, and he was talking and laughing with the warder who was bored, of course, just standing there, scratching himself.'

Mara nodded. Every school had to have a clown and Aidan was the clown at Cahermacnaghten law school.

'And then Aidan challenged the warder to a proverbs contest and the winner was to have a pint of ale from the nearest tavern. So Aidan started off with that old one in that Latin book that your father brought back from the time he went on his travels to Rome – *Linacre's Latin Grammar* – "Where is no fyre, ther is no smoke". And the warder said, "One good turne asket another", and Aidan said, "Many hondes maken lite werke", and they went on like this for ages until Aidan came out with "Better ys late thane never", and the warder couldn't think of any more. He said that he would give Aidan the money to go to the tavern for a drink, but then Aidan said that if he would give us a look at his prisoner then we'd pay for a drink for everyone, including him. And that's how we saw Sheedy.' Fachtnan finished, giving her a slightly apprehensive look and explaining that he had just got small beer for the boys and confided Fiona to Moylan's care before going into the alehouse.

'That was very clever of Aidan,' said Mara appreciatively. 'Did Sheedy know you? I suppose it must be well over a year since he disappeared.'

Fachtnan shook his head. 'Not at all,' he said sadly. 'He's completely out of his mind, Brehon. We must do something to rescue him. The warder said that he would definitely hang. There's been a lot of thieving from the shops recently – people say that it is those Spanish sailors who are in town – but no one has been caught except poor Sheedy, of course.'

Mara thought about the matter, watching the seagulls squawking overhead, flying towards the harbour. What would be the best course of action? Here in Galway she had no status. In fact she was probably doing an imprudent thing in even visiting the city. Not only was she a Brehon – and Brehon Law was proscribed and detested by the English, but in addition she was the wife of a Gaelic king. Could she perhaps be captured and held to ransom, thrown into the squalor of the city gaol, placing an obligation on Turlough to come and rescue her and her scholars?

'Ah, here are some fellow guests,' called back Lawyer Bodkin.

He dropped Fiona's arm and hurried back to Mara. 'Here is Mayor Lynch,' he said and then hastened forward. Mara watched his hurried gait with interest. The lawyer was fighting his way through the crowds on the pavements while the mayor stood still and awaited his arrival.

Mayor Lynch obviously lived up to the old name of 'sovereign' and expected greetings from all of his subjects. The busy evening crowd had already parted to allow him and his family to walk in the centre of the pavement and most bowed and doffed caps as he passed. He showed no signs of acknowledging these salutations, though his wife and son bowed and smiled from time to time.

Mara made a sign to her scholars and waited, her mind alert and interested. What sort of man would he turn out to be? The mayor and his family had hardly paused to greet Lawyer Bodkin, but were coming towards them — a tall, very thin man, fairly elderly, a plump middle-aged woman and a boy of about Fachtnan's age.

The boy took Mara's attention. He was so vibrant, so full of life, gleaming like polished copper, a tall boy with curly, chestnut-coloured hair, a bright alert face with a grin stretching from ear to ear as he surveyed the group with frank curiosity. He was wearing a bright red jerkin, a crisp white shirt with Spanish lace work showing and he had a jaunty red cap with a kingfisher's feather stuck into it.

'Greetings! Welcome to Galway!' he called out excitedly and then gave a shamefaced, guilty look at the frowning face of his father.

And yet, what had been wrong with the boy's impulsive speech, thought Mara as she eyed James Lynch carefully. *A hard, cold man* had said Ardal O'Lochlainn, and Ardal was a man who never spoke without due consideration of his words. She smiled politely and waited for introductions. Mayor Lynch gave her a courteous bow in acknowledgement of Henry Bodkin's words, but did not return her smile. He had a pale face with pale grey eyes and a thin, pinched mouth. He did not speak and did not offer to shake hands, but his wife, introduced by Lawyer Bodkin as Mistress Lynch, had taken Mara's arm impulsively and said immediately, 'Please call me Margaret. What beautiful hair you have!'

Like her son, thought Mara, smiling as she mentioned her own first name, and decided to return the compliment by admiring

Walter. As a mother herself she guessed that would be a more valued remark than a mere exchange of flattering remarks about clothes. Margaret was richly dressed with a hood embroidered with pearls and an exaggeratedly wide skirt made from expensive brocade; the clothes, even in the streets of Galway, were worthy of remark, but the praise of her son brought a glow of pleasure to her powdered cheeks.

'My Benjamin,' she said half-laughing at herself, but beaming proudly at the youngster. 'You must know, Mara, that Walter is the youngest of my children. Nine girls, one after the other, all of them married, and I thought I had finished breeding, but then came the son. You can't imagine what I felt.'

'My son is only eighteen months old, but I think I can imagine how proud you are of your son,' returned Mara, touched by the woman's open affection for her handsome boy. The father, too, despite his cold manner, was keeping a careful eye on his son and appeared to be mentally comparing him to the law school scholars who surrounded him and were chatting with various degrees of proficiency in English.

'You must come out on The Green and practise some jousting,' Walter was saying. 'Did you bring your swords?'

'He's such a gentle boy,' said his mother indulgently as her son was excitedly regaling the law school scholars with his tales of daring while walking backwards down Quay Street in front of the boys. 'He wouldn't hurt a fly,' she added with a fond smile as he took from his belt a very handsome dagger, its ebony handle embossed with silver, and waved it in the air, miming the action of stabbing someone in the chest. 'You should have seen him yesterday morning when he discovered some boys stoning a kitten. He climbed after it right up to the roof of St Nicholas's, ruined his hose and his second-best jerkin, carried the little thing down and brought it home. He found a box and lined it with sheep's wool and fed the kitten with milk until its sides bulged. It's beside the fire in the kitchen at our castle at this very moment and it looks as if it will stay there for ever – if it was anyone other than Walter, the cook would give notice and leave, but he can do no wrong in our servants' eyes. You should have seen him with tears in his eyes, putting ointment on the little thing's cuts and bruises!'

'That was kind,' said Mara appreciatively. She thought that young Walter Blake would get on well with Fachtnan, who was

also a gentle and kind boy. From behind her she could hear the
heavy, sombre tones of the mayor discussing market rights with
Lawyer Bodkin. 'I suppose your husband is proud of him also,'
she ventured.

Margaret sighed. 'They are so unalike,' she confided. 'Of course,
Walter is a "Blake" through and through. Takes after my family.
I'm a Blake, you know. And you wouldn't believe it; every single
one of my nine girls was a Lynch from the moment they opened
their eyes. Always knew the right thing to do. Never spoke
without thinking. All made good marriages, too.' She sighed
heavily and then called out merrily, 'Mind your steps, fool boy;
your uncle is right behind you.'

Valentine Blake looked quite like his sister Margaret. He was
a plump man, richly dressed, good-looking, but lacked the amazing
burnished beauty of his nephew. He, too, was fond of the boy
and was playfully shaking him by the shoulders as he turned a
smiling face towards his guests.

'I shall have to call you Mistress Mara,' he said with amusement
when Lawyer Bodkin introduced her carefully as 'my lady judge'.
'I can't possibly address a young and beautiful woman as "judge"
when it brings such an image of fusty old men to my mind.'

'Well, call me "Brehon" and then there will be no complica-
tions,' invited Mara. She eyed him severely. She was not willing
to surrender any part of her status in deference to the views
of the anglicized inhabitants of this alien city. It was important,
she thought, that James Lynch, the mayor, should recognize
her status and appreciate that she was well qualified in law.
Valentine Blake was a charmer, of course, and used to ladies
falling for his attractions. He was teasing his sister now about
sending Walter on a long sea voyage to toughen him up and
laughing at her protestations that Walter caught cold easily.

'You should be like those Roman mothers who exposed their
baby sons out on the hillside – the ones that survived were the
only ones that were worth rearing,' he said.

'Spartan mothers, I think,' put in Mara. Walter's mother was
looking quite distressed, her eyes filling with tears at the thought.

'Spartan? Oh well . . .' Valentine was not really embarrassed
by his mistake, but he made a big show of hiding his face in his
hands and shaking his head disbelievingly – all to the amusement
of the young people.

'But there was a Roman, Lucius Junius Brutus, who agreed to the execution for conspiracy against the Republic of his own two sons,' said Hugh consolingly.

'Yes, there was nothing soft about these ancient Romans,' agreed Mara. It was brave of Hugh to speak out, she thought. His English was very much poorer than that of the other scholars, but he himself was often teased by Moylan and Aidan for mistakes like that so he probably felt sorry for Valentine. He was a nice boy, not as clever as the others, but blessed with a sensitive nature.

'Walter and I will take off one night in my ship and fight the Ottomans; these wretched Turks are spoiling the trade,' declared Valentine with an arm around his nephew's shoulders. 'That's right, isn't it, Walter? And then you'll have a use for that fancy dagger that I brought you. Now let's follow James. The Brownes will soon be here.'

He ushered them down the road towards the water.

Blake's Castle was very splendid. In fact, thought Mara, it was the most splendid and the largest building that she had seen that day. It was newly built, her host had told her, and even in the dim light of evening, the white surface of the limestone walls, towers and battlements shone and glittered – almost as white as quartz. It was in a wonderful position, with the restless blue and white inlet of the Atlantic Ocean as a backdrop and surrounded by neat gardens, well walled and guarded from any marauders. Above its gates was a stone shield, with the figure of a cat standing out in bold relief and painted black. Beneath it were the words "*Virtus sola Nobilitat*" pricked out in gold and black, and Mara wondered cynically whether it was true that virtue alone ennobled the merchant princes of Galway, or whether successful trading played its part.

The interior matched the glamour of the exciting exterior of the building. As Mara walked through the front door, held open by her host, she stopped abruptly and gave a quick gasp of astonishment. The hall was magnificent. An enormous, mullioned window of clear glass was set into the western wall and its diamond-shaped panes framed vignettes of the turbulent, white-capped green waves and of the colourful sails and small black boats that rode them.

'Got this marble all the way from Connemara – brought it down in my own ship,' said Valentine as Mara's eyes went to the spectacular floor which mirrored the colour of the ocean outside the windows. The whole expanse was tiled in grey-green marble, flecked here and there with subtle pinpoints of cream.

'It's perfect,' said Mara admiringly. She bent down and touched the glossily smooth surface. Brigid would like this floor, she thought. Her housekeeper always complained about the work of keeping clean the rough, flagstoned slabs that formed the floors of the school and the Brehon's house at Cahermacnaghten.

'Valentine was always a boy who wanted perfection,' said Margaret fondly. 'Second best was never good enough for him. Spoilt, he was, with myself and my sisters like little mothers to him.'

'Some people have to accept second best if they don't have the means to achieve perfection,' observed her husband drily, but his words were almost drowned out by Walter who was exuberantly welcoming his new friends to his uncle's house.

'How do you like the way that I have placed the mirrors, Mistress Mara?' asked Valentine eagerly, ignoring the dour expression on his brother-in-law's face.

'I like the effect,' said Mara. 'They bring so much extra light indoors.' What an unpleasant, carping individual was this James Lynch, she thought. Or was he perhaps jealous of the display of wealth here in this wonderful castle. She looked around with a smile of admiration.

Here and there mirrors with gilded frames were placed on the walls, tilted at an angle so that they reflected the green of the marble. Heavy oak court cupboards, dark with polish, were placed against the white walls, but the room was dominated by that magnificent floor – almost as though the ocean was brought indoors. Mara gazed into one of the mirrors and was confronted by the thin face of the mayor of Galway, standing just behind her, and bearing an expression of contemptuous disdain. His own house, she reflected, as she met his eyes, was probably not as beautiful as this.

'Up here,' said Valentine, smiling happily and indicating a short, wide flight of stairs at the back of the large entrance hall which led up to a tall, mullioned window overlooking the broad river that entered the sea at Galway. A cushion-strewn bench stood in front of the window and the staircase itself then branched off in two different directions. Still keeping her arm tucked into Mara's, Margaret Lynch led her up the stairs and steered her in through a door on the right-hand side.

'Come on, boys, and girl, of course.' Valentine, already inside the room, bestowed a warm smile of admiration on Fiona who responded with an amused grin.

'Where's your ship moored, Mr Blake?' Shane was asking, but Mara didn't hear the answer. Her eyes widened at the sight of the lovely room ahead of her. Once again the floor was of the cream-flecked grey-green marble, but here it was dotted with colourful woven rugs in rich shades of raspberry-red and sea-blue. The walls of the long room were panelled in golden wood that smelled of lavender polish. Small, precious tapestries hung on the walls, and sconces of sweet-smelling beeswax candles were placed in front of more gilt-framed mirrors.

In one corner of the room a group of prettily dressed girls, in stiff brocaded dresses, and with matching hoods set on top of their long hair, hung over a harpsichord, where a slightly older girl was lightly touching the keys and singing a low, plaintive melody.

'This is my wife Cecily,' said Valentine as the girl at the harpsichord stood up and came towards them. 'And these are my daughters, Anne, Elizabeth and Catherine.'

Cecily murmured a greeting to Mara. She looked hardly older than her three stepdaughters and seemed happy to rejoin them while Valentine took Mara on a tour of his magnificent room.

He was entertaining company, she thought. He had a story to tell of each item that he had collected. She listened, but she was more interested in James Lynch, the mayor. From time to time she glanced over at him, but there was little other than a faint shade of boredom to be read from his face. Margaret, on the other hand, seemed to be fond and proud of her brother, hanging on his arm and prompting him to tell stories about the Turkish boat which had sold him his rugs and the Spanish town where he had found an exquisite tapestry of a unicorn.

'Once I saw it, I had to have it,' said Valentine enthusiastically, gazing fondly at his treasure.

'Didn't bother asking the price, I suppose,' put in James Lynch quietly, looking with disdain at his brother-in-law.

'Who could bother about a price for a thing as beautiful as this?' Margaret spoke quickly. Her face when she looked at her husband was defiant and, somehow, angry.

'Were you brought up here, Margaret?' asked Mara, hoping to dissipate an awkward moment between husband and wife. 'What a lovely place it is.'

'On this spot, but in a much smaller place – Valentine is the one who knows how to make money. My father imported skins and leather but that was not so successful with a countryside in the hinterland full of cattle,' said Margaret. Her voice was full of pride when she added, 'When Valentine took over the business he started to import salt from Portugal. No one had thought of doing that before so it has been a huge success.' She lowered her voice and whispered in Mara's ear, 'I'm hoping that he will agree to taking Walter under his wing.'

Every topic of conversation came back to Walter almost immediately, thought Mara with a suppressed smile. She looked across at Valentine who, having shown his treasures, was teasing Jane Bodkin about having Hugh as her new young man – he had even brought a flush of colour to the old lady's thin cheeks. Yes, Walter would probably get on better with his uncle than with the sour, thin-faced father.

Nevertheless, thought Mara as she accepted a seat on the embroidered cushioned seat in front of one of the two windows beside Margaret, James Lynch is the man that I must turn my attention to. Valentine Blake, his expenditure and his personality, all that is really of no interest to me; it's James Lynch that I need to woo if I am to rescue an unfortunate countryman of mine from the cruel and unjust courts of Galway.

Mara furtively scanned the forbidding countenance of the Mayor of Galway, while listening to Margaret's stories of Walter's good nature and love of his mother with an attentive face and half an ear. What were his interests? she wondered. How can I open up conversation with him?

'And your husband, James, what is his business?' she asked when eventually she managed to find an opening.

'Coal and fish,' said Margaret merrily. 'You must come and visit us, Mara. I can guarantee that you will never be cold and we don't always have to eat fish!'

'And Walter is not so interested in coal and fish,' queried Mara, looking across at the handsome young man. He was chatting in a friendly way to Fiona. Fiona, of course, was a beauty who turned all heads, but he didn't seem as interested in her as his uncle, Valentine, who was still eyeing her with an appreciative smile.

A moment later Mara saw why Walter was not impressed by Fiona.

Four

The oath of allegiance to the king of England to be administered to all who live in Ireland:

'I become faithful and true ligeman unto kyng Henry the viith kyng of England and of Fraunce and lord of Irland of lif and lym and erthly worship and feth and trought. I shall beer unto hym as my soveraigne liege lord to lyve and dye agentst all maner creatours so god help me and his seyntes.'

The steward had just announced the next guests, the Browne family. Valentine, his wife and his daughter went forward to greet them. Mara studied the newcomers with interest. Philip Browne had an amiable face – the usual dark hair and white skin of Galway people – his wife very much darker – this must the Spanish wife – one boy who looked like his father and another who looked as though he had come from southern Spain with the dark, almost Moorish colouring of that region.

But Walter Lynch had eyes for only one person in the family party. He left Fiona abruptly.

Catarina Browne was looking even more beautiful than she had done when Mara had met her on The Green. She was dressed in an elaborate Spanish gown made from red silks and satins and trimmed with the same colour of velvet, each individual cloth bearing its own shade. The effect was of a shimmering sweep of intense red light and the rosy glow seemed to be reflected in the adoring face of the boy who stood before her, carrying her hand to his lips in a courtly gesture.

'My little Scottish primrose has been abandoned by your son for the Spanish rose,' murmured Mara in Margaret's ear. Fiona had tossed her blonde head and turned back to the other boys, giggling with Aidan over some silly joke.

'Walter's been in love with Catarina since he was five years old,' said Margaret. She tried to sound apologetic, but a smile of pride and triumph curved her lips. 'It will be a good match. Philip Browne is a very successful merchant and Catarina will have a fortune from her mother. The Gomez family from Cadiz,' she said settling into a comfortable gossip mode, 'is fabulously rich. There was no heir for years and Philip Browne hoped that his son might inherit the Spanish fortune through his mother, but when David was ten years old Señor Gomez married again and had a son – Carlos. He, of course, will be a very rich young man,' she said enviously, 'but Isabella has her own fortune and that will be for Catarina.'

'Is this the first visit that Carlos has paid to Galway?' Mara thought that the hopes of an alliance between young Walter Lynch and the well-endowed Catarina might not work. The girl seemed to be paying more attention to her cousin Carlos than to him and when she did address a remark to Walter, it seemed to be made in a rather condescending fashion. Boys and girls, brought up together, did not always marry. Carlos did not have the shining beauty of Walter, but, although probably only a year or so older, he had an air of authority, of experience, and, of course, the glamour of his Spanish gold to set him up as a serious rival.

None of my business, thought Mara and with a murmured excuse to Margaret, she got up to inspect a flamboyantly decorated wall-hanging of Spanish leather, which was displayed quite near to the cushioned bench where James Lynch was sitting, and then, when he made no move to her side, she gave up the pretence and sat down beside him.

'So much to see here in the city of Galway,' she said. 'I was admiring your very fine walls earlier when our host took me up to The Green.'

The mayor looked at her suspiciously. 'We have to maintain them well,' he said stiffly. 'We are surrounded by a hostile people.'

'And then this very fine harbour,' said Mara, ignoring his attempt to start an argument.

'Talking about the harbour, James, just as we were passing on our way into here, there was a very fine ship from Spain arriving,' called out Philip Browne, rather rudely interrupting an anecdote about Walter's babyhood which Margaret was relating to him and his wife. He crossed the room, studied the mayor's face from under his eyelashes as he added maliciously, 'Plenty of taxes for you, my friend. I'd say that there was as much as a hundred tuns on board.'

Mara absorbed this with interest. A hundred tuns meant about two hundred thousand gallons of wine. The tax on this must be absolutely enormous. James Lynch, however, showed just a placid satisfaction.

'Good,' he said, almost to himself. 'So that's arrived. That means we can get building.'

A splendid place like Valentine's palatial residence, wondered Mara, but then, almost as though the strange man sitting beside her had read her thoughts, he said to her abruptly, 'I want to build a grammar school for the town. They have them in all the major towns in England – they even have one in Dublin. This will be built beside the church and will educate the sons of the merchants and will have free places for ten poor, but deserving, town boys.'

'And will be known as the James Lynch Foundation,' said Valentine. His tone was teasing and Mara thought he might be revenging himself for some of his brother-in-law's remarks earlier. It was obvious that there was little love between them. Not a likeable man, James Lynch. Philip Browne, also, was eyeing him with a look of dislike.

'Not James Lynch anything,' said the mayor stiffly. 'This school will be named the St Nicholas Grammar School and it will take boys up to the age of fourteen. They can progress from there to a university in England, or a law school, or into a trade in the town.'

'Pointless waste of money – ten free places. How can the town afford to keep this going? You won't be mayor for ever, you know, and you will leave a burden on your successors and their children. Valentine, do you approve of this absurd business?' Philip Browne sounded so angry that the two young men and the four girls at the top of the room, stopped talking and turned around to listen. The law scholars politely turned to look out of the window at the back of the room.

'I've told him that,' said Valentine, smiling good-humouredly, 'but let's not think of it now.' He picked up a small bell of chased silver and rang it. A man, dressed as a steward, appeared and bowed towards the mistress of the house, murmuring something.

It was, however, Valentine, who ushered everyone into the dining room, seating Mara beside himself, and Fiona on his other hand, and sending the angry-looking James Lynch to sit beside the amiable Cecily. In a few minutes all were seated around a long table spread with a purple tablecloth which showed off the elaborate silver plates, silver knives and silver drinking goblets.

Both young men, Walter and the Spanish boy, Carlos, drank fairly heavily throughout the meal. They were placed on each side of Catarina, which perhaps had been rather tactless of the host. Mara was sorry that this was not an informal household where when the meal was announced people moved to sit beside who they chose to talk to. Mara had wanted to place herself next to James Lynch, but had to make do with his wife Margaret who was on her other side – and she was the better talker of the two.

However, when Valentine's wife, Cecily, claimed Margaret's attention for a moment, Mara immediately took the opportunity of leaning across the table to address James Lynch.

'Tell me some more about your grammar school,' she said.

He shrugged. 'Nothing much to tell; we have to get the building up before any plans for the teaching are made.'

'And you will have no difficulty with the town council?'

Once again he shrugged, a look of faint amusement in his eyes this time. 'No,' he said. 'They will do what I suggest.'

And he cast a challenging glance across the table at Philip Browne.

Not a man to cajole or establish a relationship, she thought. However, as a lawyer, she was trained into taking different approaches to a problem. She had tried being friendly; now she would try a different tack.

'I had a very interesting afternoon in Lawyer Bodkin's chambers,' she began, trying to make her voice sound authoritative and intellectual. 'He was kind enough to lend me his law books. It was fascinating to pick out the differences between your law and ours.'

'Your law,' he queried with an ironic lift of his eyebrows. His thin lips were twisted into a sneer. The pause he made and the puzzled tone of voice were all deliberately affected, thought Mara. She said nothing, just gazed steadily at him and after a moment his eyes dropped. 'Oh, *brewone* law,' he said, deliberately mispronouncing the word, and when she still kept her lips closed, he looked at her with an air of curiosity.

'Yes,' she said sweetly when she judged that sufficient time had elapsed, 'of course, here in Galway you are rather cut off from the rest of the west of Ireland, are you not?' And she saw with satisfaction how his face darkened. She had evoked the familiar nightmare for the dwellers of the city state of Galway. There were about three thousand people with English names and English lifestyles, living inside its strong walls, but outside those walls were millions with names prefaced with an O' or a Mac who, though denied the opportunity, according to one of the statutes, "to strutte nor swagger through the streets of Galway", were nevertheless an ever-present threat. From across the table she saw Lawyer Bodkin look at her with slightly widened eyes.

But I've done the right thing, though, thought Mara. This is a hard-hearted, self-satisfied man. Not a man to be appealed to. Not a man to take compassion on poor old Sheedy who had lost his wits and who stole a pie because he was starving. No, this was a man to be threatened.

'I think we have an acquaintance in common,' she continued, looking challengingly at Mayor Lynch. 'The Lord of Clanrickard is a great friend of my husband.' And if that reminded him of Ulick Burke's last daring raid on the Lombard Street in the heart of the city, well that might be all to the good, she thought as she turned back to Margaret again.

'You must see the Shrove Tuesday celebrations tomorrow evening, Mara,' the latter was saying. 'I would ask you to supper at our place, but it is so much more fun to go out on to the town streets. Your young people will love it. We're hoping that the weather will keep fine. The whole of the city is like one huge fair – lanterns everywhere and food cooked at every street corner.' She sighed heavily and added, 'But my husband does not like that sort of thing, so these days I stay at home and just look out from the top windows.'

'Your son would enjoy it, though,' said Mara with a smile.

'Oh, I would not burden him with his old mother these days,' said Margaret with a fond smile. 'He and Catarina will be together.'

'Why don't you come with us?' said Mara impulsively, and then looked across at Lawyer Bodkin. 'My scholars would enjoy these Shrove celebrations. Would we disgrace you if we went?'

'Of course not, I would be delighted to escort you,' he said, and to her surprise he looked quite animated by the thought. 'I haven't gone for the last few years because Jane has taken a dislike to the crowds but you need fear nothing for your young scholars. The behaviour is usually very good and the mayor –' he looked across at James Lynch – 'always ensures that all available constables are on duty. I will escort you ladies if necessary, but I do assure you, my lady judge, that there is nothing to fear and Mistress Margaret and you would be perfectly safe together.'

'Well, let's just go together then,' said Mara, turning back to Margaret. 'I will enjoy your company and we can gossip about our sons, and you will show me all the sights of Galway.'

'That's very kind of you,' said Margaret appreciatively. 'Last year I was to go with Valentine and Cecily, but she gave birth to their son two weeks too early and so was laid up for Shrove Tuesday. Of course, Valentine has his daughters by his first marriage,' she looked down the table at Eliza – she's married to one of the D'Arcy family – he's away at the moment – but you can imagine what it was for him having a son! He just worships that child.' She raised her voice, looking teasingly down the table at her brother. 'Valentine, are we going to see little Jonathon? I can't believe that we are almost at the end of a meal at Blake's Castle and the young prince has not yet been displayed to your guests.'

There was no doubt that Margaret and James Lynch were an ill-assorted pair, thought Mara, after she had duly admired the strong, handsome one-year-old child, who arrived so quickly in the dining room that his nurse must have been awaiting the summons. Margaret continually tried to repress her exuberant friendliness and high spirits when she saw her husband's cold eye on her, and young Walter cast frequent guilty looks down the table at his father – especially whenever Catarina's attention was taken up by her wealthy cousin, Carlos Gomez.

It would be a great blow to James Lynch and his prestige in Galway city if this match between the heiress, Catarina Browne, and his only son were to fail. He was not a man to dismiss the matter with a tolerant shrug and Mara found herself feeling rather sorry for Walter. Judging by the looks exchanged between Carlos and Catarina, she reckoned that the poor boy was not only going to be disappointed in love but was going to be blamed by his father for his failure.

However, all of this was none of her business and she turned
back to James Lynch and treated him to a learned lecture on the
writings of the ancient Greeks on the finer legal points of 'laws
in conflict'. This took his attention and he surveyed her with
interest. She guessed that his own education had not included
any knowledge of ancient civilizations – it was interesting how
passionate he was about offering the opportunity for education
to the sons of the citizens of Galway – in any case, Mara was
someone who loved to impart information.

It was ironic, thought Mara, that she was giving a lecture on
Roman law to a man who was trusted by the city of Galway to
judge cases in that law. He was totally ignorant of anything other
than his own privileges and prejudices, she thought, feeling deeply
shocked that such a man would hold the power of life and death
over his fellow citizens, but not allowing her feelings to show on
her face. From time to time she appealed to Henry Bodkin and
he did not fail her, deferring to her superior knowledge and
flattering her. He was amused, she thought, and wondered how
much a clever, learned man like he had suffered by being placed
lower in the court than a completely unqualified magistrate, like
James Lynch.

'Of course,' she said, lightly, 'when it comes to laws in conflict,
the Romans had gone into this matter with even greater thor-
oughness and had laid down the important principle that all court
matters should be easily understandable to the defendant as well
as to the plaintiff and officials of the court. I understand,' she
concluded, 'that the law here in Galway is known as the law of
the king and of the emperor, so Roman law is probably very
important to you. Lawyer Bodkin was telling me that the court
trial of a man speaking only Gaelic will take place tomorrow;
now Roman law would give him, as a stranger—'

'But this man Sheedy had no right to be in our city – no one
gave him permission to enter,' James Lynch interrupted. The
mayor, she thought, was beginning to sound rather defensive.
Most of the table was listening now. Walter Lynch had given up
trying to talk to Catarina Browne and was eyeing her with an
expression of awe and apprehension. Philip Browne was looking
maliciously pleased. He had been overruled peremptorily about
this projected grammar school and seemed delighted that the
mayor was getting the worst of the argument. Valentine Blake

exchanged a quick grin and wink with his sister Margaret as Mara waved aside the last point.

'I think that it was the Italians who said that a shipwrecked sailor had to be afforded all possible aid if the language of the court was not his own language. In fact,' she said with conviction, 'now that I come to think of it, that may be how this man arrived in your city. He may well have been lost overboard from a ship and washed into the shore by dead of night, and crept through the city gate more dead than alive,' she finished, rather pleased with the picture that she created. 'And thus his arrival in Galway city could be said to be by *force majeure* – or, as we would put it, by an act of God, and God, as we are taught to believe, is merciful.'

'I don't pretend to be able to interpret God's instructions; I just listen to the evidence and pass sentence,' said James Lynch in a tone of voice which said that this was going to be his last word. 'And now,' he looked across at Valentine Blake, 'perhaps we could have the next course. I don't wish to be out late tonight. Tomorrow will be a very busy day for me.'

Mara eyed the implacable face across the table from her and felt a measure of despair for a life depending on any mercy that might be forthcoming from James Lynch.

Five

Scat. Hiberniae. 14 Hen. III.
(From Blackstone's Commentaries, 1765–1769)

At the time of this conquest the Irish were governed by what they called the Brehon law, so stiled from the Irish name of judges, who were denominated Brehons. But King John in the twelfth year of his reign went into Ireland, and carried over with him many able sages of the law; and there by his letters patent, in right of the dominion of conquest, is said to have ordained and established that Ireland should be governed by the laws of England:

But to this ordinance many of the Irish were averse to conform, and still stuck to their Brehon law: so that both Henry the third and Edward the first were obliged to renew the injunction; and at length in a parliament holden at Kilkenny, 40 Edw. III, under Lionel Duke of Clarence, the then lieutenant of Ireland, the Brehon law was formally abolished, it being unanimously declared to be indeed no law, but a lewd custom crept in of later times.

'As far as I can tell, under the English law system, the defendant gets a chance to make a statement before the jury – a matter of twelve men from the town selected to listen to the proceedings – to say whether the culprit is guilty or not.' Mara was giving her scholars a rapid lesson in English law as they stood huddled against the stone-built customs house beside the port of Galway. The icy wind sweeping in from the inlet from the sea ensured that they had complete privacy at this spot and she had something important to say to them. She had refused the rather reluctant offer of Lawyer Bodkin to accompany them this morning and had told him placidly that they would sit in the spectators' gallery.

'That's odd – twelve men who are not lawyers,' said Fachtnan with surprise.

'The lawyer explains the law to the mayor or sovereign and he explains the position to the jury,' said Mara. She frowned slightly. 'In a way,' she said reluctantly, 'I suppose it should be good, an ordinary man's point of view, but—'

'But these ordinary men are probably all too scared to go against someone important like the mayor – he seems to be a sort of king here, doesn't he? It wouldn't work on the Burren, anyway. Everyone would want to know what you thought before trusting their own opinion – not that they would be scared or anything . . .' interrupted Moylan, his sharp eyes sparkling.

Mara laughed. 'I think you are probably right,' she said, but then quickly grew serious again. 'Poor old Sheedy! I think that there is no chance that I can speak for him. My qualifications as a lawyer will not be accepted by the court. The only possibility for us is to rely on this speech that the defendant is allowed to make before he is finally found guilty or not guilty. I propose to offer you, Hugh, as a translator.'

'Me, why me?' Hugh turned red with embarrassment and astonishment.

'You are well liked here in Galway,' said Mara diplomatically. She had chosen Hugh as his English was the least proficient of all her scholars and whenever he stumbled she could interfere and make explanations. She guessed from what Fachtnan said that Sheedy was even more insane than when she had pronounced him to be a *dásachtach* and outside the reach of the law so far as any wrongdoing was concerned. Brehon law was most clear and explicit on this point, even going so far as to make it an offence for any sane person to incite a *dásachtach* into committing an offence and saying that 'the rights of the insane take precedence over other rights'.

The courthouse in Galway city had a queue in front of it when they arrived. This afternoon and tomorrow would be a holiday and it looked as if the townspeople had already begun their Shrove celebrations. A noisy crowd of young boys whose badges declared them to belong to the guild of tanners were wrestling with each other in the queue. Mara gave a long look at them and regretted declining Lawyer Bodkin's offer to escort them. She had no desire to seat herself and her scholars among this unruly mob.

However, at that moment they were approached by a steward who bowed respectfully and said the mayor had observed them from his room and wished to offer them accommodation in the courtroom if they were minded to watch the trial.

And thus they were ushered into an empty courtroom, and shown a bench where the scholars could sit. The steward carried over a heavy oaken chair ornately upholstered in brocade for Mara. She took her seat, spread her skirts and smiled her thanks to the steward, dispatching a polite message of thanks to the mayor.

'Lawyer Bodkin sent a message to the court this morning,' he said chattily. 'He told me that you were a lady lawyer and that you were a guest of his and that your lads –' his eyes slid over Fiona, blinked, and then he hastily corrected himself – 'your pupils would benefit from seeing a trial conducted in . . . I mean . . . conducted in our manner.'

'Yes, indeed, it should be most beneficial to them. The judge sits there, does he?' Mara indicated an elaborate chair sumptuously upholstered in red velvet. 'You have a lawyer for a judge, I presume,' she added, as he seemed surprised by her words. She was interested to hear what his reactions would be to that statement.

'No!' He seemed quite appalled at that. 'That chair is for his worship, Mayor Lynch; these two chairs are for Bailiff Blake and Bailiff Skerrett – the mayor is the judge and he sits there, and the jury sit over on that bench to the side so that they are near to the judge and he can tell them what to make of the evidence.'

'And the prisoner?' asked Mara.

'Over there.' He indicated a tall, box-like enclosure. 'Of course, when they are really vicious, like some of those wild O'Flahertys, then they are brought into the court in cages.'

'In cages!' exclaimed Shane.

'That's right.' The steward smiled kindly at the boy. 'You'd have liked to see that, wouldn't you? But this man that is being tried today is just a poor old fellow. The case will be over in two shakes of a lamb's tail.'

And then he was off, promising to bring back a hot brick for the lady's feet.

'Brehon, what am I going to do if what Sheedy says doesn't make sense? What am I going to say?' Hugh was working himself up into a state. His freckled face alternatively flushed a bright pink and then paled. He ran his fingers through the copper curls which had taken the fancy of Jane Bodkin. The other scholars looked at him with commiseration.

'I'll do it if you like,' offered Fiona.

'No,' said Mara decidedly. 'You speak English with a Scottish accent and Shane speaks it with a northern accent. I taught Hugh and he speaks in a way that will be understood by all in the court.' And if this left Fachtnan, Moylan and Aidan, all of whom had been taught English by her, to be quite unaccounted for, well, no one, she hoped, would be brave enough to point out that fact. Hugh had brought up a good point, though, and she was glad of a few minutes' privacy in the unoccupied courtroom to answer it.

'All I want you to do, Hugh, is faithfully and conscientiously to translate each word that Sheedy says into English – even if it doesn't make sense. If you are unsure – just repeat the word and look across at me for help.'

Moylan's eyes sparkled with intelligence at those last words, and he and Fiona glanced at each other mischievously.

'What the Brehon means, Hugh,' intervened Fachtnan hastily, 'is that she can trust you just to give Sheedy's words. If it was Moylan, well, he'd have to make things sound better. You know the way he is always saying "let me rephrase this" when someone says something at law school, and then if it was Aidan, he couldn't resist the temptation to make a joke.' Fachtnan gave a humorous glance at the two older boys and they both grinned.

Mara found herself, not for the first time, thinking what a very good Brehon Fachtnan, with his talent for diplomacy, would make if he were able to pass his final examination. A law like Brehon law which had no gaols, no hangings, no whippings, had to be administered purely by the consensus of the people of the kingdom. Tact, diplomacy and an understanding of human nature were essential qualities for any candidate for the post. Every one of the numerous small kingdoms in Gaelic Ireland had to have its Brehon; eventually Fachtnan would find a post, but in the meantime he had a lot of studying, not easy for him, to go through.

'And Fiona would not be able to resist flirting with the judge,' said Moylan, entering into Fachtnan's intentions with his usual ready wit.

'Perhaps he likes young boys better,' said Fiona wickedly with a sidelong glance at Mara, and smiling teasingly at Hugh.

Luckily at this moment the steward came back carrying two hot bricks. One he tucked under Mara's feet and the other was placed beneath the silken tasselled cushion that lay on the floor before the mayor's feet. None were brought for the bailiffs or for the lawyers

'I'm going to open the doors now as soon as the constables come in. There's a lot of riff-raff around. The apprentices have the day off and the shop boys have been given a few hours off as they will be on their feet until midnight with the Shrove Tuesday celebrations. Don't you take any notice of them, my lady judge – anything I can get you before I go? Glass of wine? The mayor is just taking one now and it's very good wine – not Spanish or Portuguese wine, good French stuff – all the way from Burgundy.'

Mara regretfully declined the wine, though she was pleased to hear that James Lynch was even now sipping his burgundy. It should make him more good-humoured, she thought as she watched the crowd pour into the onlookers' gallery above her head. She didn't recognize any of them. Young Walter obviously had no interest in seeing his father at work, or perhaps a boy who pitied and cared for an abused kitten would dislike to see a sentence handed down to a man whose only crimes were hunger and a lack of wits.

'All rise!' bellowed the steward, and suddenly the noise in the gallery ceased as they all rose to their feet. A small procession came from behind a velvet curtain and took their places on the stage.

James Lynch looked much the same as he had last night – the wine seemed not to have taken any more effect on him than had his abstemious consumption in his brother-in-law's house. His grey eyes were cold and his thin mouth was hard as he took his seat and placed his feet on the warmth of the silken cushion.

His cousin, Thomas Lynch, the senior lawyer in the city, was a much smaller man, small and very thin, also older. A man on the verge of retirement, she thought, and hoped that this might provide Lawyer Bodkin an opportunity for advancement. He sat down on his less prestigious chair and then the two bailiffs took their place. Valentine Blake looked much the same as he looked last night, a pleasant cordial fellow. He bowed and smiled towards Mara and her scholars. He was a man with a smile for everyone, she noticed, even including the crowd in the gallery who responded with a few excited whispers.

'Bring in the prisoner,' barked Thomas Lynch, and Mara thought

how different everything was to her open-air court in the Burren
where proceedings always started with a greeting from her to the
assembled people.

Poor Sheedy was dragged in by two of his gaolers. He looked
tiny, hunched and bent – almost like a captured spider. Once the
door to the prisoner's dock was bolted from the outside his arms
were released. Instantly he covered his eyes with them and cowered
away into the corner of the box. The warders forced him forward
again and held him facing the lawyer, though they allowed his
arms to stay covering his face. Thomas Lynch eyed him with
contempt, but his worship the mayor just stared ahead in a bored
fashion.

'Who speaks for the sovereignty of Galway?' roared the steward,
and a lawyer in a gown came forward and bowed to his senior.

'I do, My Lord,' he said.

The mayor turned his eyes on him, 'Call your first witness,
Lawyer Joyce,' he said.

So this was William Joyce, inhabitant of the chambers above
Lawyer Bodkin.

'Call Grocer Joyce,' called the steward loudly.

'Another Joyce!' whispered Moylan.

The steward bawled out the name and a large, pleasant-looking
man came from behind the curtain, bowed to the mayor first and
then the judge and took his place in the witness stand. He kissed
the book held out to him by the steward of the court and muttered
some words after him.

'What's that for?' whispered Fiona in Mara's ear.

'Kisses the Bible and swears to tell the truth.' Mara wondered
whether it would be a good idea to introduce something like that
into Brehon courts but then decided against it. Kissing the Bible
and swearing to tell the truth would probably have little significance for a man or woman who had good reason to lie and would
be unnecessary for those who wanted to tell the truth in the first
place. This was a city where religion and the church were of great
importance, she mused. It was interesting that their laws were so
savage and inhumane. Rome, she knew, criticized the slackness
of the church in Gaelic Ireland, where many of the priests married
and had children – had sons that inherited their fathers' position
in the church. The present bishop of Killaloe in the kingdom of
Thomond was the son of the previous bishop and he had several

children, all of whom had made good marriages due to their father's position. The bishop of Galway, or warden as he was known, was a much-feared man, appointed by Pope Julius II, nicknamed 'the fearsome pope'. The clergy of St Nicholas were to be 'learned, virtuous and well-bred, and were to observe the English rite and custom in the Divine Service', according to Pope Julius.

Grocer Joyce gave his evidence clearly – an honest man, if not a compassionate one. He saw Sheedy come into the shop, watched him walk over to the table, seize the pie and go out with it. When he got to the door Sheedy was already running away with the pie in his hand and he shouted to a constable to run after him.

'What was the value of the stolen article?' asked Lawyer Joyce in the tone of one who knows the answer already.

'One shilling and sixpence, and good value, too,' replied the grocer with a decided nod. Did the man know that these words were condemning a fellow creature to a terrible death? wondered Mara. The answer had to be yes.

'Do you see the man who stole the pie in this court?' asked Lawyer Lynch, intervening with the impatient air of one who wants the trial to end as soon as possible.

'I do, My Lord.' Grocer Joyce, a man of few words, pointed out Sheedy, still cowering away from the light from the large thick candles.

And then two shop apprentices gave their evidence and also the wife of the shopkeeper across the road. The jury nodded to each other and exchanged smiles with her. Probably they were all shopkeepers, thought Mara.

Lawyer Lynch then summed up the case from the evidence gathered by his junior. The prisoner had stolen a pie worth more than one shilling as had been attested by witnesses of good character. There was little else to say so he sat down, still looking rather bored.

And then the moment came. The mayor addressed the prisoner. 'Your name is Sheedy O'Connor?' He said the words in tones so loudly that they echoed off the tall ceiling and startled Sheedy into raising his head.

For a moment something which appeared to be normality seemed to come into the old man's eyes and then they dulled again. He dropped his head back down on to his arms which were now propped up by the bar of the prisoner's dock. The mayor carried on without a second glance.

'Sheedy O'Connor, you have been accused of the crime of stealing a pie worth one shilling and sixpence. Have you anything to say before sentence is passed?'

Sheedy said nothing and did not lift his head. The mayor nodded at the warder in an irritated way.

'Answer his honour!' Sheedy got a vicious dig in the ribs which made him look up again.

'I'm hungry,' he said in Gaelic.

'Nothing to say, your honour,' said the gaoler promptly, and the mayor fumbled in a box that lay on a small table beside him.

That was enough for Mara. She got to her feet instantly. 'My Lord,' she said in a loud clear voice, 'allow me to help to translate. Your prisoner merely said that he was hungry.' Without giving him time to answer she beckoned to Hugh and swept down to the front of the court with him. Purposefully she had spoken in Latin. If Lawyer Lynch, like Lawyer Bodkin, had qualified in one of the Inns of Chancery, he would have been trained in that language. He appeared to understand, but the mayor stared at her in puzzlement and leaned back to confer with Lawyer Joyce. The two bailiffs leaned over to listen in. Valentine Blake, she noticed, had a broad grin on his face. Mara did not look at them, but turned an earnest glance on Lawyer Lynch.

'Although a lawyer myself,' she said still speaking in fluent Latin, 'I do realize that I am not qualified to take part in this trial but if you will accept the services of this young boy then he will do his best to interpret for the prisoner, who, I suggest, has no knowledge of English.'

She placed the blushing Hugh at a distance from Sheedy so that he could not be accused of conferring with the prisoner and then returned rapidly to her place.

There was some low-murmured muttering going on between the dignitaries of the court. She thought that Valentine Blake appeared to be trying to persuade the others, making large, open-handed gestures and smiling. She felt a rush of gratitude towards him. It was kind of him to be concerned about a poor old man like Sheedy. The others turned and stared at Hugh who looked, with his small, slim figure, to be even younger than his fourteen years and who was blessed with an amiable, open-faced charm. After a minute the mayor said in English, loudly and clearly, 'The services of the young translator are accepted.'

'Perhaps the question might be repeated to the prisoner,' suggested Valentine Blake. The mayor gave his brother-in-law an angry look, but said nothing. Valentine Blake nodded in a kind way to Hugh and Mara nodded as well.

'Sheedy, have you got anything to say about taking that pie from the shop?' asked Hugh in Gaelic. The boy's voice shook, but that would do no harm. 'I asked him if he had anything to say about stealing the pie,' he said to the mayor timidly.

At the familiar sound of the Gaelic, Sheedy raised his head.

'Hungry,' he wailed and Hugh translated.

Now all eyes were on Sheedy and he responded by looking around the big room in a confused manner.

'I am the king, the king, the king,' he said in a sing-song voice, looking across at Hugh and nodding his head as Hugh turned the Gaelic words into English.

Then came a flood of broken phrases. The word 'hungry' recurred again and again. Hugh had to struggle to keep up. His face was flushed scarlet and his eyes were large with apprehension, but he kept drawing out the English words to the best of his ability. Mara had thought that she would have to intervene, but was happy to see that there was no need to do so. Neither the lawyers, nor the mayor had liked her fluent Latin, she surmised. Best leave it to Hugh who was shining with earnestness and with perspiration.

'Me a king; me hungry; me fox,' muttered Sheedy continuously.

Hugh translated, adding timidly, 'In our law a hungry fox, that is a hungry man, must be fed, your worship.' Mara's eyes shone with pride in him, one of her least able boys. She swore inwardly that, by hook or by crook, this gentle, diffident boy should be got through his examinations.

Then Sheedy began to scream, 'Water, me choking, drown him, drown him.'

'He's mad,' shouted a brave apprentice from the gallery. There was a chorus of laughter after that and Sheedy stopped screaming and smiled gently up at the gallery. 'Me king, me king of Galway,' he said proudly, and this time he waited for the translation before going back with the monotone mutterings about hungry foxes.

And then, quite suddenly, he stopped. He put his head down on his arms again and it almost seemed as though he had fallen into a sleep.

'Have you finished?' enquired the mayor. The warder kicked Sheedy and Hugh repeated the words, but Sheedy said no more.

'He's mad,' repeated the voice from the gallery.

'The court will be cleared if there are any more comments,' said the mayor. He paused and then said solemnly, 'I will now sum up.

Members of the jury, I advise that you pay very good heed to my words.'

He then went on to say that the crime was clearly committed by the defendant – the evidence was overwhelming. It had been witnessed by three people of good character; it had not been denied by the defendant, 'In fact he had the pie in his possession when he was overtaken by the constable.' Mara listened to him with growing apprehension.

He paused then and directed a sharp glance at the gallery. 'No medical evidence has been presented to the court about the defendant's state of mind. We have provided him with a translator, rather unusually in a city where no one, who does not speak English, has a right to be present, unless they are in the service of someone who will speak for them. We have listened carefully to what he has had to say and I am sure that the young translator rendered his words faithfully. I can find no denial, no new evidence in the prisoner's words. So, members of the jury, the decision is now yours. Do you wish to retire?'

There was a short whispered conversation between them and then the foreman spoke up. 'No, your worship,' he said.

Mara's heart beat fast. Was that a good sign or not?

'And have you all agreed your verdict?'

'Yes, your worship.' Fiona's hands were clenched and Hugh had gone very white. Mara signalled to him to return to his place beside her.

'We find the defendant guilty of stealing a pie to the worth of one shilling and sixpence,' said the leader of the jurymen. He hesitated, and looked at his fellow jurors. 'But we would . . .' he said and then stopped. The chief lawyer impatiently gestured to him and he sat down abruptly. The judge received his words impassively. He turned and began, once more, to root around in

d that man, though found guilty by the judge, being generally
d to possess no greater understanding than a beast, was granted
pardon by . . .'" she turned back to the book and read
ith a flourish.

urdus Tertius Rex.'"

Richard the Third,' translated Hugh.

we go across to London and talk to King Henry, eighth
name?' asked Moylan hopefully.

would be the right thing to do,' said Aidan, nodding a
approval of this proposal to extend their holiday
ely.

sn't the mayor the representative of the king?' asked Shane.
d us that didn't you, Brehon.'

's right, Shane,' said Fachtnan, seeing that Mara was busy
thoughts. 'I would think that the mayor could grant a
rdon to Sheedy if he wished to do so.'

is wonderful,' said Mara eventually. She paused and thought
her moment. 'We will do nothing today,' she said decid-
far, we have avoided causing any great annoyance to
ynch and this must continue. Hugh did well today – I
he would, and as usual I am glad to be proved right,'
t on, pretending not to notice the smiles exchanged
Aidan and Fiona. 'If we meet the mayor tonight during
se of the festivities then you will all greet him politely
due remembrance of his high office here in Galway.
w I will take this law book and go to see him at the
l. A royal pardon, that's what a man who is known as
can grant.'

ets of Galway that night were a wonderful sight. Every
of the tall tower houses and stately homes of the city
p with candles. Torches made from pitch tar, harvested
e trees, flared from iron holders in every corner of the
d there were musicians everywhere.

rent music to ours, but very pretty,' said Hugh approv-
using beside a man and listening intently to the song.
n an arm was flung around his shoulders and a strong
oice was singing the words, harmonizing with the lute
n a few minutes, the boys and Fiona, all trained to
e verse, had joined in also.

the box on the table beside him. This time he found what he
was looking for and donned a black cap.

'Sheedy O'Connor,' he said. 'You have broken the law of this
city state of Galway and have stolen goods to the value of more
than one shilling. I therefore recommend that you be hung by
the neck until you are dead.'

There was a dead silence in the court. Even the rowdy apprentices and the shop boys celebrating the beginning of the festival
were silent. All eyes were fixed on Sheedy who lifted his head
once more and then gave a friendly, childlike wave to Hugh.

It took all of Mara's self-control to stay silent. Valentine Blake
was looking appalled, and despite the fact that bailiffs were supposed
to say nothing, he was whispering urgently in his brother-in-law's
ear. Even the senior lawyer, Thomas Lynch, looked at the mayor
as one who could change the sentence that had been delivered.

From the gallery an ugly murmur had begun. The same brave
voice called out for the third time, 'The man is mad.' And the chant
was taken up by other voices. 'Mad, he's mad,' said the voices.

'He should be sent to the good nuns on Nuns' Island,' called
a woman's voice.

Then the mayor stood up. He waited calmly until the voices
stopped and the wave of muttering subsided, and then he spoke.

'The sentence is ratified,' he said. 'It will take place in one
week's time on Gallows' Green outside the eastern gate.'

With deadly accuracy an egg hit him right in the middle of
the face and then the uproar began. Cabbage stalks, filthy pieces
of mud-soaked linen, a piece of an old shoe were flung at him.
The mayor stood firm, thin lips pressed together, cold grey eyes
unwavering.

'Constable, clear the gallery,' roared the senior lawyer, but
already, appalled at what they had done, the crowd had begun to
tumble out on to the street.

'Come,' said Mara to her scholars. 'There is no more that we
can do here today. But rest assured, I will not let this matter lie.
We have one week, and with God's help we can achieve much
in a week. That man will not get away with this.'

Six

Stat. Hiberniae. 14 Hen. III.
(Blackstone's Commentaries *continued*)

And yet, even in the reign of queen Elizabeth, the wild natives still kept and preserved their Brehon law; which is described to have been 'a rule of right, unwritten, but delivered by tradition from one to another, in which oftentimes there appeared great shew of equity in determining the right between parties, but in many things repugnant quite both to God's law and man's.' The latter part of which character is alone allowed it under Edward the first and his grandson.

Mara borrowed four books from Lawyer Bodkin's scanty library and she and her scholars spent the afternoon going through them in a small back parlour which Jane Bodkin made available to her, placing on the large table a tray of quills and ink jars, as well as refreshing drinks and small cakes, and giving orders for a large bucket of coal to be brought up before withdrawing respectfully. There was no doubt that the good manners of the scholars, well schooled by Mara, had made a big impression on Jane and there probably would be little difficulty if they prolonged their stay. Indeed, she had already cordially issued an invitation and her brother had echoed it.

However, was there anything they could do for poor Sheedy?

The scholars were perusing the books in pairs, pausing from time to time to make a note. No one spoke and even Aidan curbed his sense of fun. The scene this morning had appalled them all.

'A seven-year-old can be brought before the court and sentenced to whatsoever punishment fits the crime,' said Shane in tones of awed disbelief.

'Unless he be a clergyman,' said Aidan, who was sharing a book with him. He stared at the words in puzzlement. 'A clergyman is a priest, isn't he? How can a seven-year-old be a priest?'

'I think it just means able to read or write – attending a clerical school,' said Mara.

'So if a clergyman, even if he is a ful[l] a murder, he is just branded on the t[ ] amazement. 'No fine or anything!'

'I think that was a law brought in by H[ ] it, Brehon?' said Moylan. 'I remember r[ ] it. Wait a minute! Here it is. He was fo[ ] bishop Thomas Becket.'

'And now it's Henry the Eighth,' said H[ ] a cake. 'Wish I had known about tha[ ] pretended that Sheedy could read.'

'Not in a court of law; no one shou[ ] law,' said Mara sharply, and then she loo[ ] and said earnestly, 'Hugh, you did all t[ ] of you. And look how the ordinary peop[ ] By giving Sheedy's words, simply and [ ] anyone of sense that the man was mad. [ ] were convinced by your words. Do yo[ ] cried out the truth? The man is mad, t[ ]

'Funny the way they number their ki[ ] Eight Henrys so far, isn't it?' observed A[ ] attention from Hugh who looked close[ ]

'I knew a man once who did that w[ ] his first cow Buttercup and all her daugh[ ] were Buttercup the First, Buttercup the [ ] Mara cheerfully. 'Have you found anyth[ ]

'Just something from the Ancient Gree[ ] a neat note and looking at her hopefull[ ]

'I'm afraid—' began Mara but then Fi[ ]

'I've found something – wait, let me [ ] I think that is right.' She looked with a [ ] fellow scholars.

'This is dated 1484 in the reign of R[ ] three of them, then,' she said with a qui[ ]

'That's less than thirty years ago,' said [ ]

'And Richard the Third was the king [ ] to Galway and all those valuable right[ ] prisage to be at the disposal of the ma[ ] people of Galway should think very high[ ]

'That's even better then,' said Fiona. [ ] with excitement and there was a tremor [ ]

'Come with me, all of you. I'll show you the city,' said Walter Lynch, flashing his irresistible smile at Mara, and then turning to the musician, he said, 'You come, too, good fellow, here's something for you. Let's go to the Brownes' place. I want to serenade my cousin.' Something that flashed like gold was slipped into the man's hand and Mara saw his eyes widen at young Walter Lynch's generosity.

The tower house belonging to the Browne family was near to St Nicholas's Church. Walter arranged his singers and the lute player on either side of the steep steps and then waited expectantly. First came Philip Browne, his son David and his Spanish wife Isabelle. The high sides of the stone balustrade hid the musicians and they did not look down, but came straight across to Mara, inviting her to accompany them to the service at St Nicholas's Church.

'In a moment,' said Mara, indicating the young people across the road. 'I must tell Fachtnan where I am going and leave him in charge of the other scholars.'

'They will be quite safe,' assured Isabelle. 'The mayor pays the constables a double wage tonight to make sure that all is well within the town.'

'Any rowdy young people usually go outside the city walls, to The Green or down to the meadows by the sea; that's right, David, isn't it?' Philip Browne dug his son in the ribs.

'Not me, sir,' said David. 'I'm supposed to look for a wife tonight, or so my father bids me,' he confided in Mara, lowering his voice to a mock whisper. 'The trouble is she has to be wealthy as I am not a very good merchant, not like my Spanish cousins.' He laughed heartily and Mara suspected that he was not that poor. He was certainly very richly dressed.

'Ah, here they come, the pair of them!' said Philip as, above the laughter and the noise, he heard the sound of his front door opening. He and his wife turned to face their house and at that moment the lute player strummed a few notes and began to sing, accompanied by the other young people. Walter Lynch swept off his hat and perched on top of the stone balustrade, singing lustily:

'Greensleeves was all my joy;
Greensleeves was my delight;

Greensleeves was my heart of gold;
And who but my lady Greensleeves.'

But then his voice faltered. He got down from his perch and stood rather miserably at the bottom of the steps.

Catarina was not alone. Her arm was tucked into the arm of her handsome and very rich cousin, Carlos Gomez. For a moment Mara thought Walter would turn and disappear into the crowd, or perhaps rejoin her scholars, but Catarina was too quick for him.

'Walter!' she cried. 'How lovely! Did you arrange that? And how did you know that I was going to wear my green gown? You've been bribing my maid, haven't you?'

And he probably had, thought Mara with amusement. Catarina wore a Spanish style of gown with the bodice and skirt fashioned from pale green silk, shot with silver, and the sleeves were made from brilliantly moss-green velvet. Her fur cloak was pulled well back in order to display the dress and it hung in graceful folds down her back from her shoulders.

'Oh do get them to sing it again,' called Catarina. She was enjoying the picture she made as she stood there with her arm tucked into that of her Spanish suitor, while her childhood sweetheart stood humbly at the bottom of the steps. A crowd had gathered as if a play were about to be performed.

'Carlos brought her that cloak as a gift from Spain,' confided Isabelle. 'It's made from the finest miniver. She's a lucky girl.' Her eyes were thoughtful as they looked across the street and saw what a little tableau of opulence the girl and her wealthy cousin made, standing there together in front of the ornate doorway, its two marble pillars framing the pair and the studded oak door forming a background to them.

And then the song finished. Catarina, still keeping a firm hold on to her cousin, came down the steps and tucked her other arm into Walter's. As they went down the narrow pavement the crowds stepped on to the street to allow them to pass.

Well, thought Mara, to herself, I can foresee this ending in trouble.

'Mara!' called a merry voice. 'My lady judge! I've been searching for you. Lawyer Bodkin told me you had just left. Have you forgotten that you promised to come with me to visit my favourite pie shop?'

'How could I!' exclaimed Mara. She would be delighted to go with Margaret, who was chatty and amusing, whereas the Browne family were a little dull – and a pie shop sounded to be more fun than a church. 'Just let me have a word with my scholars first.'

She crossed the street, conscious of the fact that Margaret's greetings to the Browne family were quite subdued. Walter's doting mother did not like her son's place beside the beautiful Catarina to have to be shared with Carlos Gomez.

'And Fiona, you must stay with the boys at all times. There will be lots of drinking and stupid behaviour going on,' she finished, conscious of her responsibility towards a pretty girl like Fiona.

'Of course,' said Fiona virtuously. She made herself as tall as someone as tiny as she was could possibly manage and flirtatiously took Moylan's arm, and Fachtnan's also, gazing adoringly from one to the other and vigorously fluttering her eyelashes.

'You're not big enough,' said Aidan, surveying her critically. 'You just look silly down there between the two of them. And, to be very honest,' he added, 'you're not as beautiful as Catarina, anyway.'

'Just you wait until you next need help with a Latin translation!' said Fiona, narrowing her eyes menacingly at him while Fachtnan glanced down at her, smiling lovingly. He looked away, flushing slightly when he saw that he was observed and Mara sighed.

Life was difficult for young people, she thought. Handsome young Walter was in love with Catarina but, she guessed, Catarina was more interested in Carlos Gomez; Fachtnan was in love with Fiona who had just a comradely affection for him. And back in the Burren waited Nuala, the young physician who adored Fachtnan, without any hope, now, of his returning her feelings.

What a tangle, she thought, as she handed over some silver coins to Fachtnan and crossed back to join Margaret and make her apologies to the Browne couple.

'Little minx,' said Margaret angrily as they went down Gate Street together.

'Who, Fiona?'

'No, of course not, she's sweet and just having fun. It's Catarina. She has an eye to the whole of the Gomez fortune instead of

being content with a slice of it. Mark my words; she'll throw
over my Walter if she gets a chance to have Carlos.'
    'Are the family of Carlos so rich, though?' asked Mara.
    'My dear! Immensely! You have no idea! Such a fortune!'
    'Well, Walter's very young,' said Mara consolingly. 'He'll find
another girl. He's a handsome lad. My Fiona was eyeing him
yesterday before Catarina came on the scene.'
    Margaret shook her head. 'Walter is a boy whose feelings go
very deep. He's such a sensitive boy. I think it will break his heart.
It's not the fortune that Catarina will bring; I don't think that he
cares tuppence for that. Though, to be honest,' she added, 'I'm
pleased about the fortune because the prospect of it stops my
husband nagging at the boy to make something of himself; to set
himself up as a merchant even if he doesn't like the fish or the
coal business. James gets very disappointed and displeased with poor
Walter and I'm the one that has to keep the peace between them.'
    Not an easy father, perhaps, to disappoint and displease, thought
Mara, but she kept her thoughts to herself, and questioned
Margaret about the pie shop.
    'It's just down near the inlet from the sea on Bridge Gate
Street. It's a very respectable place, I can assure you, owned by
one of the Blakes – a man called William Blake – and the Blakes
are always respectable.' She laughed merrily at the thought of that
and then said, with an anxious glance at Mara, 'You're not worried
about going to a pie shop unescorted, are you? I can assure you
it's quite safe. My husband has paid for extra constables to be on
duty tonight and he himself walks the streets continually on an
evening like this. It's very important to him that Galway is a
well-run city. He won't tolerate any rowdy behaviour within the
walls.'
    'Marvellously well-kept streets,' said Mara politely, surveying
the clean, well-brushed pavements, and the street with its kennel
running freely down the centre. Compared to the country lanes
that she was used to it was smelly, but three thousand people
were a lot to be herded up together in such a small space. A bit
like this new practice of keeping pigs in a pig sty rather than
allowing them to roam through woodland, she thought, and
listened politely to the details of how much money James Lynch
spent on maintaining the streets.
    'This is why he's been elected year after year,' said Margaret,

'Go ahead and find us a table at Blake's pie shop,' said Margaret, while Mara reflected on the warm-hearted charm of the Blake family. Valentine had spoken lightly of his baby son, but it was obvious that the child was deeply loved. Why on earth had Margaret married a cold man like James Lynch? As they had passed through the junction between Bridge Street and Market Street she had glimpsed his tall, spare figure making its way down the pavement, looking neither to right nor to left – not even acknowledging the salutes of those who had drawn back in order to allow him to pass.

'Valentine adores that little Jonathon,' confided Margaret as they made their way slowly down the street, pausing to greet almost every second person. 'Of course, like myself, he had a string of girls in his first marriage. You should have seen him when the little fellow was born. You won't believe this, but he was crying with joy!'

Valentine had secured a table by the time they arrived. To Mara's surprise the tables were not inside the pie shop, but arranged around several charcoal braziers in a small, walled yard beside the shop. Their table was in a prime position with its back to one brazier and another straight in front of them. Large square blocks of limestone were heating under each brazier and serving boys, their hands well protected with wads of sacking, placed them at the feet of the customers. The walls were high enough to keep in the heat and the starry sky above made a magnificent ceiling.

Valentine was not alone. Beside him was Walter; a rather silent Walter who was drinking heavily, slopping wine from a jug into a large goblet. There were two empty wine jugs already on the table and Mara saw his mother's eyes go straight to them while she embraced her son with a fierce hug.

He smiled at that and was not too drunk to rise politely and greet Mara, but he was unsteady on his feet.

'You need something to eat,' said Margaret, sending an apprehensive glance towards the street. 'Don't let your father see you like that.'

'I've ordered two pies,' said Valentine reassuringly. He sniffed at the almost emptied jug. 'Portuguese wine!' he exclaimed. 'You'll have a sore head in the morning, young man, if you drink any more of this stuff,' he said warningly. 'That's six times stronger than ordinary wine!'

with wifely pride. 'People know that he's not like some of tl
other mayors.' She lowered her voice. 'You should see the Athy
tower house. Richard Athy was mayor for three years before Jam(
was elected. He was in a small way before he had a few years a
mayor, and now he's importing horses from Spain and sellinį
them all over Ireland.' She gave a hasty look around and hisse(
in Mara's ear. 'Not a penny spent on the streets and the wall!
during that time, but a fine new house and business built foı
himself.'

Mara nodded and murmured some remark about admiring the
walls during her walk yesterday to The Green. She had also,
during that walk, seen the splendid Athy tower house which was
probably the tallest house in Galway and was set inside some
magnificent-looking gardens. Although she wasn't here to take
sides but, if possible, to rescue her fellow countryman, she encouraged Margaret to go on talking about her husband. The more
she could understand James Lynch the easier it might be to
successfully sue for a 'royal pardon' on behalf of poor insane
Sheedy. A man who wanted to be just, wanted to do the right
thing, she mused. It might be possible to talk to him privately
– perhaps he might issue that royal pardon to celebrate some feast
or other, or something like that. He would need some such face-
saving excuse. It would be out of character for him to admit that
he had made a mistake by passing that death sentence. She would
stay a few extra days, she decided. The Bodkins had seemed
genuine when they issued the invitation. The scholars were
enjoying themselves and it was good for them to see a different
mode of life and to realize the importance of safeguarding the
ancient Brehon law of their forebears.

'There's Valentine,' exclaimed Margaret. 'How now, Brother,
what have you done with your lady wife?'

'Little Jonathon isn't well and she didn't want to leave him
said Valentine. He was well dressed in a black velvet padde
doublet, embroidered with gold and matched with black hos
The flamboyant garments enhanced his dark good looks. 'O
it's nothing!' he continued hastily. 'Not even a fever – just sn
fling and feeling sorry for himself, poor little fellow. I hate to
him like that. Cecily told me to go out as I was fussing too mʲ
over him and making him feel worse. Good evening, Brehc
you see that I remembered your title!'

'I'm not a child,' said Walter angrily. 'As for my father; I don't care that much for him.' He snapped his fingers contemptuously in the air and then hiccupped abruptly.

'Here comes the pie,' said Margaret, gazing anxiously at her beloved boy.

Easy to see what had happened, thought Mara. The older and more experienced Carlos had probably got tired of the threesome – perhaps taunted young Walter – and then if Catarina had laughed, well, that would have been enough for a sensitive boy. He would have taken himself off and sought comfort in wine. Mara wished that her scholars had been with her. Fachtnan would have been good with Walter – although they were much of an age, Fachtnan was mature and sensitive in his dealings with the young.

'Oh, what a lovely pie!' she exclaimed aloud when the food arrived. Walter would be better without the attention of three adults focused on him so Mara spent the next few minutes admiring the pie and asking for details of its filling.

It was a large, round pie, placed on an even larger round plate. The swirling patterns of the plate – Spanish, guessed Mara – were echoed in the curved slices of apple and pear which crowned the pie, radiating out from the centre until they touched the crisp, golden pastry shell. Valentine cut it into large slices and ladled one carefully on to Mara's plate. She tasted it appreciatively.

'Delicious,' she said. 'What on earth is in it? There are so many flavours.'

'Goods from all over the world,' said Valentine gaily, while Margaret popped a square from her own slice into Walter's mouth. 'There's cheese from the town of Brie in France, oranges from Spain and wine from Portugal, saffron and ginger from the east, pheasant from England.' He spun out the list of ingredients to an almost impossible length, while Margaret tried to feed a bit more pie into Walter and Mara savoured the rounded full-bodied taste from the jug of wine that Valentine had ordered.

'And salt from Valentine Blake,' said Margaret, but at that moment, Walter snatched the jug of strong Portuguese wine from the table, upended it over his mouth, put it back and staggered off.

'Oh dear, oh dear, I do hope that James will not see him like that,' said Margaret with a sigh.

'Leave him alone,' said Valentine. 'Enjoy your pie while it's hot, and your wine, of course. Every young man gets drunk from time to time.'

'I'm just afraid that he will meet them again and that he and Carlos will come to blows,' said Margaret.

'Probably the best thing that could happen, you know. Carlos Gomez is not a bad fellow. Responsible sort of man, too. He handled that affair of the captain of his father's ship, that Alfonso Mercandez, very well.' He turned to Mara and continued in a whisper. 'Carlos found that Alfonso Mercandez has been stealing from his father for years – getting merchants in Galway to pay high prices for the goods that he carried and then subtracting a large chunk before he brought the money back. Of course, the Gomez family are very rich but no one likes to be cheated. Carlos mentioned it to him – he lied and pretended that he knew nothing – but as young Gomez said to me, he decided that it would be best to leave the matter until they returned to Spain and he had all his father's account books. In the meantime, of course, he has been going around discreetly questioning people like your friend Lawyer Bodkin about the actual prices they paid for horses and other goods.'

'I don't care how clever and discreet he is,' said Margaret unhappily. 'I don't want my Walter getting into a fight with him – not tonight of all nights. James would never forgive him, or me, either, if his own son was one to break the peace.'

'I'll go and search for him and put his head under the nearest pump once I've finished my pie,' promised Valentine. 'You take our visitor to see the apprentices' mystery play in the churchyard and I'll scour the streets. Once I have him sobered up a little I'll join you there.'

Jane Bodkin was already in the churchyard waiting for the play to begin, though she explained that her brother was not too keen on plays and found them rather tedious. As they had promised, a bench was reserved for their visitors and a few minutes after Mara arrived, Fachtnan appeared. As they made their way forward, Mara counted heads and was relieved to see that all six were present. Their cheeks were flushed by the excitement, but Fachtnan assured her that they had had no more than a goblet of hot, spiced wine flavoured with the oranges from Spain and Portugal whose exotic taste and smell seemed to be everywhere on these Shrove ceremonies.

'It's the story of the three kings visiting the child Jesus,' explained Jane, leaning across so that the younger boys could hear her. 'The goldsmith's and silversmith's apprentices take the part of the kings. Master Tanner is Herod and his apprentices are the soldiers. One of the innkeepers in Galway always plays the innkeeper part, directing the strangers to the stable, and then the wool merchants' apprentices play the part of the shepherds.'

Philip and Isabelle Browne were sitting just opposite to them. Margaret had joined her husband in the front row, but Mara could see that she continually looked over her shoulder as though waiting to see Walter appear.

The Brownes, also, were looking around and seemed relieved when Catarina appeared. She was alone, though. Either Carlos had decided that he was not interested in the play, or else Valentine Browne had perhaps taken the two young men off to sober up and perhaps even to fight off their differences.

Whatever had happened, neither Carlos Gomez nor Walter Lynch had appeared by the time that the play had finished.

Seven

Annals of Clonmacnoise
(13th century)

The Brehons of Ireland are divided into several clans and families as the McKiegans, O'Davorans, O'Brisleans, McTholies and Mac Clancies. Every kingdom has his peculiar Brehon dwelling within it, that has the power to decide the cases of that country and to maintain their controversies against their neighbour-countries, for which service they hold lands of the lord of the kingdom where they dwell.

'Sleep in tomorrow morning – we won't breakfast until about ten o'clock,' were Jane Bodkin's last words to her guests on returning from the play that night. 'Henry's not home yet,' she had said slightly disapprovingly, noting the candle left on the table near the hall door after the others had taken theirs. 'I suppose he is talking with friends in one of the inns; the men often don't bother going to see the play – of course, it's the same play every year,' she had added as she took her own candle and made sure that her guests had everything they required.

Mara, however, had her own internal clock that woke her at seven in the morning whether winter or summer. She decided to get up and rekindle her coal fire herself. The ewer of water on the pot stand was still faintly warm and once the flames began to leap up it soon heated enough to make washing pleasant.

Mara's mind was busy with thoughts of James Lynch. What was the best way to approach him, she wondered? Would it be a good idea to take her scholars, or to go privately by herself? The latter, she decided. From what she had seen of him so far he was a self-contained, private person. He had taken no part in the merriment of the night before, had not even gone to see the play, but had ceaselessly patrolled the streets. Her last glimpse of him had been at the market place where his icy voice had penetrated the drunken laughter of some young men and had caused them to move swiftly away, heading towards the town gate

– no doubt planning to carry on drinking in The Green, or somewhere else well outside the city walls.

Logic, precedents; that would be the way to approach this man, she decided. He had his virtues; Mara believed what Margaret had said about her husband's probity – this was a well-maintained city. When she had walked around with Henry Bodkin she had noticed that there were men at work on the walls, men at work on the pavements, on the roads and also on the ornate gardens outside the city where the trees were neatly pruned and the paths well swept.

A man like James Lynch would not be moved by a plea for mercy, but he might be influenced by a well-reasoned argument which was based on the laws that he upheld and was backed by a judgement given by Richard III, that English king, who had founded the prosperity of the city of Galway. The man, judge though he professed to be, was quite ignorant of the law which he was sanctioned to uphold, but would he be willing to learn from an outsider?

Mara took a quill, ink horn and some vellum from one of her satchels, lit a second candle and sat down at the small table and opened one of Henry's law books. After half an hour she had a page of notes which she gazed at with satisfaction. By herself, she decided. This was a man who would not like witnesses to his change of mind.

And if she succeeded then she would return to the Burren on the following morning. She was lonely for the fresh air, the open spaces and the swirling limestone mountains. Hopefully they would take Sheedy with them. Her son-in-law, Oisín, kept a string of pack ponies, one of which she could, she was sure, even in his absence, borrow in order to take the poor old fellow back to his own environment where the law would protect rather than accuse him.

By this time there was a cautious stirring on the stairs and when Mara went to the door she saw a maidservant emerge from Fiona's room with a bucket of fresh coals in her hand. She smiled at the girl and went in to find that Fiona, to her surprise, was not yawning in her bed, but already up with a wrapper around her and was standing at the window.

'Brehon, come and see. It's a holiday today; I'm sure of that. Someone was talking about that last night; being pleased about not having to get up for work. Today is Ash Wednesday, so everyone should be either in bed recovering or at church receiving the holy ashes, but the streets are full. The whole city seems to be in some sort of fuss about something,' she said with a puzzled expression. Mara crossed over to stand beside her scholar. Her own rooms faced the inlet from the sea, but Fiona's was full of the morning light and Lombard Street lay beneath her windows.

There was something odd about the crowd. Mara felt her own brows knit. If, indeed, this was a holiday, she would have expected to see people chatting, laughing, perhaps some yawning – a few with sore heads. But the people in the street below them huddled together in small groups, whispering, glancing over their shoulders, their eyes wide with shock. Sometimes a newcomer joined a group, was told some news and then a hand was clapped to a mouth in a gesture of horror.

Cautiously, Mara pushed open the casement window between the stone mullions – the diamond-shaped panes of glass were thick and full of bubbles. It was difficult to see properly through them.

Just as she did so a woman wearing an ornate purple hood had joined a group standing directly in front of Bodkin's tower house. Her voice floated clearly up in the still, frosty air.

'What are ye all—' she began her question in a loud, cheerful voice, but then one of the other women in the group seized her wrist and said something into her ear, then stood back to see the effect of her words.

'Whaat? Murdered?' shrieked the woman in the purple hood, and the others hushed her instantly. One of them glanced up, saw Mara at the window and they all moved rapidly down the street. Mara closed the window and looked at Fiona.

'Murder?' she queried.

Fiona nodded. 'That's what she said.' Her voice was airy and unconcerned. 'Let's hope that it was that mayor, James Lynch,' she said lightly. 'I'd have no sympathy for him. Poor old Sheedy. The jury were going to recommend mercy, but he shut them up. If they hang Sheedy, then, in my mind, James Lynch will be guilty of murder, and it's no good you talking about a conflict of laws, Brehon. Do you remember what Cicero said about all law being based on natural law, *lex naturalis*, and that the laws of men must be derived from the laws of God? Well, God would not condemn to death a poor old man whose wits are wandering for the theft of a pie.'

'I'm glad you know your Cicero so well, but while we are inside the city walls of Galway be careful to voice thoughts like that just to me. I hope that there was no talk about this matter when you were out last night.'

'Fachtnan shut Aidan up and we all took the hint,' said Fiona with a shrug. 'It would be rather exciting if the mayor were murdered, though, wouldn't it, Brehon?' she added as Mara went out of the room.

Mara went down the winding stone staircase with a smile. Fiona was irrepressible. Totally spoilt by her father; Robert MacBetha had cheerfully acknowledged when he had brought her to Mara's law school on the Burren that, 'You'll get more work out of her than I'm managing to do these days.' Robert and Mara were the same age and had worked side by side at her father's law school, competing with each other, neither allowing the other to gain too much of an advantage. Unfortunately there was no one to compete properly with Fiona, these days. If only she had come when Enda, Mara's star pupil, had been there. His family had money troubles and Enda had left the law school once he had gained the minimum law qualification and begun to practise as a lawyer in the kingdom of Thomond. Moylan was sharp and quick-witted but did not have Fiona's brains, and Fachtnan, though intelligent and hard-working, had great memory problems.

But then she forgot about Fiona as she went into the dining hall. Henry Bodkin and his sister Jane were there and judging by his cloak and the flush on his cheeks from the cold air, he had just come in from the street. Indeed, she had noticed an icy draught from an imperfectly closed front door as she came down the stairs.

Henry Bodkin had been speaking quietly, but Jane reacted just as the women in the street had done. She had gasped, clapped her hand to her mouth, opened her eyes very widely and had gulped out, 'Murdered!'

The word hung in the air for a moment and then the lawyer nodded; nodded slowly and with a heavy air of regret about him.

Mara hesitated at the door. This was, she reminded herself, none of her business. If it were back in the kingdom of the

Burren that this word had been uttered, she would immediately have had to get to work, going herself to see the body, summoning witnesses, gathering evidence with the aid of her young scholars, putting her brains to work and never ceasing her efforts until the killer was brought before the court beside the ancient dolmen of Poulnabrone.

However, a little curiosity was permissible, she decided, and now was the time to ask before the scholars arrived downstairs.

'You seem worried,' she ventured, looking from one to the other.

Jane Bodkin turned a shocked face towards her. Her large, short-sighted eyes filled with tears.

'His poor mother,' she gulped and went out of the room, pulling out a linen handkerchief from the large pocket that hung from her waist.

Mara turned enquiring eyes on her host. *Poor mother* – not *poor wife*, nor, *poor children* . . .

'There's been a murder,' he said, 'or rather –' he corrected himself – 'a killing. A terrible ending to last night's festivities!' He broke off as loud shouts came from outside the half-closed front door.

'Excuse me,' he said and made rapidly for the front door. Mara followed him, snatching her own cloak from the row of hooks in the entrance hall. As she did so, there was a clatter of feet on the stairs and the six scholars, led by Fiona came running down into the hallway. They too would have been watching from the window and they instantly took their own cloaks, and followed her out into the street.

Lombard Street was now almost empty. The few people who were still there were hurrying towards Gaol Street. There was a noise in the distance, a rhythmic thudding, something that Mara could not identify instantly. At first she thought it might be horses, but this sound was more muted. And then there was another sound that rose, high and clear, above the mutters from the crowd.

'Left turn!' yelled a voice and then, 'Eyes right!'

'Soldiers!' breathed Moylan. He and Aidan pushed in front of Mara and began to make their way through the crowd. Mara followed in their footsteps, feeling slightly apologetic as she saw people on the pavement step out into the road in order to allow them to pass.

By the time that they reached Gaol Street itself, the crowd was huge. A few constables were doing their best to confine the people to the pavement, but they kept spilling back out again on to the road. Mara hesitated, wondering whether she should call the boys back. But once again, the strangeness of their clothes caused people to turn around and stare and this allowed the two boys to struggle to the front and the others to follow them. And then they could see everything.

The soldiers were in two groups, very smart in white coats with a green stripe on the sleeves. They marched precisely and rhythmically in front of one man, a man not in uniform, but wearing the sweeping fur-trimmed gown of office with a gold chain around his neck and a flat black cap on his head. The Mayor of Galway, James Lynch, had just come from his house on the corner of two streets. He held his head high and looked neither to right nor left, but kept his eyes fixed straight in front of them and his feet moving to the pace of the soldiers.

And behind him came four soldiers dragging a wretched creature, bareheaded and without a cloak, his hose soaked in mud and bearing some ominous dark red stains across what had once been a white shirt, his matted hair fell in dank locks across his face, but that was not enough to hide his identity from the crowd and a loud gasp went up.

And a name was sent from mouth to mouth.

The prisoner was Walter Lynch, only son of the lord mayor of the city of Galway.

For a moment, Mara thought that there must be some mistake. The change between this poor creature and the tall young man that she had seen yesterday was enormous. He had been so vibrant then, so full of life, gleaming like polished copper, she had thought at the time. Now the curly chestnut-coloured hair was dull and matted; the jaunty red cap with a kingfisher's feather stuck into it had been lost. The bright alert face was puffy and white and the red jerkin and crisp white shirt were smudged with bloodstains.

Mara watched in horror as the soldiers turned down towards the prison. A sharp command was given; the door was pulled open by the gaoler. He looked sleepy and unkempt, but even from a distance Mara could see how he straightened himself at the sight of the lord mayor and the troop of soldiers. She was too far away to hear what was said, though the crowd stood so still and soundless that the noise of seagulls overhead suddenly seemed almost unbearably intrusive.

The mayor appeared to be speaking, giving orders; looking straight at the gaoler and then at the sergeant-in-command. Never once did he look at the wretched face of his only son.

And then he stood back, waved an imperative arm and the boy was dragged into the prison. The sergeant and two men went with him and returned a few minutes later.

The troop turned and marched back, making a smart left turn when they reached Lombard Street.

'They'll leave him in there for a day or two, and then he'll be released,' said a voice from behind Mara. It was, she saw from the corner of her eye, the woman in the ornate purple hood. 'Stands to reason, doesn't it? The mayor's own son!'

'What happened?' asked Mara, turning around in a friendly fashion. 'We're strangers here,' she added apologetically.

'God bless you; so you are.' The woman beamed at her. 'I'm one of the Blakes, myself; one of the poor relations, you could say, but that's a nice boy and it was just one of those unfortunate things. I don't suppose that he meant to kill him, you know. Too much drink taken; that was the problem.'

'It was a fight, do you think?' asked Mara easily. She was beginning to guess.

'They're bringing the body to St Nicholas's Church,' said the woman, beginning to shove her way to the left in order to follow the soldiers into Lombard Street.

'We'll go in front, Mistress Blake, and make way for you,' said Moylan gallantly. 'Come on, Aidan.'

'Nice, well-mannered boys,' said her new friend. 'They were at The King's Head Inn last night – you know, Stephen Lynch's place. Everybody praised their behaviour and how they did not drink too much. I'm Mistress Athy, really,' she added. 'I married an Athy, but you know what they say, "once a Blake; always a Blake". Lord love you, the city is full of Blakes.'

'Well, I'm glad you think my boys are well behaved,' said Mara, doing her best to lead back to the subject of young Walter Lynch. 'Of course, like all boys, they are better behaved if they don't drink too much . . .'

'Well, you're right about that; that's just it; that's what happened last night – too much to drink. She's a cousin of mine, Margaret, the lad's mother, but she gave him too much money. Ruined, spoilt, he was. Couldn't deny him anything!' She raised her voice. 'Into Market Street, lads, that's where they are bringing the body.'

There was no need for her to say that. The troops had already marched into Market Street and the crowds had followed. At a word from the sergeant, the soldiers formed two lines on the upper part of the street, leaving a narrow passageway between them and pushing back the crowd against the doorways opposite to the church. At the gate to the church, the bishop stood, his vestments fluttering in the slight breeze, and after a moment's hesitation the mayor crossed over and stood beside him.

'Here it comes,' hissed Mistress Athy. Her ears were sharp and had caught the first sound of marching feet. A second later that was drowned out as the church bell began to toll. Mara counted the strokes and saw that everyone around almost held their breath as they did likewise. Some used fingers to help them in the sum, but all came to the same conclusion.

'Twenty years old, God have mercy on his soul!' sighed Mistress Athy. 'They found him lying dead on the ground just outside the windmill above Lough Atalia, you know. And –' she hesitated, looked around, and then continued in a sibilant whisper – 'they do say that young Walter Lynch was only a few yards away, lying dead drunk on some sacks inside the windmill.'

And Walter had been smeared with blood, thought Mara. What an end to that night of merriment.

A murmur rose up from the crowd. A new detachment of soldiers had joined the first group – all but four of them, who marched at the back of the regiment.

And this four carried a plain stretcher – no coffin.

The body lay completely exposed on the stretcher. There was no covering over the face that was still contorted in its death agony, and no covering over the body – just the clothes in which he had died, soaked in blood and bearing traces of dark mud.

And from the centre of the chest protruded a dagger.

The blade was buried deep, but the ebony and embossed silver of its hilt gleamed in the pale sunshine of this February morning.

Mara drew in a deep breath and from all around her she heard the echoing of its sound as a sigh ran though the crowd. It was

Walter Lynch's dagger and it was buried deep in the chest of the Spanish boy, Carlos Gomez.

'The captain of the Gomez ship wants to take him straight back to Spain,' whispered Mistress Athy. 'The carpenters and smiths are hard at work making a coffin lined with lead so that the body can be taken away on the evening's tide.'

The body was followed by the captain of the ship, some of the sailors and by four other mourners. Isabelle Browne, the dead boy's aunt, was almost prostrated by grief, clinging to her husband Philip's arm and weeping profusely, her dark-skinned face red and blotched with tears. Behind them came their children Catarina and David.

Catarina, unlike her mother, was not weeping. She was dressed in deepest black – the robe hung loosely on her – probably borrowed from her mother – but Catarina wore it with dignity, her shoulders square and her head held high. Her black hair was covered by a black lace Spanish veil and she had drawn one edge down over her forehead and eyes. She walked steadily, the tips of her fingers just touching her brother David's arm. She did not look to right or left until she came to a standstill behind her parents as the bishop offered his condolences to the relations of the slain boy.

It was only after Philip and Isabelle had moved forward to follow the body into the church that she spoke. She dropped her hand from her brother's sleeve and turned to face the two men, the bishop, and the lord mayor who had stood stony-faced, erect and silent during the condolences.

'If there is any justice in this city of Galway, then the man who did this should be hanged,' she said, her voice ringing against the stone building beyond and her words crystal clear to the shocked crowd.

A murmur rose up as she mounted the steps to the church. Was it a murmur of sympathy, of understanding, of pity for a beautiful young girl?

Or was it, wondered Mara, the forerunner of a blood lust which has gripped crowds from time immemorial?

Eight

Crích Gablach
(Ranks in Society)

All cases of killing must be thoroughly investigated by the Brehon. Only when those investigations are complete may the trial be held.

In the case of a murder, if the fine administered by a qualified judge is not paid within a period of two months by the guilty person or by the clan then the victim's kinsmen are permitted to carry out a blood-feud to exact vengeance on behalf of the dead man.

The church service – the prayers for the dead – had just finished when James Lynch left his place beside the pulpit. He had stood there very quietly for the whole service, never moving, never hanging his head or averting his gaze.

Now, without a word to the bishop, he climbed the pulpit steps and faced the congregation in the packed church. When he spoke his voice was low, though pitched to reach the back of the church and showed no emotion

'In view of the wish expressed by the relations, friends and servants of the dead man to send the body back to the unfortunate parents in Spain as soon as possible; a journey which will take at least two weeks and perhaps longer if winds and tides are not favourable,' he said in an even, remote tone of voice, and paused slightly before resuming. 'Bearing in mind all of these considerations I give notice here that the trial of the man accused of this murder will take place today at twelve noon. The proclamation will be cried at all street corners and I hereby order any witnesses with relevant testimony to present themselves here at that hour.' He paused and then said drily, 'As many of the public as can be accommodated will be admitted to the trial and in order that this may be possible and that justice may be seen to be done, my lord bishop has given permission for the trial to be held here in the church of St Nicholas of Myra.'

There was a sudden movement; a word bitten back, a hand

upraised and a man stepped from behind the holy water stoop. For a moment Mara hardly recognized him and then saw that it was Valentine Blake. The smile, the carefree air, the easy good-natured pleasant face that he normally presented to the world was gone. This man was blazing with anger.

'Your worship,' he called. 'Is it fair to rush the course of justice in order to accommodate a man who wants to sail today? The young visitor from Spain, so unfortunately slain last night, can and should be buried here in Galway, where his grave will be respectfully tended and his parents welcomed to our city if they wish to visit. In this way time can be given to the investigation into the killing.'

The silence was so intense after these words that it seemed as though the whole church held its breath and waited for the answer.

But there was none. James Lynch gave his bailiff one glance, then stepped down the steps to the pulpit and marched straight down the middle aisle of the large church and through the western door.

Slowly and hesitantly, one by one, some people came up, touching the stretcher reverently and then crossing themselves, muttering a prayer as they did so.

Mara followed them, slipping out into the aisle as unobtrusively as she could manage, while making a sign to the scholars to remain in their places.

It's none of my business, she told herself once more, but still she could not subdue her instinct to know all. The corpse, she thought, when she reached the top of the queue was a piteous sight, the front of the body soaked in blood and the back, as far as she could see, caked in mud and grass. No one had attempted to wash or to compose the dead young man. Even pieces of gravel still remained in the sticky blood at the back of his head.

When her turn came she reached out and touched the dead hand that was flung to one side of the stretcher. She kept her own hand in position for a moment while she uttered a Gaelic prayer in a penetrating murmur. Let the others in the queue think that holding a hand was a native Gaelic custom, she thought, as her mind registered the impressions. The face was set in contorted lines of pain. Carlos had been conscious of being stabbed. He had seen his killer, she thought, looking into the sightless eyes.

The hand was as stiff as a piece of stone. *Rigor mortis* had set in strongly despite the cold night. Carefully, she examined the dagger and the angle that it had entered the chest. Carlos Gomez had been dead for about twelve hours, she reckoned. The fingers were locked stiffly into position.

She had seen something else, also. The dead man's dagger was still neatly tucked into its hilt on his belt. Mara bent over the corpse, praying softly and making the sign of the cross over the dead man's chest. Adroitly and working from the shelter of her large, flowing sleeves, she managed to withdraw Carlos's dagger from the hilt. The steel shone clean and unmarked in the light of the candelabrum placed beside the body. Hastily she returned it and moved on and took her place in the returning queue. This was no drunken fight, she thought, that had resulted in the death of one of the protagonists. This, indeed, was murder.

But why had Carlos, a strong, fit-looking young man with a bold, resolute face, allowed someone to come up and stab him in the chest, right in front of his eyes, without making any effort to draw his own dagger?

Mara cast a quick look over her shoulder. The woman behind her in the queue was talking over her shoulder in sibilant whispers to a friend.

'Where was he found?' she was saying. Mara listened eagerly to the reply and nodded her head when she found that it had been on the shore of Lough Atalia.

'Just beside the windmill,' said another voice – 'just lying there above the water. The miller found them at dawn – the two of them. The Spaniard was as stiff as a poker and young Lynch was fast asleep.'

Strange to go to sleep after committing a murder, thought Mara. Why didn't he leave the place as soon as possible – put a distance between himself and the body? Still, perhaps Walter Lynch had collapsed from the effect of alcohol. Mara crossed herself and continued to follow the people making their way out of the church, giving a quick signal to the scholars to join her. She had found out what she wanted to know.

By the time they came out of the church town criers were already broadcasting the news at the street corner.

'Anyone with any knowledge of the whereabouts of the late Carlos Gomez or of Walter Lynch during the hours of nine in the evening and seven of this morning must go to the courthouse and give evidence.'

'Let's go back to the Bodkin house,' said Mara. Henry would not be at work today so it would be interesting to talk to him.

'We saw Walter a few times during the evening, but I'm not too sure about the time,' said Fachtnan hesitantly. 'He was pretty drunk; he could barely stand. The last time we talked with him was quite late. He came up to us when we were chatting to a man called Richard Athy and his family. There were young children there so I took him away. I wanted him to go home but he broke away from me. He seemed to want to be on his own so I let him go.'

'Then you must go and give your evidence at the courthouse,' said Mara instantly. She would find it easier to talk to Henry alone; he was a reserved man and would be wary of giving his opinion in front of sharp young ears. Quickly, she doled out some money to Fachtnan and told him that he could take the others to Blake's pie shop after they had given their evidence. The terrible news of the morning had meant that they had all missed breakfast and they were probably already quite hungry.

Henry was there when she arrived at the Bodkin tower house. She saw his tall thin form standing at the window of the parlour as she came up the steps and he, himself, came to open the door for her. He looked drawn and tired, she thought, as she followed him into the parlour, refusing all offers of food and drink and shutting the door firmly behind her.

'What will happen at court this afternoon?' she asked. 'Who will be the judge?'

'It has to be the sovereign, the mayor,' he said. 'Our system is the same as the city states of Venice or Verona where the duke is always the judge.'

'What happens if he is ill?'

'The case is postponed.'

'So he will sit in judgement of his own son. What will the charge be?'

Lawyer Bodkin hesitated for a moment and when he spoke he did not really answer her question. 'You are the second person that I opened that door to during the last half hour,' he said. 'The first was Valentine Blake. He asked me to act for his nephew; to be a defence lawyer in this case. Do you have such a thing in your law system?'

'We do,' said Mara. 'Anyone who is summoned to appear before a court of justice has a right to have a lawyer with him to argue his case.' She did not add that it had not happened in one of her courts for at least ten years. The people of the Burren were willing to accept her judgements and the punishments that she handed down.

But what if the punishment was not a fine, but a condemnation to death by hanging? Then the situation might be very different. She thought of the huge responsibility of condemning a man to die, and of no possibility of ever remedying a mistake. The memory of that body, covered in tar, and hanging from the gibbet near to the eastern gate of the city made her feel slightly sick. She looked at Henry Bodkin. What did he think of this matter, she wondered?

'Did you accept the office?' she asked.

'No,' said Lawyer Bodkin. He spoke slowly and with hesitation. 'No, I didn't. I suggested that he ask Lawyer Lynch. He's the boy's cousin.'

And was also the cousin of his powerful father, James Lynch, the sovereign prince of Galway, the equivalent of the mighty Duke of Venice of whose powers over life and death her father had spoken in awed terms when he had returned from his pilgrimage to Rome many years ago. Mara thought the words but did not utter them. Her host looked drawn and almost ill. She remembered Jane commenting on his late arrival home at the end of the Shrove festivities and wondered whether he had drunk too much. Or was it just a natural reaction to the terrible news of the morning.

'I felt that the whole thing was too hurried for me,' he continued after a minute. 'If I take on a case, I like to think about it, to uncover evidence if need be, to have conversations with my client. Apparently – I was not at the church myself – but Valentine Blake tells me that the trial has been fixed for twelve noon today.'

'Are you good friends – you and Valentine Blake?' asked Mara sympathetically, seeing the drawn face before her wince as he uttered the word 'trial'.

'Neighbours, rather, and we often share the hire of a ship. If I bring horses from Portugal, his salt acts as ballast in the hold and gives more room for the animals, or at least that's how it

used to be before these present problems in Portugal.' He had
shrugged at the idea of being a friend, but his eyes showed pain.

'What will the verdict be? What can the verdict be?' Mara
amended her words as he shrugged slightly at her first
question.

'Guilty, or not guilty.' After a minute, he added, 'I haven't
known any other – and it is normally guilty.'

'But there can be a recommendation for mercy?'

'There has to be, of course!' Lawyer Bodkin seemed pleased
that she had brought up that possibility, though surely that should
have occurred to him before since they had discussed this provision when talking about the case of Sheedy. She had even shown
him the case from the time of Richard III.

'I haven't known it; but, of course, that would be the way to
go about it.' He must have sensed her surprise because he seemed
to feel that he had to explain why he had not mentioned this
possibility, citing his tiredness and his shock at the news
as excuses, and then finished up by saying, 'I might just stroll
down to see Thomas Lynch and put that idea in his head.'

Mara declined a half-hearted invitation to go with him on the
grounds of having some shopping to do before their return
tomorrow. She thought she would see how her scholars were
getting on. There were only about ten streets in the city of
Galway; she would surely meet them sooner or later.

'I'm sorry that Jane will not be able to go with you; she . . .
she is unwell. This terrible news has upset her badly.'

Mara was secretly relieved that there was no sign of her hostess.
The last thing she wanted was to go around the streets of Galway
with Jane twittering in her ear. However, she did wonder at this
excessive sensibility. The women on the streets and in the church
this morning were shocked; shocked but not prostrated. Jane had
commented severely on how Walter was spoiled by his mother
and had not expressed any interest in young Carlos Gomez. Why
was she so upset that she had to take to her bed? Jane Bodkin
was not the sort of woman who would lightly neglect her guests.

There was an enormous queue stretching right down Courthouse
Lane. Mara walked the length of it, people drawing back to allow
her to pass and eyeing her with curiosity. The news of the lady
judge appeared to have spread through the whole city and everyone
seemed to think that she was going into the courthouse. Even

those who were already wedged into the doorway stood back to allow her to pass through.

Mara declined their courtesy with a shake of the head and explained that she was looking for her scholars.

'They've already come out, Mistress,' said one man. 'Look, the young fellow with the red hair and the other dark lad – they're over there at the fish market.'

Shane had been talking to a fishmonger, but had now joined Hugh who was conversing earnestly with a dark-skinned man wearing a pair of gold earrings and a flamboyant red cap. It was the Spaniard she had seen earlier following the body of Carlos to the church – probably the captain of the ship. A well-off man, this captain of the ship – the gold in those earrings was considerable and gold rings flashed from his fingers as he waved his hands in talk. This man was unlikely to be an ordinary sailor; he carried his wealth on his person, perhaps, but even so he was wealthy. Perhaps, like some sea captains, he had a share in the enterprises of his masters.

Hugh was certainly growing in confidence on this visit to Galway. There had been a time when Mara had wondered whether she should break the news to his father, an ambitious silversmith, that Hugh was unlikely to pass the difficult examination to be a Brehon, but now she was glad that she had waited. The boy was improving so much as his confidence grew and she would keep him. Even if, like Fachtnan, he needed an extra year, then that was of no importance. He would make a good lawyer and possibly even a Brehon. He, more than Shane, who had always been clever and quick-witted, seemed to be leading this conversation with the ship's captain, asking questions, obviously stumbling over their translation, but carrying it all with such an air of good-humoured charm that the man was friendly and responsive. He, in his turn, was laughing and apologizing for his bad English.

Mara turned away hurriedly and melted back into the market-goers. She would hear about it later and in the meantime it would be a mistake to interrupt this conversation. She wandered back up through the streets. There was little air of festivity this morning. There seemed to be only one subject of conversation and that was the slaying of Carlos Gomez. There was a little knot of people at the four crossroads where Little Gate Street and Great Gate Street joined on to Skinner's Street and High Middle Street.

'He was drunk,' said one woman. 'People do terrible things when they are drunk.'

'God help him; he didn't have enough sense to go and hide. Just went and lay down inside the windmill not a hundred yards from the body. He was fast asleep when the constables found them. They had to shake him awake. That's what I heard anyway. Nice young lad. Always polite and well mannered! Just drunk, I suppose!'

'Drunk or not; he killed the Spaniard. It's lucky for that young fellow that he is the mayor's son,' said one man grimly. He raised his voice. 'I suppose he won't hang, like my cousin's son who was hanged because he killed a man in a fair fight.'

His voice was so loud that several passers-by turned to look at him and a moment later Mara could see why he had spoken in such raised tones.

James Lynch, the mayor, was walking up the street, probably coming from the gaol or from the courthouse. When he reached the four crossroads junction, he stopped by a large tower house at the corner of High Middle Street, took a large key from the purse on his belt, inserted it into the ornately studded door, went in and closed it behind him. His face looked the same as always and, although he could not have failed to hear the words, he betrayed no sign of emotion.

But, thought Mara with a surge of pity, what about his wife Margaret, the adoring mother of the boy who now lay in that filthy gaol? Mara could hardly bear to think of how she must be suffering. She wished that there was something she could do. Was the poor woman sitting inside, weeping? Perhaps waiting for her hard-hearted husband to come home? Perhaps she was even now looking out from that window beside the framed panel which was dedicated to Henry VII, king of England when James Lynch first became Mayor of Galway. Mara stayed for a moment, her eyes on the strangely carved gargoyles that protruded from above the windows on the top storey of the house, and her mind busy with questions about what she could possibly achieve if she interfered in this matter.

'Walk with me, Mara,' said a voice from behind her. And then, a little impatiently, 'I can't keep calling you "my lady judge" and I can't get my tongue around "Brehon". Let me call you Mara. Please, Mara, please walk with me. You are a stranger here and you are not caught in the tangles of relationships.'

'How are you feeling?' Mara compassionately studied the face of Valentine Blake.

'Bad!' he said abruptly. 'Will you come with me? I want to go to the King's Head. That's probably the last place that Walter visited before he went outside the city. I've been trying to trace him, to see if anyone was with him. And I'm looking for that Alfonso Mercandez, the Spaniard, the captain of the ship belonging to the Gomez family. I want to speak to him.'

'Do you think that Mercandez might have something important to say? Do you think that Walter may not have committed the killing?' asked Mara, but Valentine shook his head.

'I'm afraid that might be too much to hope for. But if he was there; if he could have followed the two lads; perhaps give evidence that Walter was badly provoked. There's no doubt that both of them were drunk. Carlos was as bad as Walter. I heard that the innkeeper at the Unicorn down by the docks had to separate them. Catarina went home in disgust because of something that Carlos said to her in front of Walter; I met her in tears myself. But did they stay together when they left the city?'

'Why the King's Head, then?' asked Mara.

'Nearest inn to the gate leading out towards Lough Atalia,' he said briefly. 'I want to ask the landlord whether they were there last night.'

He was silent for a moment as he fell into step with her and they paced the street together. Most people turned to stare at him and a few greeted him sympathetically. He was well known and well liked in the city, it appeared, and probably everyone knew of his close relationship to the boy who was being spoken of as a murderer.

'I must see Alfonso Mercandez,' he burst out after a few minutes' silence. 'Why has he to take the body back to Spain? Why has he to go on this very day? Other foreigners are buried in Galway – and Carlos has an aunt and two cousins living here. This matter should not be rushed. I can't think why James is about to allow this to happen.' Valentine Blake violently kicked a loose stone out of his way. He ran his fingers through his head of bushy curls, so like that of his unfortunate nephew, and stared at Mara with a look of bitter despair on his face.

'What am I going to do?' he said passionately. 'I've tried to talk to James, but I think that I just made things worse. He's an obstinate devil. If he tries Walter today while this matter is fresh in everyone's mind then there will be a stink if he is released and the boy will have to leave the town. What James should do, if he had any sense, is postpone the matter for a few weeks. Allow things to cool down. Philip Browne won't make a fuss. It's a terrible thing to say, I suppose, but this last night's business will be a good piece of work for him. His son David will probably inherit the Gomez fortune now – he was in line for it before Carlos was born; I know that.'

'Perhaps the mayor fears to be blamed if he is thought to be showing favour to his son,' said Mara quietly. She could understand the feeling. Her own integrity and impartiality was very important to her. James Lynch, from what she had seen of him, was an arrogant man, narrow-minded, obstinate, but a man who would uphold the laws as laid down by the English king, Henry VII, who had ratified his appointment.

'Stupid man!' exclaimed Valentine. 'What about his wife? What about his family? What's more important than that?'

Justice, thought Mara, and then added the words 'tempered by mercy'. Mayor Lynch had shown no mercy to Sheedy but had applied justice, as he saw it, though to her it was an ice-cold unfeeling justice, to an old man who had lost his wits and had stolen to keep himself alive. His son, of course, would be a different matter to him. Perhaps Valentine Blake was suffering unduly. Perhaps the mayor would not allow the name of Lynch to be disgraced.

The King's Head was a wonderfully comfortable place. It had an enormous fire that roared up the chimney; the wooden tables were solid and well polished; chairs, benches and stools were padded by colourful cushions. Not surprisingly it was full of people. The innkeeper and his wife were pouring wine from large jugs and pot boys were running to and from the tables carrying brimming goblets and foaming pots of beer.

When they came in everyone was talking. They did not cease when Mara entered slightly ahead of Valentine, though they eyed her with a friendly curiosity. However, when her companion had hung up their cloaks and joined her, the loud voices changed to a murmur which had almost ceased by the time that they found themselves a small table by the window.

'Some wine?' asked Valentine.

'Please,' she said, and then with a memory of the mayor's drink at the courthouse, she added, 'burgundy, if possible.'

When he came back it was with a flagon of wine, a plate of crisp hot rolls and a dish of some small green fruits.

'What are these?' Mara took one up, bit into it and smiled with pleasure. The tangy, slightly salty pungency of this strange fruit was very much to her taste.

'These are olives,' said Valentine. 'Have you never eaten one before?'

'No, but I've read about them. I must buy some to take home with me. I love them,' said Mara, greedily biting into her third one. She had seen the landlord shake his head at Valentine's questions so she did not mention the matter of Walter. The chances were that if the two young men were drunk and quarrelsome they would have been refused admittance to a respectable and affluent inn like this one.

'I'll send you down a box. I get olives from Portugal from time to time. I'm fond of them too, especially nicely salted before they are potted.' Valentine was looking more relaxed now – resigned, perhaps, and the conversations from the other tables had begun again.

'Do you think that Walter killed Carlos?' asked Mara, swirling her wine and then tasting it. It was full-bodied and warming; she sipped it gratefully and then munched some bread. He had not answered, but a faint frown darkened his face again. She decided not to repeat the question but took another olive and then another bite of bread.

'That was good,' she said with a slightly exaggerated sigh of relief. 'I was so hungry. I've had no breakfast.'

That aroused him from his thoughts.

'No breakfast!' he exclaimed. 'Don't tell that Jane Bodkin allowed you to come out without pressing all sort of food on you.'

'She's not well; Henry said that the shock was too much for her. She took to her bed.'

'Jane Bodkin!' he called out the words in tones of a man who does not believe his ears. 'Jane Bodkin,' he repeated. 'But she's as tough as old boots. And she is as curious as a cat; I'd have thought she'd be on the town streets immediately finding out all the details. I can't see why it should be a shock to her.'

Mara agreed with him, but thought it would not be diplomatic
to say so. She recollected that Valentine Blake had called at the
household that morning in order to engage Henry Bodkin as a
lawyer for the defence of his nephew and thought she would talk
about that.

'Did Lawyer Lynch agree to act for you?' she asked, and was
not surprised when he shook his head.

'Too worried about offending his worship, the mayor,' he said
scornfully. 'I managed to get John Skerrett to act, though.'

An old man, nearing retirement, according to Henry Bodkin
– however, it was none of her business, so Mara began to discuss
the wine and to chat knowledgeably about vintages. He wasn't
listening but it would form a sociable background to his thoughts.

'You asked me whether I thought Walter killed Carlos,' he
broke into her talk after a minute. He swallowed another gulp
of wine and said appealingly, 'Was there any reason why you said
that? Can you think of any other possible explanation?'

'Tell me what happened.'

'They were both very drunk,' he said despondently. 'Everyone
in the town knows that. I met Catarina walking all by herself, in
floods of tears. She had left them quarrelling and had run away. I
gathered that Carlos had said something very offensive to her when
she tried to make peace between them. I took her to her door
and advised her to go to bed and to forget all about them. But
when I went back to the Unicorn they had disappeared. I tried
this place, but they weren't here, either. And I'm afraid that I gave
up then,' he shrugged uncomfortably. 'I was tired of the whole
affair so I just went off and had a walk down by the docks to clear
my own head before going home to bed.' He paused, and said
quietly, 'If only I had stayed looking for them, followed them out
of the town, dragged them both back by the scruff of the neck
– well, this may never have happened.'

'I don't think you can blame yourself,' said Mara. 'Young men
get drunk; it's part of growing up. These two young men were
both spoiled and had too much money. That added to the problem.
It's no good now to dwell upon the past.'

'Walter had blood all over his clothes when he was found, you
know, and of course his dagger was driven deep into Carlos's
chest. I heard the constable say that it looked as if they both fell
asleep and then Walter woke and stabbed him, and then went

into the windmill and fell asleep. Carlos's dagger was quite unmarked.'

Mara nodded. If Carlos had been still asleep when the deadly attack was made, well that would account for the dagger being plunged into the chest rather than the back; it would also account for the fact that the Spanish boy's dagger remained unused. On the other hand, her own impression from the dead man's face was that he had seen his end coming and had been on his feet when the dagger entered his chest. Still, she could be wrong; she wished that a physician that she trusted could have seen the body.

And then, of course, there was the matter of the back of Carlos Gomez's head. What had happened to that?

'If only there was something that I could do, now,' groaned Valentine. He gulped down his wine, but shook his head when the innkeeper came forward with another flagon. 'Can you think of anything?' he asked, looking at her appealingly. 'Lawyer Bodkin was telling us that you solved a case where a mine owner that he knew was murdered. He said that he was astonished when he heard the solution and that you must be very clever to have guessed it.'

Mara was chary of giving him too much hope. If only she were back in the Burren, where her word was law, then this case would be tackled methodically, witnesses would be interviewed by her scholars, the whole matter debated in the schoolhouse at Cahermacnaghten, maps laid out, information neatly collated and available to her and, above all, she would have time to think, time to make sure that no mistake was being made. A case like this could take up to three weeks to solve – more if needed.

The trial of Walter Lynch would be held in two hours – and what lay beyond? – the hangman's noose?

Valentine Blake jumped to his feet. 'I must find that ship's captain!' His voice was husky and strained with emotion. He looked like a man in a state of utter desperation. 'I must find him and force him to agree to allow Carlos to be buried here in Galway. We must have more time before the trial and judgement. If necessary, I'll throttle him with my bare hands.'

Nine

Commentaries (Acts 22:24-5), New Testament

This plea ('Civis Romanus sum', 'I am a Roman citizen') by St Paul – when threatened with scourging – sufficed in ancient Rome to stop arbitrary condemnation, bonds and scourging. Every Roman citizen had a right to appeal and to have that appeal heard by the Emperor. No Roman citizen could be condemned unheard; by the Valerian law he could not be bound; and by the Sempronian Law it was forbidden to scourge him or beat him with rods. When the chief captain commanded that Paul 'should be examined by scourging', Paul asked a centurion: 'Is it lawful for you to scourge a man that is a Roman, and un-condemned?'

Mara, left to herself, sipped her wine slowly, nibbled her olives and watched the pale gold sand slip slowly past the narrow centre of the large hourglass that stood on the shelf above the innkeeper's head. The church bell had sounded the eleventh hour when they had entered the inn and the landlord had just tilted the glass. Now more than half the sand had descended into the lower half of the glass. There must be less than half an hour to go before the court would sit. And as yet there had been no public announcement of the postponement of the trial. Valentine Blake had either failed to find the Spanish sea captain, or else had been unable to persuade him to agree to the burial of Carlos in the city where he had met his death.

Reluctantly she got to her feet, smiled across at the landlord, collected her cloak and went out into the street. She hated the thought of it but she had to go to this trial; nothing in her life and training had made her feel that she could evade responsibility. A daring plan had come into her mind and she resolved that if the opportunity arose, she would not hesitate to rise to her feet. But perhaps she would not need to do this. First she would have to make an attempt to see this John Skerrett and make sure that he was going to put the possibility of a royal pardon in front of the judge. James Lynch was a difficult man, a cold, hard man, as Ardal O'Lochlainn had said, but he was also a very upright one. Whatever was done had to be done in public so that his honour would be salvaged.

People were already huddled in groups at the back of the church when she arrived. Some men were working in the upper half of the church and amongst them she recognized the steward who had given her a seat the day before at Old Sheedy's trial. She walked boldly up to the chancel of the church and accosted him.

'I'm afraid that I didn't thank you for that hot brick yesterday,' she said, giving him the benefit of her warmest smile. 'Goodness, what a lot of work you have to do today! How on earth are you going to manage?' With a shock of horror she saw that the dead body of Carlos was still on the top step to the altar. It had been placed within a wooden lead-lined coffin, but the lid was lying beside it, the body exposed. No attempt had been made to clean the body or cut away the blood-soaked clothing and a few blue-bottle flies buzzed sleepily around it. Mara tore her gaze away from it and looked back at the steward.

'We've got these twelve chairs for the jury. At first I put them in two rows, but now I've rearranged them in a semicircle so that they can look at each other when significant pieces of evidence come up.' He gazed at the artistic arrangement of chairs with satisfaction before going on to show her that his worship the mayor would sit on the bishop's throne. The prosecuting lawyer, Lawyer Lynch, and the defence lawyer, Lawyer Skerrett, would speak from the pulpit.

'Pity we don't have another pulpit so that the witnesses can speak from there,' he said with disappointment, 'but I've done my best by putting that box over there beside the tomb. The witness will have to stand on that and then most of the church will be able to see them. I had a word with the bishop about them standing on the tomb itself but he wasn't happy.'

Mara gazed at the semicircle of chairs, trying to visualize how the jury would react to this strange trial held only hours after the murder was discovered and where the judge was the father of the accused. And what did the bishop think about the whole affair? After all, she said to herself, Christ flogged the

moneylenders from the temple. What would he think of a man
being tried for his life a few feet away from the sacred altar? That
was, of course, assuming that the jury found him guilty and that
his father could think of no excuse for pardoning him.

'Will they be the same men in the jury as yesterday?' she asked,
and he shook his head.

'A cousin of Philip Browne is the foreman,' he said. 'Most of
the others are of the name of Browne as well – merchants, mainly.
He was allowed to pick them.'

And of course, they will be keen to have a quick solution to
the killing in order not to anger their powerful relations, Philip
Browne and his wife Isabelle. Mara thought the words but managed
only to nod in response.

'And what about a dock; what will you do about that?' She
looked around at the arrangements with what she hoped looked
like a smile of approbation.

'They're bringing down a cage from the courthouse,' he said
with the air of one who has a limitless fund of good ideas. 'I
thought that would solve the problem. Would you like to sit over
there in the aumbry by the window, my lady? You'll have a good
view of everything there.' He pointed to a small niche in the wall
with a marble shelf which could be used as a seat. It was a dark
corner with no lights nearby and so was a wonderful place to see
without being too conspicuous.

'I was hoping to have a quick word with Lawyer Skerrett about
a legal matter,' said Mara tentatively, but the steward shook his
head.

'His worship the mayor and the two lawyers will walk up from
the courthouse so that they arrive as the bell sounds for noon,'
he said to her disappointment. 'You'd better take your seat now,
my lady, because someone else might take it.'

There was truth in what he said. The large church was filling
up fast. She would just have to rely on Valentine Blake remembering to put the point. Mara thanked the steward with a smile
and moved away.

By this stage Mara had noticed that her scholars had entered
the church; she counted heads rapidly. Yes, they were all there.
However, she made no sign to them and was pleased to see that
Fachtnan ushered them into a space about halfway down the
church. She doubted that they would be called as witnesses; they

would have had nothing of any importance to relate, and she was not keen to involve them in her plans. The mood of the city was volatile. It was unclear what result was hoped for from this trial and, indeed, it was quite unclear to her what verdict would be arrived at by a judge who happened to be father to the accused man.

If this trial of a near relative had happened in any of the Gaelic kingdoms, she mused as she took her seat in a marble alcove – if this had happened in Burren, for instance – she would have sent for the Brehon of Corcomroe and asked him to hear the case; and, of course, the same would have happened anywhere else. The kingdoms mostly had friendly links with some nearby neighbour and so there would have been no problem.

However, English-speaking Galway, ruled by English laws, was quite isolated. It would take a week or two to get a judge from Dublin and even so the court procedure would have been different. In Dublin the law was exactly the same as in England, but traditionally Galway was ruled by Roman law. It was only in the last few years that English law had begun to prevail. The law of the king and the emperor, she thought, and resolved to make her own knowledge of Roman law be, at last, of some use to her.

Mara looked around her. She noticed Henry Bodkin standing quietly and unobtrusively in a dark corner. Jane was not with him. She must still be unwell otherwise curiosity would have brought her. After all, the Brownes, the Lynches and the Blakes were all close friends to herself and to her brother.

Then there was a stir amongst the crowd and a murmur. The Browne family had arrived – all four of them; Catarina with her face cold and resolute, David looking around him eagerly, Isabelle shedding tears into a lace-edged handkerchief, her husband ill-at-ease and slightly embarrassed. They marched up towards the top of the church and people stood by to allow them a place just before the altar. Valentine Blake greeted them as he came in, but all, except Philip, looked away and did not return his salutation.

From her half-hidden position Mara scanned Valentine's face, but read no hope in it. His brows were set into a frown and his lips were tight. He had not gone to sit by the altar, a place that his position as bailiff would have merited, but seemed determined to remain in the body of the church and to dissociate himself from the trial. She wondered whether he had managed to even talk with the Spanish captain. She had noticed Alfonso Mercandez, the Spanish captain, come in a little earlier and his face, also, was set and resolute, and he avoided looking at Valentine. He was in a difficult position, she acknowledged. He was employed by the Gomez family and if he arrived back with the bad news, but without the boy's body, there would probably be recriminations and he might well lose his position.

There was no sign of Margaret and Mara hoped that she would not come. She did not know how any mother could witness her son in such a plight without breaking down and this would add to her husband's severity.

The cage for the prisoner had arrived by cart. She had heard the horses squeal as their feet slipped on the icy cobbles outside the church and then the two great doors at the western end of the church were thrown open. A double line of soldiers marched in, fanned out, then turned to face each other so that they formed a well-guarded passage in the middle aisle. The cage was carried solemnly up between them and deposited in front of the altar, just beneath where the coffined body of Carlos Gomez lay. It was a heavy iron cage, a cage for a wild beast, a place where a man could crouch, but not stand.

A gasp had come from the assembled crowd when the cage had been carried in and then there was a dead silence – everyone straining his ears until the expected sound arrived – the well-disciplined tramp of marching feet.

They were taking no chances with Walter Lynch. Mara saw with pity how the young man, still besmeared with blood, puffy-eyed and white-faced, was loaded down with chains, manacled and shackled and led like a captured wolf up between the two lines of soldier and was thrust into the cage. Once again Mara prayed that Margaret was not present. This sight would be enough to kill any mother. A sigh went through the crowd and several women took out handkerchiefs.

And then the soldiers stiffened. It hadn't needed any command from their superiors. The heads were immobile, still turned to the middle aisle, but the eyes were slanted towards the west door.

There, in all the splendour of striped robe, coif and cap, came his worship, judge of the court, the sovereign mayor of Galway, James Lynch followed by his officials and behind them the two lawyers, Lawyer Thomas Lynch and an old man bent and frail. Mara's heart sank. This must be Lawyer Skerrett. He did not look as though he had the energy or the stomach for a fight.

'All rise!' bellowed the steward, and the crowd rose to their feet obediently. Mara did not rise. She had decided that a movement would only call attention to her.

The wretched prisoner crouched in his cage and sobbed loudly, while his father took his seat on the bishop's throne and called for the submission by the lawyer speaking for the sovereign state of Galway.

'My Lord,' said Thomas Lynch. 'This is a crime committed in a drunken rage. It offends against the laws of hospitality, as the victim was a young man from the country of Spain visiting cousins in the city of Galway. The sovereignty will bring evidence to show that the accused was seen fighting with the victim on many occasions during the evening that preceded the crime.'

He then sat down. Mara began to feel hope rising. It was a very mild introduction, better than she could have hoped for. The word 'murder' was not even mentioned. Her eyes sought Valentine Blake's and saw him lift his head and gaze towards the altar area. There was a candle quite near to him and she thought she could read the dawning of hope in that uplifted face, which was so like that of his unfortunate nephew.

And then witnesses were called one by one. First came the constable who had found the body and after him a long procession of townspeople. Few had much to add to the fact that there were numerous fights between the two young men throughout the evening. One witness, the Grocer Joyce, added, 'To be sure, your honour, young men are always fighting on Shrove. I broke up three fisticuffs myself. Master Walter meant no harm, I'd say.'

Not relevant, thought Mara, and looked at Lawyer Lynch, waiting for him to ask for the last remark to be stricken from the record, but he said nothing and it was left to the presiding judge, Mayor Lynch, himself, to say those words. His tone, when he spoke, was dry and indifferent and never once did he glance at the wretched boy crouching in the cage.

The Spanish captain was called next and he marched up and took his place firmly on the large box, kissed the Bible, swore to tell the truth, and nothing but the truth, and then said loudly and dramatically that he had seen Walter pull out his knife and threaten Carlos Gomez with it. He had intervened and persuaded Walter to put the knife back into the pouch on his belt.

'Did you not think to take the knife away from him,' asked Lawyer Skerrett. This was his first intervention and he did it in a quavering unsure voice.

Alfonso Mercandez turned to him. 'I was ordered to go away and I went. Señor Gomez was my master and I obeyed.'

Go on; ask him if Gomez had been fighting, had also pulled a knife. Mara willed the words to reach Lawyer Skerrett, but he sat down looking uncertain.

After this there was more of the same. The crowd shifted their feet and sighed. Although a few braziers had been lit, the church was icy. Even in her double-woven, fur-lined cloak Mara was cold and wished that the obliging steward had the facility to supply hot bricks as he had done at the courthouse.

But then the steward called for Mistress Catarina Browne and everyone grew still again.

Catarina took her place on the witness box with great composure, still clad in those over-large black garments of mourning. A tall, strong-looking girl, thought Mara. What a pity she had not taken the knives off those two boys instead of dissolving into tears and going home. Her own scholar, Fiona, though almost a foot smaller and far slighter, would have done that and then no harm other than two sore heads in the morning would have occurred.

Catarina's evidence was colourless, no mention of the storm of tears that had sent her running up the street towards her home. She did mention meeting Lawyer Bodkin though, so the next witness to be called for was Henry and he came forward in his lawyer's gown, looking trim, neat and self-contained, and told the court that he had followed the two young men out through the eastern gate and had tried to reconcile them.

'And what was the result of your intervention?' asked Lawyer Lynch in the bored tones with which he had conducted the whole of his interrogations.

'Carlos Gomez turned back with me and re-entered the city,' said Lawyer Bodkin.

Ask him about this! Mara silently implored Lawyer Skerrett. Put it into the jury's mind to wonder why Carlos, once back inside the gates of the city, had returned later to the company of

Walter. Did not that seem to show that they were not on such bad terms after all? Indeed, Henry Bodkin himself looked expectantly at the lawyer for the defence as if he expected a question, but there was no movement from the old man, who seemed to be contemplating the toes of his well-polished boots, and Lawyer Bodkin, after a bow towards the enthroned judge, left the witness box and returned to his place.

And then Lawyer Lynch summed up – a transparent case whose details were known to most of the town, he said. The accused and the victim had quarrelled all evening and this quarrel had ended in tragedy. The evidence lay – and he pointed dramatically at the body in the coffin – in the fact that the accused man's dagger was found stuck into the heart of the victim.

That dagger had been, thought Mara suddenly, rather carefully inserted for such a drunken man. She wished that she had access to some medical person, but her memory of the knife seemed to show that it had avoided the ribs and had been inserted below the breast bone. Chance perhaps, but perhaps not. If she were the lawyer for the defence she would bring that out. After all, Walter was not the only drunken and belligerent young man that night. Shrove, was, according to her host, famous for fights and once the combatants had been shepherded away from the city streets they were allowed to settle their differences in their own way.

Lawyer Skerrett's summing up was even feebler than she had feared. Only in the last moment did he say, 'I ask for a plea for mercy on the grounds of the young man's youth and previous good character.'

'He's older than my fifteen-year-old cousin who was hanged for killing a man ten years older than himself in a fair fight,' said a voice from the back of the church, and the judge frowned.

'Silence in court,' bellowed the steward.

'Shut up,' roared many voices, and only desisted when the judge threatened to clear the court of bystanders.

'Has the defendant anything to say?' queried the judge, looking languidly up at the great stained glass window behind his head.

The defence lawyer glanced hopefully at the cage but the wretched boy still wept noisily and said nothing. 'No plea is entered, My Lord,' he said eventually and sat down heavily.

'Members of—' began the judge.

Swiftly Mara got to her feet. What she was going to do had no legal precedent, no possible validity and its efficacy would depend on how many words she managed to get out before she was silenced. English, she thought, and a flow of words as fast as she could manage to utter with clarity.

'Your worship and gentlemen of the jury,' she said rapidly, 'I do not know the custom of your courts, but if it may be permitted to an outsider like myself to speak . . . It is possible, your honour, that the accused does not know whether he is guilty or not. If he slept all night in a drunken stupor then only God alone will know whether at one stage of the night he woke and committed the murder, or whether some other person, maliciously inclined, killed Carlos Gomez and smeared the accused man with the bloody evidence from the wounds of the dead man. I submit, your worship,' she went on even more rapidly, 'that the only possible verdict is that of an acquittal or a retrial when more time for evidence gathering has been afforded.'

And that must be well under one minute, she thought triumphantly as she bowed respectfully to the judge, to the jury – who looked astonished and were obviously wondering who she was and where she had come from – and smiled sweetly into the bewildered face of the elderly Lawyer Skerrett.

'The last intervention will be disregarded and not recorded in any court record,' said Mayor James Lynch, rising and addressing the jury with more emphasis than usual. 'Members of the jury, you also will disregard the words that you have just heard and will not, in any way, bear them in mind when you come to give your judgements.'

But they heard them all the same, thought Mara triumphantly. Whose influence would bear the most heavily on their judgement? However, she had given the judge a chance to save his son from a hasty condemnation and he could declare a mistrial and give a date for a new hearing.

However, her heart sank as she heard his summing up, heard the merciless phrases drop one by one from the judge's lips: evidence of bad-feeling, of quarrels, striking and irrefutable evidence which was obtained at the scene of the murder.

'I will enumerate that evidence,' said James Lynch, his voice strongly ringing through the rafters of the church.

'Firstly: The accused was found lying beside the dead man.

Secondly: The accused was found to be covered with the blood of the dead man which gushed out during the fatal blow. No wound was found on the accused, so we know that the blood was the blood of the victim. Thirdly: The fatal wound was inflicted by the accused's own dagger which has been identified by members of his family. Fourthly: You have heard evidence of enmity and bad-feeling between the accused and the victim.

'Members of the jury, the accused had the means, the motive and the opportunity to perpetrate this heinous crime; how say you? Is he guilty or not guilty?'

No one spoke, no one moved. The jurymen looked at each and then looked at the floor beneath their feet. The boy in the cage ceased to sob.

'Do you wish to retire to consider your verdict?' The voice of the judge seemed to bear down heavily upon the jury. They shifted uneasily. Several cleared their throats. They leaned in closely to each other and began to converse in loud whispers. Mara was so near that she could see the expression on their faces. Not anger, not pity, more a sort of embarrassment. The foreman appeared to be arguing with some who shook their heads and then shrugged their shoulders. One man at the end of the row said something emphatically. Mara caught the word 'trade' and knew that the game was up. These men were traders, merchants, and whatever was bad for trade was bad for them. The son of a powerful and very rich Spanish trader had been murdered and a victim had to be offered to assuage the wrath of the bereaved family.

'We are agreed, your worship,' said the foreman, standing up and bowing respectfully.

'And how say you; guilty or not guilty?' enquired the judge impassively.

'Guilty, your worship,' said the foreman defensively, eyeing the judge carefully.

James Lynch showed no emotion. He leaned over, took the black cap from the box on the table beside him, placed it carefully on top of his greying hair and said solemnly, 'Walter Lynch, you have been found guilty of the wilful murder of Carlos Gomez and I sentence you to be hanged by the neck until you are dead. The sentence will take place in five days' time in order to allow you to have due time to repent of your sins before you face your Maker. And may God have mercy on your soul.'

'My Lord,' shouted Mara at the top of her voice. 'The law of Galway, I have heard it said, are the laws of Galway are the laws of the king and the emperor. One Roman law is relevant here. Lex Valeria in his book: *de Provocatione*, dating from the sixth century before Christ says, and I quote: "And by that law it is granted to every Roman citizen the legal right to appeal against a capital sentence, defined and confirmed the right of appeal." St Paul, himself, My Lord, pleaded that law.'

For a moment she regretted having wasted time in giving the whole law and the reference, but her rigorous training in the law had been too strong for her.

'Surely . . .' she said with a break in her voice, 'surely you will give the prisoner leave to appeal.'

'Turn that woman out of the court,' said Judge James Lynch, hardly raising his voice above it's usual cool, calm cadences.

'You're a cold-hearted devil,' roared out Valentine Blake, and his words seemed to be a signal to the rest of the church as most of those present leaped to their feet. 'You cold-hearted devil! You should be driven out of this city.'

His words had no sooner ceased to echo around the church when the cry was taken up. First one or two – it was hard to know where the chant started – and then, here and there, and soon from every corner of the large church, more and more until the entire church joined in the chorus.

'Out, out, out,' they shouted and drummed their feet on the tiled floor. 'Out, out, out.' *Dum, dum, dum.* The sound of the words and of the actions was like that of drums beating, and it continued, getting louder and louder. Almost the entire church took up the chant. Even respectable women were slapping their hands and drumming with their feet.

Lord Mayor James Lynch faced them dauntlessly, his eyes angry, his face pale, but with no sign of fear. The lawyers and the jurymen withdrew back towards the altar and then vanished through the door to the sacristy, but the judge did not stir.

'Resign!' shouted one voice, and this was taken up by others, but the majority kept to the simple and effective rhythmic chant of 'Out, out, out.'

'Soldiers, clear the court!' called Mayor Lynch, and made a signal to the waiting troop. Mara did not hesitate. Her first duty now was to her scholars. Rapidly she went down the church until she reached them, glancing over towards the small chapel of the Blessed Sacrament on the north-western side of the church. It was empty and lit by just one tall candle, but it would provide a quick exit if the door happened to have been left open.

The noise was so great that she had to signal, but Moylan picked it up instantly and the others were alert and quick thinking. She saw them move, slide through and thanked God for their quick wits. They followed her instantly up the aisle and through the dark chapel, still smelling of incense from the last service there. The door was unlocked and they quickly passed through it.

'Back to the Bodkin tower house immediately,' she said as soon as they were outside. She was in danger; she knew. There had been a note of real menace in James Lynch's voice. He would not hesitate to throw her in prison. And what about her scholars? Had she endangered them also?

'Through the graveyard, Brehon,' said Moylan. 'There's a gate to Lombard Street from there.'

Mara began to breathe more easily. The crowd from the church would spill out into Market Street. The well-trained troops would clear them from there, either back up the town towards Gate Street, or else down to Lombard Street, in order to allow the soldiers to escort the prisoner back to the gaol. But by that stage she would have her scholars safely under cover inside the substantial walls of the Bodkin tower house.

And she also would be under the protection of a prominent citizen of Galway.

Not one of them, she resolved, would stir outside the door that night.

But what about that poor boy? What about Walter Lynch, only and beloved son of his mother, who had been denied the right to appeal against his sentence and had been condemned to a death on the gallows?

Mara resolved that she would not give up the fight. Somehow or other, her brains, her courage and her knowledge of the law would have to achieve the impossible. How could she restore Walter to his mother and get Sheedy out of that filthy gaol?

Ten

Medieval Law
(*From* Blackstone's Commentaries)

The customs of London differ from all others in point of trial: for, if the existence of the custom be brought in question, it shall not be tried by a jury, but by certificate from the lord mayor and aldermen by the mouth of their recorder; unless it be such a custom as the corporation is itself interested in, as a right of taking toll, &c., for then the law permits them not to certify on their own behalf.

Jane Bodkin, herself, opened the door to them. Her face was pale but she was composed and hospitable, and asked eager questions about how the trial had gone. It was obvious, though, that her mind was elsewhere and she jumped nervously when a squeaking hinge heralded the opening of the door to the outside.

'Henry!' she exclaimed thankfully, but she did not move towards the hall, just busied herself with pouring small beer for the scholars and offering them tasty slices of ham pie to go with it. The verdict of guilty against the son of the presiding judge seemed to upset her less than the talk of the unrest in the church and she was eager to hear all about it, exclaiming with horror at the sacrilege. Or perhaps, thought Mara, trying to be just, she could not face the thought of the boy whom she had called 'the loveliest baby' being hanged on Gallows' Green.

Henry Bodkin's face lit up briefly when he came into the parlour and saw his guests.

'Good,' he said with satisfaction. 'I saw you go through the chapel and hoped that you were safe. That was well thought of. Things are getting serious in the town tonight. Tempers have been stirred and I cannot see this state of affairs being easily resolved. He was a popular young man and I always liked him,' he added with an air of regret.

'I can't bear to think of him,' said Jane soberly. 'And his poor mother, too. Tell me, Henry, is there anything can be done to save him?' Her eyes met her brother's and for a moment there was a slight tension in the air. Almost, thought Mara, as though Jane felt that Henry was not doing enough for Walter. Perhaps she deplored his refusal to act for the young man. That was the trouble with these old bachelors, she thought, with a moment's irritation. They were selfish and they never wanted anything to disturb the easy, pleasant tenor of their days. If Henry had taken on the case, she could have helped him; could have been at his elbow suggesting things; could have put her scholars to work. Even with a couple of hours only in which to work, perhaps they might have come up with enough evidence to cast a doubt in the judge's mind, enough evidence to have justified the postponing of the trial.

Although, thought Mara, I can understand his reasoning. Yes, the matter was too hurried. Yes, no lawyer wanted to be rushed into making a case with only a couple of hours of preparation. Yes, this was a particularly dangerous and difficult case with the whole of Galway city taking part and with the judge of the court happening to be the father of the accused man. No wonder that Henry Bodkin had not wanted to touch it. But still, what was a professional reputation worth when placed on the scales against a young man's life?

'Mara says that there was a riot beginning in the church.' Jane Bodkin shuddered, and then said with disgust, 'What a place to hold a trial! It should have been at the courthouse, not inside a consecrated building.'

'I think that Mayor Lynch was determined that justice should be seen to be done,' said Henry Bodkin quietly. 'The church was the only place that would be big enough to accommodate most of the citizens.'

'He probably thinks of himself as a sort of God anyway,' said Fiona, with a freedom of speech that none of the other scholars would have assumed in front of strangers. Though Mara always encouraged them to speak their minds to her, she usually reproved any such outspokenness in public.

However, this time she did not rebuke Fiona, even with a look. She was curious to find Henry Bodkin's opinion of the judge's action and looked at him expectantly.

'Difficult to know what else he could do with the evidence,' remarked Henry Bodkin, with an indulgent smile at Fiona. 'But I grant you it was a piteous sight.'

'He didn't have to yield to pressure to hold the trial today, though, did he?' said Mara smartly, looking an invitation to the boys to join in the discussion. 'What do you think, Fachtnan?' she added.

'The law of God should be above the law of man,' quoted Fachtnan. 'I think he showed no mercy to Walter. How could he have done that to his own son?'

'You forget Abraham who was willing to sacrifice his son, Isaac,' said Henry, pulling his beard with an amused smile.

'Abraham! I should hope we are a little more civilized than that these days,' said Fiona disgustedly. 'At least we Brehon lawyers are,' she added with a challenging look.

'Your lawyers are civilized, yes,' said Henry, with a courteous half-bow to Mara, 'but can a society be civilized if it allows thieves and murderers to walk free after the payment of a fine?' His eyes were amused as he watched Fiona's indignant face, but his words had a heartfelt ring about them.

'That's an interesting thought,' said Mara judicially, 'and yet perhaps if we can move from Abraham to the New Testament, we see that Jesus preaches forgiveness for a sinner who has shown repentance. And,' she added triumphantly, 'during all my years as a Brehon I cannot remember an incidence when a murderer, tried and sentenced by me, reoffended. The fine is so heavy that his or her kinsmen become responsible for behaviour in case they should have to pay out again. The person who has killed may walk free; but they are watched by the community in which they live.'

'But—' began Henry Bodkin, but at that moment there was a loud frenzied attack on the door of the house, the knocker banging against the iron plate in an urgent summons.

The steward of Henry's household was already at the door, a drawn dagger in his hand. He peered through the small window to one side and then said with shocked tones, 'It's Mistress Lynch.'

'Open up; quickly, man!' Henry Bodkin himself was at the door and he caught Margaret as she stumbled over the doorstep and slumped into his arms. Her face was streaked with tears, her hair tumbled, her dress stained with streaks of mould and her headdress missing. The well-dressed, well-groomed wife of Mayor Lynch looked like one of the boatwomen from the fish market.

'I tried to get into Blake's Castle,' she gasped, 'but Valentine is not there. He's out in the streets. I didn't want to stay with Cecilia. She could not protect me if James came looking for me. He will want me to stay at home, to stay quiet, to do nothing, but I'm not going to do that. I'm not going back to James. I've been afraid of him all of my life. I've been a coward and I've betrayed my son. But I am not going to be like that any more. Now I will rescue my boy if it costs me my life.'

Her eyes met Mara's and she held out a hand. 'Thank God you are still here. You must help me. You must. Walter did not do this thing. He would not. He could not.'

'Come into the parlour,' said Mara soothingly. It was not polite to take the lead in someone else's house but the two Bodkins seemed to be frozen. Neither had moved nor said anything.

'I . . . I can't bear it,' sobbed Margaret hysterically as Mara put an arm around her waist and half-supported, half-carried her across the hallway and into the warm parlour. 'My son! My only son! His own father to condemn him to death!'

'Some wine,' said Mara sharply, aiming the order to a space halfway between Fachtnan and Henry Bodkin, but it was her scholar who poured the wine from its flagon on the fire hob and brought the goblet across to her. Mara held it in her hand and said in a low, soothing voice, 'Drink this. You must be brave for Walter's sake. We will talk about it in a minute and will see what there is to be done.'

Something in those words seemed to quieten Margaret and she made an effort to sip. She tried to speak, but Mara held up an authoritative hand.

'Not yet,' she said firmly. 'Drink your wine first. We must be very calm and very practical. Remember that there are five days before the execution. Your son will be safe for those five days. A lot can happen during that time.'

Margaret gulped at the wine and then seized Mara's hand. 'Will you help me?' she implored. 'You won't go back to your own kingdom and leave me, will you? You will be able to prove to James that his son did not do this terrible thing. James will listen to you; he despises me. He thinks that I am silly and hysterical. You're clever; you will be able to find a solution.'

Mara's eyes met Henry's as he stood on the other side of the sobbing mother. *If there is a solution*, his eyes seemed to say and she nodded at him. The horror of the trial lay in its indecent haste and in the fact that it was the father of the boy who had pronounced the fatal sentence on his only son; not in the verdict itself. Very few courts in England would have given a different verdict. The evidence against Walter Lynch was overwhelming – even she, in a Brehon law court, might have felt forced to name him as the guilty party if no new evidence came to light after weeks of careful investigation.

Warm-hearted Fiona, however, had no such hesitations and doubts. She knelt on the floor beside the poor woman and seized the cold hand, rubbing it between her own two warm ones.

'We'll help,' she said impulsively. 'We'll all put our brains together, won't we, Brehon? Some of us,' she went on in her usual airy fashion, with a sidelong glance at Moylan, 'don't have many brains, but every little helps.'

Margaret gave a gulp and half-smile and Fiona went on swiftly, 'Now tell us why you think that Walter didn't do it?'

This direct approach seemed to work with Margaret better than silent sympathy or the shocked exclamations from Jane Bodkin. Her eyes were still brimming with tears, but she tried to sit a little straighter and smiled affectionately at the girl.

'If only he had been with all of you last night!' she said, gulping back a sob. 'He liked you so much and he would have been safe and happy with you. I know he didn't do it. Walter could not kill anything. He was such a gentle boy. He was always concerned and anxious if any person or animal was injured in any way.'

'He said nothing when he was asked if he had done it.' Fiona's eyes were sympathetic but her tone was firm. 'Why do you think he didn't deny it, if he had not done it?'

'I don't know,' wept Margaret. And then she mopped her eyes and tried again. 'At least I do. The boy is terrified of his father. James has been so strict with him. He loves him, but he thinks that Walter has a weak character and that he needs strong handling.'

'But he was threatened with death, with hanging,' said Shane in a puzzled way. 'Surely the fear of that would be worse than the fear of any father.'

Not necessarily, thought Mara. If Walter had been afraid of his father from the time that he was a little boy then he might have the habit of saying nothing when accused; might even feel that it was useless to defend himself if his father had already made up his mind. Someone like Shane, the greatly loved and much valued son of a wise and benevolent man like the Brehon for the O'Neill of Ulster, would not understand that. Aloud she said, 'I wondered whether he remembered anything from the night before.'

'You spoke up for him; my maid told me that. James forbade me to go to the trial. He . . . he,' she gulped again, and then said in a shamefaced way, 'he locked me into my chamber and took the key away and told the steward not to unlock it until he released me himself. He can't stand emotion. He's such a cold man. He doesn't understand love; he could not understand how I would happily go to the gallows if I could spare my son; how I wanted to stand beside him at that trial. He told me that I shouldn't go; that it would only upset me. I spoke to my maid through the door and asked her to go.'

'Whaat! He does think he's a god! He locked his wife in her bedroom!' Fiona was stunned at that and Mara felt a cold anger come over her. That poor woman married to that cold, hard, domineering man! She had already determined to do her best for Walter, but this story had reinforced her determination.

'How did you get out?' she asked.

Margaret gave a half-smile. 'I climbed from the window. As a girl, Valentine and I often did that and I found that the skill had not deserted me.'

Mara thought about the case for a moment. How would she approach this if it had happened in her own kingdom? Gather information, was her first instinct always – information about the accused and information about the victim.

'Does Walter get drunk often?' she asked.

'Sometimes,' admitted Margaret. 'I try to keep him away from his father when he is like that.'

'He's quarrelsome when he's drunk, then, is he?' queried Mara, but was not surprised when Margaret shook her head emphatically.

'No, never,' she said. 'He just gets silly and very, very sleepy. He would almost fall asleep standing up even if he was talking to you at the time. They say he was fighting with Carlos Gomez, but that Spanish boy was trying to needle Walter, trying to make him small in Catarina's eyes. You saw that yourself when we were at Valentine's place. Normally Walter is very good-natured.'

Mara thought back to that night. Young Walter had been

irritated by the Spaniard and annoyed at Catarina's indifference to him, but it had resulted in rather childish sulks rather than in hot temper. He had left the two together, gone off and got drunk, where another, more mature man would have ignored Carlos, treated him as a guest, but essentially an outsider.

'Let's go and see Walter tomorrow,' said Moylan suddenly. He got up from his chair and came to sit beside Fiona on the rug by Margaret's feet. 'I think someone should see him,' he said in a determined way. 'He might remember something useful. Do they allow visitors to gaols?' he added.

'I think so,' said Margaret, 'but it's no good; I didn't see him myself. James would not allow me out of the house, but I managed to get a message to Valentine and he went there. He sent me a note to say that Walter remembered nothing.'

'Yes, but that was the morning after – I'm not surprised at him remembering nothing after the way that he was drinking last night. I remember myself after the Lughnasa festival last summer . . .' He stopped abruptly and looked at Mara in an embarrassed fashion.

'Go on,' said Fiona impatiently. 'We're not stupid. We know what you are going to say. Last Lughnasa you got drunk when the crops were being cut – that's right, isn't it? Did you remember anything the next morning?'

'Not . . . a . . . thing!' said Moylan with emphasis. 'But, and this is the important thing, the following day things started to come back to me, one by one – and very embarrassing it was too, I can tell you.' His lips twitched at the memory and then he grew serious again.

'And you think that Walter might remember something tomorrow that he didn't remember today!' Margaret stared at Moylan with dawning hope in her eyes.

'Sure to,' said Moylan encouragingly. 'I wouldn't be surprised if he was to say to us that he remembered one of those Barbary pirates – you know, ma'am, the ones that your brother was telling us about; the ones that came from the Ottoman Empire and attacked his ship. Well, Walter might suddenly remember one of them stealing up on him when he was paralytic drunk and pulling the dagger from his belt and knifing Gomez. These Barbary pirates are fighting the Portuguese and probably the Spanish, too – bound not to like them, anyway. He probably wanted to pay Gomez or his father back for something – perhaps there was a sea battle where his best friend got killed by a Spaniard. Don't you worry, Mistress; I bet it will turn out to be something to do with the Barbary pirates. We'll have Walter out of that gaol by hook or by crook.'

'You're a dear, good boy,' said Margaret effusively. To his horror she bent down and kissed the top of his head. Fiona smirked at him, carefully keeping her back turned to Margaret, and Aidan choked over a suppressed chuckle. Hugh and Shane exchanged nervous grins.

'We'll try anyway,' said Moylan, a tide of embarrassment reddening his face. He leaned over, seized the poker and began to riddle the fire vigorously. A puff of smoke came out and set everyone coughing.

'Open the window, young man; you'll choke us all,' said Lawyer Bodkin good-humouredly, and Moylan, with great relief, got up quickly and went to thrust his hot face out into the cool night air.

But no sooner had he unlatched the window when all thoughts of embarrassment or amusement were forgotten. For sometime Mara had been conscious of some noise in the background but with the window opened everyone could hear the roar of a thousand voices yelling loudly. The shouts did not come from nearby Market Street or Lombard Street – they had a faraway note about them, but they were loud enough for the words to be distinguished by their ears, before Moylan rapidly closed the window again.

'Lynch out! Lynch out! Lynch out!' There was no doubt that these were the words. The city of Galway was in a state of rebellion against their mayor.

Mara's eyes met Henry's and he nodded.

'Mistress Lynch,' he said gently, 'I think that you should stay here tonight. Did you leave word with your maid about where you were going?'

'I said that I was going to my brother's place.' Margaret had undoubtedly heard the shouts but she did not appear to be perturbed by them. Her son occupied her thoughts to the exclusion of everything else. She had little pity to spare for her husband who might well be in danger at this moment.

'I'll send a note across to Blake's Castle; one of the stable boys can take it.' Henry left the room and the youngsters went on talking eagerly about Barbary pirates. Margaret's white face was beginning to get a little tinge of colour into it as she recalled distinctly seeing two dark-skinned men at the fish market early yesterday morning. Alfonso Mercandez, the captain of the Gomez family's ship, had the reputation of being a hard and ruthless man, according to what she had heard, and between them the scholars managed to concoct an interesting story where the only survivor of a pirate ship had sworn vengeance on the Gomez heir.

'I'll just go and see about a room for you,' said Jane trying to sound hospitable, but her face was strained and white and her hands trembled as she took up a candle from the table.

'I'll go with you,' said Mara. Margaret would be best with the simple and undemanding company of her scholars for the moment and she was curious about the riot. She did not follow Jane towards the kitchen quarters but crossed the hall and entered the library. Henry was just sealing a note when she entered. He gave it into the hands of a waiting stable boy and when he had gone, said with a grunt, 'Hot-headed fellow, Valentine Blake. Why did he shout that out in the church? I'd say he's out there on the streets. Dangerous sort of situation. Glad I don't have a shop. There'll be looting tonight.'

'I wondered what we could see from your roof,' said Mara. The Bodkin tower house, though not big, was tall and thin, one of the highest in the town.

'I was just thinking about that myself,' said Henry. 'Wait here for a moment until I get a covered lantern. It's getting dark outside now. We don't want to stumble on the roof.'

When he came back he carried two lanterns, one of which he handed to her. They climbed the flights of stairs side by side without a word, each busy with thoughts, until they came out on to the roof.

The evening had indeed begun to get dark. As they moved towards the crenellated edge of the roof, the bell from St Nicholas's sounded the hour of four o'clock. Mara peered out from between the upright shape of two merlons. She could see across the tops of the houses and down into the streets which were already lit with flaming torches of pitch. Lombard Street and Market Street were almost empty but Gaol Street and Courthouse Lane were packed solidly with people. They were mainly men, but Mara glimpsed the linen headdresses of a few women amongst them. All were chanting 'Lynch out! Lynch out! Lynch out! Out! Out! Out! Hang the mayor himself!' and several had cudgels which they waved in the air.

A flash of silver from Gaol Street caught Mara's eye and she leaned out a little further. Two solid lines of soldiers were drawn up in front of the prison and each soldier had a sword in his hand. The crowd surged forward towards that deadly line, but then drew back. No one wanted to run the risk of a sword in the guts and so they contented themselves with chanting and warlike cries. Mara wondered where was James Lynch while the crowd called for his blood, and then thought that she saw a tall, thin figure standing behind the soldiers. His back was to the door to the gaol.

Mara's eyes wandered over the whole city. More soldiers were marching down from the barracks near the Great Gate. For a moment the thought flashed through her mind that if the O'Flahertys or Ulick Burke of Clanrickard, whose ancestors had once owned this place, were to know about the riot, then a raid on this city with its warehouses filled with goods from Spain and from the east would yield rich pickings. To the north, west and south it was protected by water; only on the east was it vulnerable to attack.

The lights were on in the church of St Nicholas – patron saint of travellers on the sea. As Mara looked down at it, she saw a couple of priests with covered lanterns in their hands come out on to the street and look cautiously up and down. Then one turned back towards the door and made a signal. Four men, dressed as sailors, came out from the church carrying the heavy coffin cautiously down the church steps. Once they got to the bottom they quickened their steps until they reached the corner between Market Street and Lombard Street. Four other sailors waited there and the coffin was transferred to their shoulders. On they went down towards Blake's Castle and then towards the docks, changing the coffin bearers after every hundred yards or so.

There was a ship at anchor in the dock. Just a flaming torch on the corner of the custom house illuminated its drooping white sails, but as the heavy, lead-lined coffin approached, lanterns were lit on board. A gangway was hastily thrown down to connect the deck with the quayside, and up its narrow pathway the coffin was carried inch by inch. No word could be heard, but some signal must have been given because the sails were hoisted and the ship began to slip out of the harbour and down towards the open sea.

Carlos Gomez was returning home to Spain on his last voyage.

Eleven

Grith Gablach
(Ranks in Society)

Each newly elected chieftain must swear to be the king's vassal in accordance with the ancient Brehon laws, to maintain his lord's boundaries, to escort his lord to public assemblies, to bring his own warriors to each slógad *(uprising), and, in the last hour of his lord, to assist in digging the grave mound and to contribute to the death feast.*

Mara was up and dressed before dawn, and as soon as the sky lightened she went to her window. For a moment she stood there, surveying the seagulls circling around above the waters of the river's estuary. They were unusually noisy this morning – even through the dense glass of the window she could hear their strident cries. She opened the window and leaned out, enjoying their movement and excitement. They were acting as though a fishing boat were entering the harbour from the sea, but none was in sight as far as she could see. She was about to close the window again when a movement from upriver caught her eye.

A large boat, with white sails, was coming down the river. Despite the lack of wind it was moving fast. Mara could see that it was manned by a crew of young men, stripped to their shirts, and rowing so vigorously that the boat, despite its size, seemed to leap forward in the water. A minute later she was able to see more clearly – to note how the deck, the stern and the stays were all crowded with men. And to see also that a flag bearing the emblem of the Blakes, a black cat, fluttered at the prow.

Mara slipped quietly downstairs, closing the hall door noise-lessly behind her and stepped out on to Lombard Street.

When she reached the crossroads she stopped and waited. Valentine Blake was coming from the town. He looked tired, with black circles under his eyes and a fuzz of unshaven stubble on his cheeks; his clothes were crumpled and his hair uncombed.

Nevertheless, he had a certain air of buoyancy about him. She smiled and waved a greeting, and he crossed over towards her immediately.

'You're looking better this morning,' she said, feeling sorry for him and aware of his great affection for his sister and for his sister's son.

'I'm feeling more hopeful,' he admitted. 'Did you hear all that? Did you hear the riot?' His dark eyes burned with a look of triumph. 'The shouting went on all night around the gaol,' he continued. 'Surely James must take notice of that. He has to have some mercy, even if it's his own son. Can you understand a man like that?'

'I suppose he feels that it is a matter of integrity to judge every man alike, whether it is his son or a stranger,' said Mara keeping her voice dispassionate. Valentine was in a high state of nervous excitement she saw and looked as though he had had little sleep that night.

'Integrity be damned. He's thinking about his status as mayor,' exploded Valentine. 'Imagine a man putting his status before his son! I'd die first! This wasn't murder! This was just a drunken quarrel. The boy was out of his mind – knowing nothing of what he had done; no more than if he had been a certified lunatic – and thank God, we no longer hang certified lunatics! I blame myself terribly that I didn't get hold of him that night and dunk his head in a barrel. I thought he would just go home and sleep it off. He was dead on his feet when I saw him last, swaying around like a man who did not know where he was and then he sat down and put his head on the table in the alehouse and dropped off to sleep. I should have dragged him out and pushed him into his own house, but to be honest, I thought he might be better sobering up before he met his father. He's very strict with that boy. The beatings he has had – over nothing much. Hope I'm not like that with my son,' he ended, and began to walk rapidly in the direction of his castle as if he could not wait to see his baby son again.

'Margaret is with Lawyer Bodkin and his sister,' remarked Mara, matching her stride to his. 'Henry sent you a note,' she added.

'Why didn't she come to me? Has James turned on her now?' He didn't comment on the note. Had he received it, or did he come home last night long after the servants had gone to bed? Or was he only coming home just now? Mara pushed her own questions to the back of her mind and answered his.

'He locked her into her bedroom and kept her there all day; she escaped by climbing out of a window,' she said, watching him with interest.

'He's gone too far this time.' He reddened with anger and then said impetuously, 'She should leave him; take the boy, too. She's welcome to a place in my household. She and Cecily get on well. I'll come and fetch her now. What sort of state is she in?' Without waiting for an answer he started to abuse his brother-in-law.

'Mark my words; all James can think of is his status as mayor. He would think that if he freed Walter, or condemned him to just a couple of months in prison, then people would talk about him, would say that he had misused his position and that matters more to him than the life of his only son. He thinks it makes him special – a grand gesture like that – God, it makes me sick to think of it!' His face paled as he added in a low voice, 'And all because he could not bear to be called a few names.'

'Would that have happened? Would he have been criticized for it?' asked Mara with interest.

'Bound to be,' said Valentine. 'People always pass judgement on a mayor for one reason or another. Poor old Richard Athy – when he was mayor everyone was always whispering behind his back, and even calling things out after him in the street; taunting him with spending money on his fine new home instead of repairing the streets. James couldn't stand something like that; he's very proud. But to condemn his own son to death – well . . .' Valentine stared gloomily at her, his face a mask of pain and his shoulders slumped in defeat.

'Can any more be done?' he muttered, speaking to himself more than to Mara, but then his eyes sharpened as the large boat that Mara had seen from her bedroom window came into sight, gliding slowly now and pointing its nose in towards the docks, steering its way between barrels and tubs that were floating on the water of the harbour. Suddenly he changed. He pulled himself up to his full height, his face lit up with a smile and he went forward with both hands outstretched.

'Who is it?' asked Mara, keeping step with him. She was puzzled by the huge transformation in a man who, a minute before, personified despair.

'My cousins from Menlough; I had not expected them before tomorrow; they came immediately,' he said. 'We're a close family, us Blakes!' There was a wealth of pride in his voice.

'Would you like me to give your message to Margaret?' Mara asked. He had glanced hesitantly at her and she guessed that he wanted to be alone to greet his relations. He would be busy with them; the large boat was packed tightly with men, tall strong-looking men, all bearing the Blake stamp of richly-coloured faces, wide smiles and dark hair. No women amongst them, she noted. A gathering of the clan, it would be seen as in a Gaelic kingdom. To support Margaret, perhaps; or was there some other reason?

'You are very kind,' he said, and then he strode away from her, walking confidently and with his head held high, like a chief, she thought. These Blakes of Menlough were known to her from stories that Turlough and his friends often related – a thorn in the side of Clanrickard and of the O' Flaherty clan. Originally from the city of Galway, of course; some of the prolific family of Blakes had moved out to the shores of Lough Corrib and had established a power base there.

James Lynch, she thought, would not be too pleased to see them within his city walls.

At the top of Bridge Gate Street she paused for a moment. The church bell at St Nicholas's struck the hour of eight – still very early for breakfast at the Bodkin household, she thought and turned decisively to the right away from Lombard Street and towards the town. She was curious to see the shops and the surrounding streets before the damage was cleared away.

The shopkeepers were taking down shutters and talking in low voices to each other as she passed by. Several of them looked tired and there were occasional bursts of laughter followed by whispers. Mara suspected that many of these respectable citizens had joined in the riot last night; in any case there did not appear to be damage done to the shops that she had passed when she walked down Cross Street. Gaol Street was littered with stones but the gaol itself, with its barred and shuttered windows, did not seem to have suffered much harm.

It was a different story with the fish market. That was absolutely wrecked. Of course that might well be owned by James Lynch. His business was fish; she remembered Margaret saying that her husband's business was coal and fish. It was very likely that he would own the market, and if he did, the verdict by the citizens against his judgement was very clear.

The fish market stalls had not just been pushed over by a rabble; they had been systematically destroyed. The upright struts, left in position so that the waxed canvas coverings could be draped over them each morning, had been smashed to pieces and the heavy elm tables that were placed beneath them hacked with axes and knives. The barrels and tubs that stood by each stall for the fish were no longer there and several fishermen coming in with an early morning catch were looking around them in astonishment.

Mara recognized one of them, a young man from her own kingdom. 'Setanta!' she exclaimed with pleasure and went forward to meet him.

'Brehon! How are you?' He was not surprised to meet her. He and his wife fostered her small son, Conor, and they had known of her visit to Galway.

'Fun and games here last night,' he continued, looking around at the scene of devastation. 'The sea out there is bobbing with barrels and tubs. You and the scholars were safe, I hope. No problems.'

Not looting then, thought Mara, remembering the scene in the harbour – no looting, just an expression of distaste and condemnation by the people of Galway for their previously respected mayor. What would happen next? she wondered, while assuring Setanta of their safety and well-being.

He listened courteously, but it was obvious that he had some-thing to say so she looked at him enquiringly.

'The O'Lochlainn came across with me this morning,' he said, with a quick glance over his shoulder to make sure that they were alone. 'He's been staying at the Claddagh. He'd like to talk to you – he said he'd feel easier if you went back to the Burren today. He's gone down towards Lombard Street to look for you.'

'Well, I'd better walk back and see him,' said Mara. Claddagh fishing village was just across the water from the harbour. Ardal would have been within sight and sound of the stirring events of the last evening. She was not surprised that he had been worried for her safety. She would have to reassure him. 'I don't think I'll be going back today, though,' she said aloud. 'There is still unfinished business for me here in Galway.'

He bowed. To him the Brehon was a figure of authority. It was up to her to decide on what to do. 'I'll be here again in two days' time,' he said, still looking rather worried. 'If you need any help about anything, just come down to the fish market and you'll find me, or anyone will summon me. We fishermen have ways of getting in touch with each other.'

Mara wondered whether to talk to him about Sheedy, but decided not to mention the name. Setanta, though now married to a woman sheep-farmer in the kingdom of the Burren, was by origin and by upbringing from the kingdom of Corcomroe, and he would not recognize the name. It was over two years since Sheedy had disappeared from that part of the country. In any case it was probably best not to mention his name here. There was a constable striding around looking at the damage and angrily cross-questioning various bleary-eyed youths.

'It's good to know that, Setanta,' she said quietly. 'I have great trust in you and would not hesitate to ask you if I needed any help. Has there been any news of the king from Cahermacnaghten?'

He shook his head. 'No, Brehon,' he said. 'Cliona took the two children up to see Brigid yesterday afternoon and she said that there was none. Little Cormac was asking for you – noticed you weren't there. He's a clever little fellow – he and Art seem to learn new things every day. I'm teaching them to play hurling now. I've made them a little hurley stick each.'

He was as proud of the two little boys as though they – one the son of a king and the other the son of a sheep-farmer named O'Connor – were his own. Mara hoped that soon Cliona would have a child to this generous brave man. She was glad to hear that King Turlough had not yet managed to send a messenger, though. Hopefully she would be back at the Burren before he had time to worry about her. In the meantime it was good to know that Setanta would be here again in a couple of days' time. His loyalty to her and to King Turlough had been put to the proof last summer and he had not been found wanting.

Ardal O'Lochlainn was striding up and down the far side of Lombard Street, looking up at the windows of the Bodkin tower house. He was a reserved, but not a shy man and Mara was surprised that he had not gone to the house to enquire about her. However, she supposed, he might have felt that her host would not welcome visits from the 'mere Irish', as they were known, and out of respect for her he was taking his chance on meeting her. Certainly his face lit up when he saw her.

'Glad to see that you are safe, Brehon,' he said.

'I met Setanta at the fish market and he told me that you were here. You've heard of our riot last night, have you?'

He had all the details about the death of the Spanish boy, Carlos Gomez – he even knew all about Sheedy, but he seemed to have something else to say and she looked at him enquiringly.

'Let's walk down towards the sea,' she said after a minute as she saw him look up and down the narrow street and then carefully scrutinize the blank wall behind him.

There was no one around when they reached the western gate to the city. The door to Blake's Castle was closed and there was no sign of the visitors that had arrived downriver so early in the morning. However, there was a blaze of candlelight from the windows and Mara guessed that plans were being made.

But if there was a plot to rescue young Walter from the gaol tonight, what about Sheedy?

Could she – should she – interfere in the judicial process where there was such a conflict of laws? First, she thought, I will wait to hear what Ardal has to say. He is always worth listening to.

'It's to do with a man called Richard Athy, an importer of horses,' he said after a minute. And she turned a surprised face to him.

'I know the man,' she said, and waited for him to continue.

'I got this information from a fisherman,' he said, and then after a pause, 'It may or may not be correct; it did not actually come from the fisherman himself – he is away at the moment. My information came from his daughter.'

'No reason why it should be incorrect because of that,' she replied. She regarded him with interest, distracted for the moment from the affairs of the city state of Galway. Why was Ardal wasting his years with all those relationships with fishermen's daughters? she thought impatiently. There were lots of pretty O'Connor girls and O'Brien girls who would love an offer of marriage from Ardal, chieftain of the O'Lochlainns, who owned about a third of the kingdom of the Burren.

'Well, the report was that Richard Athy, on several occasions in the last year, has been meeting the Gomez ship, somewhere off the coast of Connemara, and Spanish horses have been transferred by sling between the two ships.'

Ardal was silent for a moment and then added drily, 'One feels that if Richard Athy had been purchasing horses in a legitimate way of business, then transfer into his ownership could have been managed more easily on dry land.'

'Indeed,' said Mara with emphasis. 'Well, this is very interesting to me, Ardal.' So that was perhaps what Carlos Gomez could have found out. Perhaps Walter was not the killer of the Spanish boy after all.

'I'll leave you now, Brehon, if you are sure that there is nothing that I can do for you. If you need me at any time then you can send a message to the Claddagh – any of the fishermen would take it for you. I'll wait your convenience.'

'Thank you, Ardal, I'm most grateful to you. I must stay until I can be sure that there is nothing else that I can do for poor Sheedy.'

And for Walter Lynch, she thought as she made her way back. She had no responsibility for him, but she could not turn her back on a boy who was little more than a child, and on his mother who adored him.

Everyone was at breakfast when Mara came in and apologized for her late arrival. Even Margaret was there, looking as though she had not slept, but calmer than she had been the evening before.

'I have a message for you from your brother,' Mara said to her. 'He would like you to join him at Blake's Castle.' She said nothing about Valentine's invitation to Margaret to make a permanent home there for herself and her son. There was no point in rousing false hopes in the woman at this stage.

'You will stay on here, though, won't you, Mara?' pleaded Margaret. 'I want to be able to talk to you, to ask your advice. I know that Walter did not do this thing. I am certain of it. I know that you will find out the truth. Henry told me all about you and how clever you are. Don't you think that Mara could solve this murder of Carlos, Henry?' She looked across at her host in a slightly challenging manner. Margaret, for all her gushing impulsiveness was no fool and would by now have picked up the hints that both the Bodkins thought her son was guilty as charged.

'If anyone can solve a problem then Mara can,' said Henry gravely. 'And we would be so pleased if she would extend her stay.' He said that with a quick glance at his sister who half-frowned. Jane Bodkin was probably anxious to get rid of their rather troublesome guest, who had been bold enough to tackle the mayor himself and to speak out in the courthouse and in church, but Mara accepted with smiling gratitude. For Sheedy's sake, as well as for Walter's, she would stay until she was sure that she could do nothing for them.

She turned to Margaret and offered the services of herself and her scholars as an escort to Blake's Castle. Henry, she noted, looked relieved at the prospect of Margaret's departure. The less he had to do with this affair, the better he would be pleased, she thought. He may have thought that Margaret would insist on trying to visit her son this morning, but she had said nothing. Probably it would be wiser to wait until she had her brother's company. As one of the two bailiffs in the city he would be able to bring weight to bear on the gaoler.

'I'll lend you a headdress, Margaret,' said Jane in a gush of hospitality after breakfast was finished. 'Come upstairs and choose something. I wish I had a gown that . . .' Margaret's gown was torn and crumpled but since Jane was a small, very thin woman and Margaret a large, plump one, then there would be no possibility of this. No one suggested sending up to the Lynch household for clothes, noticed Mara, and she guessed that the Bodkins, as well as Margaret, were wary of James Lynch.

'We'll wait outside for you,' said Mara, suddenly impatient of all this time wasting. Breakfast had taken about three times as long as it took in her house and she was anxious to discuss the matter with her scholars. However, she could hardly turn Jane out of her own parlour or even ask for a fire to be lit in another room, so they would have to find somewhere else where they could talk in private.

Blake's Pie Shop, she thought. Surely a piece of silver could hire a parlour there. The boys, she thought, were looking a little hungry. They were used to a much more substantial breakfast than they got at the Bodkin household, with its thinly cut slices of toast. Brigid always served up an enormous pot of porridge as well as substantial hunks of newly baked bread and slabs of cheese. Moylan, Aidan and Hugh, in particular, were growing very fast and needed a good breakfast before facing a day's work. Yes, a large slice of pie would set their brains working very well.

When they reached the corner of Lombard Street and were about to turn down towards the sea, she saw William Blake, himself, come out of his pie shop on Bridge Gate Street and walk past them with a bow, turning in the direction of Quay Street, after greeting the strangers. Margaret appeared a minute later and Mara led the way at a fast pace keeping William Blake in sight.

As she had guessed that he might do, he turned down Quay Street, walking quite fast until he reached the end of it. Then with a quick glance to left and right he crossed the road and hammered at the door of Blake's Castle. Mara congratulated herself silently on being right.

The Blakes were being summoned to a *slogád*, a hosting of troops.

Twelve

Heptad 97

There are seven qualities that make a satisfactory judge:
1. *A clear brain.*
2. *Great knowledge of the law.*
3. *Much experience.*
4. *Capacity to take pains.*
5. *Ability to see into minds.*
6. *Patience.*
7. *Incorruptibility.*

The door to Blake's pie shop stood open and there was a savoury smell of baking. Only William Blake's daughter was there, but she was effusively friendly, refusing to accept any money for the sole use of a parlour.

'If any come, then they can eat in the shop, Mistress Brehon,' she said with a quick curtsy. 'The fire is going well in the parlour and there's a pie in the oven.' She ushered them into the cosy room where half the fireplace housed an oven built from clay with an iron door. She knelt on the floor, peeped into the oven and reported that the pie would be ready in two shakes of a lamb's tail, then went out quickly and returned with an enormous cushion stuffed with goose down which she placed ceremonially on Mara's chair, and announced that her name was Joan.

'Perhaps we could have some mugs of small ale and a cup of wine for me,' said Mara, and was not surprised when the girl recited a whole list of wines for her to choose from. Galway was the largest importer of wine in the whole of Ireland and the choice was huge.

Joan brought seven small wooden platters and one large one when she returned with their drinks. She opened the oven, slid in a flat wooden spade and lifted out the pie, placing it on the large platter. With a sharp knife she immediately divided it into twelve large slices and rapidly transferred them on to the smaller platters.

'It smells wonderful,' said Shane enthusiastically. 'What's it made from, Joan?'

'A fruit called apricots and cheese from Brie,' said Joan. 'I'll bake you another in a minute or something different if you like.'

'We don't want to put you to trouble for us,' began Mara, but Joan interrupted her quickly with a flourish of her wooden spade.

'And didn't you take trouble for the Blakes yesterday, standing up there and speaking out for that poor boy Walter – a lovely fellow; the whole town is fond of him. You just tell me what you would like in the pie and I'll bake it. What about Spanish chestnuts? Have you ever eaten them?'

'Never!' exclaimed Aidan. 'But we would love to try.'

'It's very kind of you, Joan,' said Moylan, with his best smile at the pretty, dark-haired girl. He was getting to be quite a good-looking lad, thought Mara idly. He had wonderfully white strong teeth and his features were beginning to fall into place and his skin to recover from adolescent out-breakings.

'I'll slip a cocoa bean in with it,' promised Joan. 'That will bring out the flavour.'

'And some orange,' pleaded Hugh. 'We had a slice of orange last night and I've never tasted anything so good.'

'That's enough,' intervened Mara. 'We'll let you choose what to put in the pie, Joan, and I'm sure,' she added, taking a careful bite from the hot slice in front of her, 'that if it's as good as this one it will be delicious.'

'Now,' said Fiona, as soon as the door closed behind Joan, 'let's talk about the killing of Carlos Gomez, because I believe Margaret. I don't think that Walter did it.'

'I suggest that we leave Walter out of it for the moment,' said Mara firmly. The issue was too emotional a one; that attractive boy lying under a death sentence – and a horrible death, also, was bound to cloud their judgement.

'It occurs to me,' said Fachtnan tentatively, 'that there's been very little talk of the victim, of Carlos Gomez. Could we perhaps summarize what we know about him first before we begin arguing?'

'Good idea,' said Moylan, and Mara produced a piece of vellum, a quill and a well-stoppered ink horn from her satchel and looked around at her scholars.

'He was from Spain,' said Shane with a shrug.

'He was rich; at least we were told by Walter that Carlos was rich. He said that he was filthy rich,' said Aidan.

'He was thinking of setting up a business of importing horses, so that might have got in someone's way,' said Fiona.

'He was paying court – and very seriously – to Catarina Browne, who is absolutely gorgeous,' said Moylan with a sly look at Fiona. 'And,' he added quickly, 'that did not just affect Walter; apparently Anthony Skerrett, the grandson of that old lawyer, well, he was mad about her, too.'

'That's right,' said Fiona. 'We saw him looking at her across the tables when we were in one of those inns. He was clenching his fist and kicking at the table leg from time to time and muttering to the friend who was with him. He wasn't drunk either. Do you remember, Aidan? I told you to look.'

'And I said "If looks could kill . . .", I remember that,' said Aidan.

'Right, that's one name to write down: Anthony Skerrett, and the motive will be jealousy. Anything else?' Mara took another nibble of her pie. It really was delicious.

Then there was a knock at the door and Joan came in with an unbaked pie and a jug in the other. She smiled at the almost empty platters, placed the second pie in the oven and refilled the mugs with the ale.

'More wine, Mistress Brehon?' she asked, but Mara shook her head, placing her hand over her cup. The wine was very strong and she needed to keep her head clear. Fiona, she noticed, had the look of one who is thinking hard, but she wasn't the first to speak when the door closed. Uncharacteristically it was Hugh.

'I think that we should look at the captain of the Gomez ship,' he said.

'Too late, my boy,' said Moylan smartly. 'He's gone – on the high seas by now, I'd say.'

'Doesn't stop us looking at him,' said Hugh with unusual spirit. 'In fact, I think it was rather suspicious the way that he made such a huge fuss about getting away on that very day. After all, what difference would a few days' delay make?'

'In any case, that corpse will be absolutely stinking by the time he arrives in Spain; he'll be lucky if it doesn't start to leak through,' said Aidan, who was the son of a farmer. 'It was pointless, really – all this rushing away. So we have to ask ourselves why he persuaded the mayor into holding a trial and then releasing the body. I think you're right, Hugh,' he added, rather unusually for him. Aidan and Moylan rather despised the two younger boys and felt themselves to be immensely older and wiser.

'What was his motive, do you think?' asked Mara, writing busily.

'Well,' said Hugh. 'The captain seemed very keen to talk about Walter's guilt – very, very anxious that there should be no doubt about it. But I've remembered something interesting. Shane and myself were talking to one of the Spanish sailors at the Shrove celebrations and – I must say that we couldn't understand each other too well, though his English was better than the few words of Spanish we knew – but he seemed to be saying that the captain didn't like Carlos much and that Carlos had been threatening him.'

'And then he winked at us,' continued Shane, 'and slapped his purse and rubbed his first finger against his thumb, just as if he were rubbing a gold coin or something. Hugh and me thought that he was hinting that the captain had been stealing from the Gomez family and that Carlos had threatened to expose him. When he said that he went like this –' and Hugh drew his finger across his neck – 'and then he said something about the captain being *decapitado*.'

'Head chopped off, I suppose,' said Fiona.

'I remember something like that, too – about the captain. I think Valentine Blake said it to me; something about how he advised Carlos to say nothing until they were back in Spain – safely back, I think he said,' added Mara.

'But he didn't come safely back,' said Fiona.

'And Carlos Gomez wasn't really the type of person that would take advice from someone,' said Moylan. 'Valentine Blake might think that he agreed, but that doesn't mean that the suggestion was taken up. Carlos was a haughty sort of fellow. Thought he knew it all. Do you remember the way he spoke to you, Fachtnan? Like as though you were just a boy. And you were only trying to stop him putting his foot into something.'

'And he stepped in it the next minute!' Shane could hardly

stop himself laughing at the thought, but then quickly sobered up as he recalled that Carlos was now dead.

'He was drunk,' said Fachtnan, brushing it aside. 'That was why he was so rude. But I think that Carlos and the captain were on bad terms, Brehon. They seemed to give each other dirty looks whenever they met.'

'He talked big, that Carlos,' remarked Fiona. 'He kept going on about the horses that he would import and how that would make such a huge difference to the type of horses that they have here in Galway – nags, he kept calling them.'

Mara listened with interest. Her scholars were sharp and they had obviously made a lot of acquaintances during the Shrove celebrations. She was getting a very clear picture of Carlos and that was useful. On the whole, she had found that in cases of murder the character and history of the deceased was of prime importance in the solution to the killing. She decided to tell them about Ardal's words.

'Margaret Blake said something about Richard Athy setting up a horse-importing business; she said that he was doing very well with it. He struck me as an ambitious sort of man – a man to whom money and position meant a lot. And today I got some interesting information from the O'Lochlainn, who is staying at the fishing village of Cladagh.' Mara told them about the horses being winched by sling from a Spanish ship to the ship belonging to Richard Athy and they discussed it eagerly, agreeing that Alfonso Mercandez had been privately selling some of the Gomez horses to Richard Athy.

'So Richard Athy would be disgraced if Carlos got the truth from the captain,' stated Fiona.

'Also, you must bear in mind that if Carlos Gomez, with all the Gomez money behind him, started to import and sell horses here in Ireland, then Richard Athy's business could be injured,' said Moylan shrewdly.

'Would that be enough of a reason to kill a man, though?' questioned Shane. 'I wouldn't kill a man just because I was worried about my business.'

'You might if you had six sons,' said Moylan with a grin. 'Did you see the family he has, Brehon?'

'I think that is an important point, Moylan; it seems to me that the merchant families of Galway have a very strong sense of family,' said Mara, thinking of the boatload of Blakes who had arrived down the river that morning.

'They're sort of clans, really aren't they,' said Fiona. She looked around. 'We seem to have moved away from Carlos Gomez. Have we anything else that we can think of to say about him before we start looking at suspects?'

'May I sum up, Brehon?' asked Moylan, and when she nodded he rose to his feet, arranged an imaginary lawyer's gown around his shoulders and cap on his head. This practice had been started by Enda some time ago and now had become part of the ritual at Cahermacnaghten law school.

'Carlos Gomez, aged about twenty, reasonably good-looking, extremely rich, ambitious and perhaps ruthless. His plans appeared to be −' Moylan looked around and held up one hand, counting off the points on his fingers − 'One: to report the wrongdoing of the ship's captain to his father; two: to marry Catarina Browne; three: to set up a horse-importing business. And—'

But then there was a hasty knock on the door and Joan rushed in. Moylan sat down, blushing slightly.

'Excuse me, Mistress Brehon,' she said in a rush, 'have you heard the news? They are crying it at the street corners. Come and listen.'

She rushed back out again and the others followed her through the little courtyard where they had sat last night. A crowd had begun to gather around a man shaking a bell who was standing on a wooden box at the junction where the three streets, Lombard Street, Market Street and Bridge Street met.

'Hear ye, hear ye!' he called continuously and rang his bell again and again, looking all around until no more walking or running figures were to be seen. Shopkeepers in aprons joined shop boys and housewives; Mara saw Setanta at a distance with some women from the fish market.

'Hear ye, hear ye! All persons in the city to be of peaceable and civil behaviour, not to walk around the streets or rows tonight after the hour of darkness,' intoned the town crier, repeating his one sentence message again and again until the crowd started to straggle away. Several heads were together but there were no comments made aloud, and even the children were silent and anxious-looking.

Joan said nothing until they were back inside the pie shop and then she said loudly and clearly to another woman, her mother perhaps, whose head had appeared from the kitchen, 'There is to be a curfew tonight. All citizens of the city of Galway are to be indoors by sundown.' Her voice held a warning note and instantly the older woman disappeared.

'Let's see about that pie, now,' said Joan, trying to smile, but her face was anxious. Mara's suspicions about the gathering of the Blake family at their castle beside the docks grew to a certainty. Still, it was not her business. On the other hand, she decided, the affair of young Walter was her business in so much as it was the business of every human being to endeavour to save a life, if at all possible. She sat very still, gathering her powers; her knowledge of the law was of no use to her at the moment – English law reigned here – but her knowledge of human nature, the power of her intelligence and of a well-trained, well-organized mind might come up with a solution. Intuitively she had felt that Walter would not do such a deed and that intuition had been confirmed by her examination of the dead body in the church. She would say nothing of this to her scholars for the moment, she thought. Let them approach their fact-finding missions with clear and unprejudiced minds.

The pie smelled mouth-wateringly delicious and Joan refused any extra money for it – 'Just a few bits and pieces left over since last night,' she said dismissively. 'I'll leave you in peace now,' she said. 'I have an errand to do, so just let yourselves out whenever you're finished. There's not a soul will disturb you.'

And then she was off – going down to Blake's Castle with the news, surmised Mara.

'That's interesting, thinking about the dead man,' said Shane, speaking with his mouth half-full of hot pie. He chewed, then swallowed and said dramatically, 'So was the fatal blow struck because Carlos was ambitious or because he awoke jealousy?'

'Or fear,' put in Hugh. 'That ship's captain must have been scared stiff to go back to Spain with him.'

'Or was it,' continued Shane, imperturbably ignoring the interruption, 'because he was wealthy?'

'Nothing was stolen from him,' pointed out Aidan.

'That's true,' confirmed Mara. 'I saw his purse on the body.'

'I know what Shane means, though,' said Fiona. 'We should be thinking about the Gomez wealth. He was the son and heir to his father; now he's gone, who will inherit?'

'Someone in Spain, I suppose,' said Shane sadly. 'It can't be any of the sailors, so that one has to be crossed off our list. We can't investigate the people over in Spain, I suppose, can we, Brehon?'

'No, it doesn't have to be crossed off our list,' said Fiona. 'What about Catarina – the gorgeous Catarina; she was his cousin and he had no brothers and sisters; I remember hearing him saying that.' She gave a teasing look at Moylan. 'I bet you that she was the one who stuck a knife in him. She looks that type.'

'Rubbish,' said Moylan turning red. 'A girl like that!'

'She's almost as tall as you are – she's a monster,' said Fiona. 'Did you see the size of her hands? She has hands like a man.'

Mara kept a diplomatic silence while Moylan and Fiona argued, but it was an interesting point. Not only was Catarina tall and well made but she rode like an athlete and was probably very fit. After all, it didn't take much strength to knife a drunken man, especially if he were asleep. But why do it?

And then she thought of something else. Something that had been said by Margaret on that night at Blake's Castle.

'You're forgetting that Catarina has an older brother,' she said. 'David Browne was heir to the Gomez fortune until he was ten years old. Carlos was born then.'

'If he was heir then, he's heir now,' said Aidan wisely.

'So David Browne is about thirty years old. What does he do, do you know, Brehon?' asked Fachtnan.

'I haven't heard,' said Mara. 'I think,' she said rising to her feet, 'that we need to gather some more information about two house-holds. The first is the Browne household and the second is the Athy household.'

'So our suspects are,' said Fiona, lowering her voice to a murmur, 'the Spanish captain, Catarina Browne, David Browne, Richard Athy – his children are too young; the eldest is only about Shane's age.'

'I'm perfectly capable of killing a man,' said Shane indignantly, but Moylan interrupted him.

'We're forgetting all about young Anthony Skerrett.' He looked around at his fellow scholars and said defensively, 'I don't care what you all say, I think this is a *crime passionel.*'

'Don't think much of your French accent,' said Fiona scorn-fully. 'Anyway, Catarina is not all that wonderfully beautiful that everyone has to go around committing murder in order to be number one with her.'

'I think it's worth investigating,' said Mara, doing her best not to laugh. Fiona had had her own way for the last year at the law school; it would do her no harm to see that there were other pretty girls around. 'Now this is what I'd like you to do,' she continued. 'Shane and Hugh, you go and talk to the women in the fish market and see if they have any more information about the Spanish captain. The sailors might have spoken to them. Don't cause any trouble or rouse any suspicions, though. Lend them a hand at putting their stalls back up again, be friendly and don't ask questions until you have established good relationships with them.'

'And us?' queried Moylan.

'You and Aidan should find out as much as possible about the Athy household; again be tactful and careful. Chat in shops or ask for help, for directions, anything like that. And Fachtnan, I think you should talk to young Anthony Skerrett, if you can get hold of him. Compare notes about the law schools that you both attend, find out what he was doing and who he was with on the Shrove celebrations, and, I know you will do this well, Fachtnan, get some sort of impression of what he is like. It takes a certain personality to commit a murder, and also, I suppose to commit what Moylan rightly calls a *crime passionnel*.'

'And what about me?' asked Fiona.

'You,' said Mara, 'are going to come with me and to call upon Catarina Browne. I expect to hear by this evening that you are her best friend. Talk about riding. Ask her to take you on The Green; they live very near to the Bodkins; you can easily fetch your horse and join her if you can persuade her that some outdoor exercise would be good for her in her sad state. And, Fiona,' she added, 'do allow her to criticize your horse. Bear anything she says as meekly as possible, and then ask her where would be the best place in Galway to buy a new horse.'

Thirteen

Medieval Laws Based on Customs
(From Blackstone's Commentaries)

The customs of London differ from all others in point of trial: for, if the existence of the custom be brought in question, it shall not be tried by a jury, but by certificate from the lord mayor and aldermen by the mouth of their recorder; unless it be such a custom as the corporation is itself interested in, as a right of taking toll, &c., for then the law permits them not to certify on their own behalf.

Catarina was still in black when her maidservant ushered Fiona and Mara into her presence. She was no longer dressed in hand-downs from her mother, but wore a well-fitting gown of black velvet which suited her, though she did not look as splendid as she did in red. She had draped a veil of beautiful Spanish lace over her dark hair and it half-hid her face. However, even through the lace, it could be seen that her colour was as good as always, the faint glow in her cheeks enhancing the tanned skin and the bright brown eyes. There was little sign that the death of Carlos had affected her. She received her guests coolly and looked at Mara with disfavour. No doubt the intervention in the court of law had come to Catarina's ears and she was offended by it. A hard-hearted girl, thought Mara, eyeing the handsome face covertly, while Catarina exchanged a few coldly, civil words with Fiona. How could she possibly contemplate with such an unmoved countenance the terrible fate of a boy whom she had known from childhood, a boy who had grown up with her and had adored her?

Fiona was playing her part well, Mara observed with approval. She barely reached to Catarina's shoulder and that helped as she appeared more like a younger sister than a girl of the same age. She was enthusing girlishly about the report of Catarina's Arab horse and relating regretfully how short of exercise her own horse must be since they arrived at Galway.

'I wish I could see your horse,' she ended plaintively, and Mara was glad that the boys were not present because Aidan, at least, would have found it hard not to have sniggered.

'Well . . .' said Catarina consideringly. She looked down at her black clothing with ill-concealed distaste. There was no one to admire the picture of sorrow that she made and she must, by now, have judged that she had far more attractive clothes to wear. Mara guessed that her sorrow for Carlos would be short-lived; she had been flattered by his attentions and encouraged by her parents' enthusiasm. And, of course, his wealth would have been very enticing.

At that moment David Browne entered the room. Yes, she thought, he probably was about thirty years old, but bearing his years well. No Spanish beauty, such as his sister had inherited, but a chunky, square-looking young man with a shrewd eye and a smiling face. At his entrance Catarina appeared irritated. He had pretended that he did not know visitors were present; had pretended not to recognize Mara for the moment; had tried to present the picture of a languid young man about town, but those shrewd eyes belied his words and Mara saw Catarina gather herself as for a battle.

'I am going to exercise my horse; she will suffer if I leave it any longer,' she said in a challenging way to him.

His brown eyebrows rose.

'Do you think that will cause talk,' he said quietly. 'You are in mourning, you know, and the people of our blood, the Spaniards, are even more formal about occasions like this. A woman should stay indoors, hidden from all eyes until a suitable period has elapsed.'

Mara's hackles rose. She would bet that he would not refrain from exercising his horse just because of the death of a cousin.

'But Catarina is half-Irish, isn't she?' she asked in the tone of one who seeks information. And then when he said nothing, she continued, 'What an interesting evening that was – your Shrove celebrations, weren't they?' She said the words to Catarina, but kept her eye on him.

'They ended badly,' he said shortly, taking his eyes away from his sister and fixing them on Mara.

'Indeed,' she said sadly. 'What a shame that you were not successful in turning back your cousin. I saw you go after him on that fateful evening, when for the second time he went through the Great Gate to the east.'

He was taken aback at this. He eyed her suspiciously for a moment and then said, 'Yes, indeed.'

But he did not deny it, thought Mara, looking at him in a friendly fashion while suspicions flashed through her mind. So her guess had hit a target. His sister, she noticed, was also looking at him with curiosity in her eyes.

'I think, David,' she said in a deliberate fashion and with a challenge in her voice, 'I will go out. I owe it to my horse and it will be good to have Fiona to bear me company. We're very short of girls of my age in the city of Galway,' she said to Fiona confidentially. 'The young men think that they know everything and that they can be the rulers.'

'Think of me at a law school with five young men,' groaned Fiona, and Mara knowing how this one girl ruled the roost there found it hard to keep back a smile.

'I'll leave you then in good hands, Fiona,' she said. 'Perhaps David will escort me. I still find those streets quite bewildering.'

'Of course,' he said, but his voice was cold.

'You're not too busy?' she queried with a delicate lift of her eyebrows, and he shook his head, while Catarina gave an affected little laugh.

Soon they were back out on the streets, leaving the two girls together. Certainly not too busy, she thought. After all, today was a working day and he was apparently just lounging around the house and was perfectly at liberty to walk out with her. Perhaps his upbringing as heir apparent to the Gomez fortune until he was ten years old had unfitted him for the normal, everyday mercantile life of the city.

'What an appalling affair,' she said affably as she strolled down Lombard Street with him. 'Walter Lynch seemed to be such a pleasant, well-mannered young man. I find it hard to believe that he could actually have committed a murder.'

'Strange things happen when a man is foiled,' he answered.

'Foiled?' she queried. 'You mean that Carlos was going to be successful in his bid for your sister's hand?'

He nodded. 'The engagement was going to be announced on the following day. They planned a marriage at the end of Lent. Then they were going to go together to Spain for a few months.'

If that was true, thought Mara, the captain did not have much motive for the murder. If Carlos was occupied with wedding ceremonies, then he was unlikely to be pursuing his vengeance against the man – whatever the truth behind the rumours of his deceit. She looked around her, surveying the tall four-storey-high warehouses.

'Such a busy city,' she said. 'I had no idea that Galway imported and exported so many goods. What line of business are you in, yourself?'

This query took him aback. She had not glanced at him, but she was skilled in sensing sudden movements, awkward pauses. She gave him a moment to recover and then looked at him with an inviting smile.

'I've been remiss,' said David, after the silence had lasted a minute. 'I've forgotten to ask where you are going.' He hadn't answered her question but she did not repeat it.

'To the gaol,' she said in an offhand way, and then, as she watched his face darken, his lips tighten and his eyes grow angry, she said quietly, 'I want to provide that poor old man from my kingdom with some fresh clothing and some hot food. That would be permissible, would it not?'

That took him slightly aback, but then he shrugged to demonstrate his lack of interest.

'My father imports woven woollen cloth,' he said. 'You might find something to your liking in his shop or warehouses.'

No word about his role in the business, she noted. It was as she had thought. These sons of the successful traders in the city, like Walter and like David, were brought up as gentlemen and did not soil their hands with work. Walter was being pressed by his father to come into the business and was still quite young; David, though, was a grown man. Still, as far as she knew, he was now once again the heir to the large Gomez fortune, and so would remain in that happy state of having money to fulfil his dearest wishes.

If things had been otherwise, Catarina, with her dowry from her mother and with her marriage to Carlos, would have been the rich and successful member of the family. There had been a very apparent tension between brother and sister. Mara's thoughts went to Fiona and she hoped that her clever scholar was getting plenty of information from the girl who had, apparently, been betrothed to Carlos before his sudden death at the time of the Shrove celebrations.

'Woollen cloth, well, that's just what I need. Is it made up into clothes or just sold in lengths?'

'Come and see for yourself,' said David, sounding rather bored and as if he wished to be elsewhere. He led her rapidly away from Gaol Street and up Middle Street, pausing in front of a tall, ware-house-type building but with a shop front on the bottom storey.

'A warm cloak, perhaps,' she said to him, and he led the way inside.

David was greeted respectfully, but with formality by the man in charge of the shop. Mara guessed that he had not been in the shop for quite some time. He did not appear to know where the cloaks were when she addressed the question directly to him and, after a moment's hesitation, the man in charge led the way. Mara quickly purchased a cloak, a pair of hose, a shirt and warm doublet. Poor Sheedy would be more at home in Gaelic dress, but these were warm and thick and what he was wearing had been reduced to rags.

The price was high, but Mara paid without question. Lawyer Bodkin had introduced her to the bank owner in Lombard Street, a member of the Blake family, and she had changed her silver there for a large quantity of shillings and sixpences and a small amount of sovereigns, all stamped with the head of Henry VII, the father of the present king. The clothes for Sheedy took a large part of one of her sovereigns, but they would keep the poor old man warm until she was able to do something to rescue him.

David watched her purchases with astonishment.

'I hope you haven't wasted your money,' he said bluntly. 'The man will hang in five days' time.' But then his face grew thoughtful.

'The word is out that Mayor Lynch may be thinking to release his son,' he said. 'If he bends the law for that, then he might bend it for the mad man. If you are thinking of appealing for mercy for him, then you should wait and see what is happening to Walter.'

The thought had already flashed through Mara's mind that if Mayor James Lynch released his son, then he would be in honour bound to release Sheedy, also. And what would the mayor do then? Could he continue to reign? Would he be forced to resign?

It struck her that if Walter were guilty then he had done David a very good turn, without, it seemed, doing himself one. Even if his father did pardon him, Catarina was unlikely to marry a man who was suspected of killing her future husband.

'How beautiful your sister is,' she said aloud. 'I understand from my host that all the young men in the town are in love with her.'

He laughed harshly. 'That sounds an unusual exaggeration from a cautious man like Henry Bodkin; of course, Walter fancied himself in love with her, but that was only a boy-girl affair.'

'And Anthony Skerrett?' asked Mara.

'He spends most of the year in England, at Lincoln's Inn. He is training to be a lawyer like his grandfather.' David's tone was dismissive. Perhaps he did not like the idea that his sister had lots of men in love with her. Or perhaps he was jealous of her looks and her popularity.

'But at home at the moment, is that not right?' questioned Mara. English law terms, she knew, kept strictly to the exact dates for their terms, as indeed did the Irish law schools. Michaelmas Term began on the twenty-ninth day of September and the Hilary Term would begin on the feast of St Hilary, the fourteenth day of January, and would end just before Easter. The last term was the Trinity Term and that commenced on the Monday after the feast of the Holy Trinity. So what was the young man doing back in Galway eight weeks before the end of the winter term?

'That's right,' he said. And then as she raised her eyebrows slightly, he said unconvincingly, 'I've heard that his grandfather, the bailiff, John Skerrett, is not well.'

'Really,' said Mara. She had not seen John Skerrett at the trial of Walter, but he had been present at the trial of poor Sheedy and had looked as well as men aged over seventy normally look. And she said so. No doubt, David did not want to suggest that Anthony Skerrett may have come all the way from London to Galway in order to be with Catarina for the Shrove festivities.

He shrugged again. 'You may be right,' he said. 'I can't remember whether I have seen him or not.'

'I wish I had known that he was a law student,' said Mara innocently. 'My scholars would be interested in talking with him. Where does he live?'

'Near to Shoemaker's Tower,' he said briefly, and added with a tone of relief, 'Here we are at Gaol Street. You just cross the street and then go in through the doorway. You can see the gaoler standing there. You'll excuse me if I don't go in with you. I cannot abide the smell of that place.'

With a flourish of his hat and a bow he handed over the parcel and left her at the doorway to the gaol.

Mara was about to cross when she noticed that people on the

pavement opposite were drawing back, either flattening themselves against the walls, or else stepping out into the roadway. There was a faint tinkle of a small handbell and then into her sight came first James Lynch, Mayor of Galway, looking neither to the right nor to the left, but staring resolutely ahead, and then a small altar boy, ringing a bell with one hand and shaking a censer of incense with the other. Behind them came a priest in white vestments holding up a monstrance in one hand and a gold chalice in the other.

The little procession passed the silent people and turned into the gaol. Mara waited for a couple of minutes and then crossed over. As she had guessed, there was no sign of them when she entered the gaol. There was a strong smell of incense around and a minute later the gaoler came up the stairs with a large key in his hand.

'I'd like to see prisoner Sheedy O'Connor; I have some clothing for him,' she said. She put down her parcel on his table and opened it, taking a shilling from her purse while he was lifting and turning over the clothes with a dubious expression.

'Not sure if I can allow you to go down yourself,' he observed. He saw the shilling though, and she could see a hesitation in his face. 'I'll take them to him,' he offered obligingly. 'People aren't normally allowed to visit condemned prisoners.'

'Walter Lynch has just had three visitors,' pointed out Mara, moving the shilling slightly so that it caught the light from the candle and glinted invitingly.

'That's just to pray with him.' His eyes were on the shilling and she took another one from her purse.

'Exactly what I have come to do,' she said briskly, and gathered up her parcel. 'We should go down quickly so that we do not get in the way of the priest coming back up, shouldn't we?' she suggested.

That convinced him. He began to walk very quietly and carefully down the stone steps and she followed him, handing over the two shillings once he had unlocked the door.

'Look, I won't lock you in so that you can let yourself out whenever you wish,' he whispered. 'Sometimes ladies come over faint when they are down in cells like these. Not used to the smell, they aren't. Don't worry that he'll attack you when I leave; he's harmless. And he's in chains. He can't hurt you. Speak quietly, too – and don't come out until they're gone from next door.'

The walls were fairly thick and Mara could only just hear the priest's voice. He appeared to be reciting an act of contrition, preparing the lad for death, perhaps, thought Mara, appalled afresh at the notion of that young life being cut short. The words were echoed by the high voice of the altar boy. There was no sound from Walter, but James Lynch joined in halfway through with a loud steady voice.

Sheedy was sleeping peacefully. Mara did not disturb him. She had seen fairly clearly at the trial that his wits were completely gone. There was nothing that could help him except a royal pardon by reason of insanity.

And this royal pardon could be given by James Lynch as the king's representative in the city of Galway.

Mara placed the warm, thick cloak over Sheedy and hung up the hose, shirt and doublet on a nail on the back of the door. She would bribe the gaoler to bring some hot water to wash the old man and to change his clothing.

In the meantime, she would wait until the prayers next door were finished and the visitors had left. She needed to talk to Walter and see what memories might have come back. He had now had two days' sobriety after that night of drunkenness. She turned over in her mind various reasons which might persuade the gaoler to allow her access.

If Moylan was correct about how his own recollections of a drunken night did not resurface until two days later, then it would be interesting to hear what Walter's memory might now have dredged up.

The prayers were over more quickly than she had hoped. There was a sound of the door opening and a smell of incense drifted into Sheedy's cell.

'I will visit you again on the morrow, my son, and hope to find you more repentant then,' Mara heard James Lynch say, and then the sound of footsteps going back up the stairs – two men and a boy, she thought, as she listened intently to the sound. But there had been no click of a key turning. So they had not been locked in either!

As quick as a flash, Mara came out of Sheedy's cell and slipped into Walter's. She might get a few minutes' conversation with him. The gaoler would be in no hurry to lock the door. Walter, like Sheedy, would be chained up, both hands and feet, so there would be no chance of escape unless a blacksmith was summoned to strike off his bonds.

Walter, unlike Sheedy, was wide awake. His clothes had been

changed and he had been washed and shaved. A heavy sheepskin cloak hung around his shoulders and he wore stout, sheepskin-lined boots. A candle had been left in the corner of the cell and she could see him well. He was still very white-faced but his eyes were clear. He had seen her as she came through the door and she heard him draw in his breath with surprise at her presence.

'You're looking better, young man,' she said in the slightly tart tones that she would address to one of her young scholars who had been in trouble.

He smiled ruefully at her tone. 'That was Uncle Valentine. He came in at dawn this morning,' he said. 'He boxed my ears and made me strip, wash and shave and dress in fresh clothes, and told me what an idiot I was. "Get your head up and get ready to fight", that's what he kept saying to me.' He looked carefully at Mara, and then said wonderingly, 'And do you know, he didn't ask me a single question.'

Mara's heart warmed to Valentine. What the boy had needed now in order to pull himself together was simple, practical love and unconditional acceptance. That was something that he did not get from his father, she thought, but it was something that his mother's brother had supplied unstintingly.

And then she thought of Valentine as he was when she had met him that morning. So he had been at the gaol at dawn! And when had he sent a message to the Blakes of Menlough so that they had travelled down the river from Lough Corrib to arrive in the city by daybreak? The chances were that Valentine Blake had not been to bed. Had he been on the streets all night? Had the riot been spontaneous? And even if it were, had Valentine fanned the flames? Still, that was his affair; it didn't alter the help that she wanted to give to Walter.

'I'm going to ask you a question, though,' she said firmly. 'I wouldn't have asked it yesterday because you were in no state to answer it, but I am asking now. Did you kill Carlos Gomez?'

He opened his mouth quickly, and then shut it again. From upstairs Mara heard the gaoler's voice talking to the mayor and then begging for a blessing from the priest. Let him ask to receive the Blessed Sacrament, she prayed. Let them say the Rosary together – that prayer was interminable. She needed some information from this boy, something that would shed light on what happened on that fateful night. Rapidly she repeated her question.

'I'm not sure,' he said eventually.

'Not sure?' she queried.

'I don't think I did. I certainly don't remember doing it,' he said. 'I remember nothing until the constable shook me awake.' He paused and then frowned. 'At least nothing important,' he said then.

'Tell me what you remember; I'll be the judge of whether it is important.'

'I just remember waking up and finding my cloak spread over me and then I went back to sleep,' said Walter.

'And why did that surprise you?'

'It's just that I had a memory of searching for it and not being able to find it.'

'Ah,' said Mara. 'And that is all that you remember?'

'That's all,' said Walter. He began to look a little miserable.

'Let me give you some advice, Walter,' said Mara rapidly, with one ear inclined towards the conversation between the priest and the gaoler above. She took the boy's hand within her own two hands and said emphatically, 'Under no circumstances confess to a murder that you may not have committed. Make no acts of contrition, either to your father or to the priest, or even to the Lord above, as you never know who may be listening. If you don't remember killing a man, then deny you have done so. You would remember if you did a thing like that,' she said bracingly. 'Keep that in your mind and keep your courage up. Now I must go, but I will try to see you again.'

Quickly, Mara opened the door, pulled it closed noiselessly behind her and then re-entered Sheedy's cell. The old man still slept, now cosily warm, she judged by the slight flush of colour in his cheeks.

In a way, she thought as she watched him, his plight might be more dangerous than that of Walter. The boy had powerful friends in his mother's family – the Blakes were roused for action and would not allow this affair to go ahead without protest.

But was James Lynch vulnerable to pressure? Or would he just go ahead with this unnatural execution of his son?

When the gaoler came in, Mara was sitting peacefully in the corner of the room and her eyes were shut as if in prayer. She heaved a big sigh and opened them when he set down the candle.

'May the Lord have mercy on his soul,' she said as she followed him upstairs, and negotiated a sum which would ensure that Sheedy was kept clean, warm and well fed for the few days of life that were still left to him.

On the way out she paused and examined some large dents in the heavy, studded door.

'What happened to your door?' she asked innocently.

'That crowd last night, drunk they were, most of them – trying to keep up the festival for a second night,' he said. 'I couldn't see much myself, inside here, but I can tell you that I feared for my life for a while when I heard the blows on the door. The mayor was good though. Had a troop of soldiers down here before they could do much! He's just told me that he will send them out to clear the streets at sundown as the curfew bell is ringing, and then they will stand guard outside the gaol for the night.' He lowered his voice. 'He's a hard man, the mayor, but he's a very just one. The law is the law; that's what he said to me. The citizens and people like me must be protected from those who would break the law. Even if one of them is his own son! You have to admire a man like that – well that's my view anyway, but there's plenty would disagree with me. They say he'll have to resign!'

The law is the law, said Mara to herself as she walked away. She had lived all of her life as far back as she could remember with that saying. Her father, a man admired by all for his firmness of principle, could well have said that. There was no reason why Walter, though the son of the judge, should not be found guilty by a just law. But was this law just? And had it even been followed? Did English law countenance the holding of a trial hours after the deed was committed? The evidence against Walter was evidence of circumstance only. And even if he had committed the deed, it was obvious that the boy had been drunk and incapable – out of his mind, as her scholars would say. What was it that Fiona had read out from the book of English law? Mara murmured the words to herself: 'And that man, though found guilty by the judge, being generally considered to possess no greater understanding than a beast, was granted a royal pardon by Ricardus Tertius Rex.' This applied to young Walter – out of his mind with drink – almost as much as it did to poor Sheedy.

I must do my best for both, thought Mara.

Fourteen

Utopia
(Thomas More's novel which describes an ideal society)

'Instead of inflicting these horrible punishments, it would be far more to the point to provide everyone with some means of livelihood, so that nobody is under the frightful necessity of becoming first a thief and then a corpse.'

Thomas More (1474–1535), student at Lincoln's Inn from
1496–1500

Fachtnan was sitting beside the window of a large inn called Blake's, which was situated across the street from the magnificent Athy tower house and quite near to the back of St Nicholas's Church. Beside him was a young man and they seemed to be chatting amiably. Mara hesitated for a moment, but Fachtnan smiled a welcome so she went to join them. Fachtnan, even as a young boy, always showed good judgement about the right thing to do and she assumed that he had reached the end of his conversation.

'This is Anthony Skerrett, law student from Lincoln's Inn, Brehon,' said Fachtnan, punctiliously introducing them to each other once she was inside the building.

'Welcome to Galway, and welcome to Blake's, the best drinking place in town.' Anthony was a rather square-looking young man with black hair cut very short, grey eyes and resolute chin. He looked full of character and intelligent. Fachtnan was drinking small beer, but young Skerrett had a cup filled with a dark red wine, which he sipped slowly and with the air of one who appreciates fine wines.

'Do let me get you something to drink, Brehon,' he said, seeing her eyes go to the cup.

'I mustn't stay,' she said. 'We are due back at the Bodkin household for a meal shortly so I must walk up to The Green and escort back Fiona, one of my scholars.'

'Yes, I've heard that you have a girl law student,' he said with an amused smile. 'By Jupiter, that would wake up the law school at Lincoln's Inn.'

'You would find it hard to keep up with her sharp wits,' agreed Mara affably. She knew that was not exactly what he had meant, but was unwilling to acknowledge that it was odd for girls to study law. 'She's riding with Catarina Browne at the moment,' she added.

She was not surprised when he immediately tossed back the remainder of his wine and rose to his feet. His face had lit up at the very name of Catarina.

'You must allow us to accompany you, there,' he said politely, and shook his head at the girl beside the bar. 'No more, Anna; we must be off,' he said, his smile discreet and restrained. Not a young man to flirt with girls in taverns, thought Mara.

Nevertheless, Anna was looking after them regretfully as they left. There were no other customers at the inn and a pair of personable young men was company for her. In fact, thought Mara, there was no other member of staff, either, no male member of the Blake family, here at this inn; just as there had been no males at the pie shop. Even Blake's blacksmith business at Lombard Street, she had noticed, had held only one rather young boy anxiously tending the fire.

'That was kind of Catarina to take your girl student riding,' said Anthony as they went out into the street.

Mara smiled but made no reply. She was busy looking around the streets. Soldiers in pairs tramped around, walking belligerently down the centre of the roadway, looking intently down alleyways and lanes. Constables, armed with short stout truncheons, stood in doorways or else walked slowly amongst the people, eyeing every face that passed as if looking for trouble. She listened with half an ear to Anthony telling Fachtnan about Catarina's new horse and about her excellence as a rider. There was no doubt, she thought, the young man was very much in love. He was at that stage of infatuation where he found excuses to drag his loved one's name into everything irrespective of the subject. Fachtnan's remark about the fine clock outside the tower of St Nicholas's Church brought forth an anecdote of how he was once late for a meeting and how Catarina had taken him down to the church to prove how late he was; the mention of Lawyer Bodkin reminded him that Catarina had predicted that the lawyer would now import horses of Arab breeding; and the sight of a beautiful length of red silk displayed in the window of a clothier made him stop, with his eyes widening as he told Fachtnan that he thought Catarina would love that colour.

So could it have been he who killed Carlos in order to eliminate the opposition; or was a young man with a steady, square jaw and a pair of intelligent eyes really the type to commit a *crime passionel*? A man who was legally trained and probably schooled to hold his passions at bay.

'Anthony was telling me about the dinners at Lincoln's Inn, Brehon,' said Fachtnan. 'Tell the Brehon about it, Anthony.'

'Well,' said Anthony, 'as we, the students, are eating our dinners, there is a scroll of vellum, tied with tape, placed in the centre of the table. As soon as the meal is over, one of the sergeants of law stands up, unties the vellum, unrolls it and then reads a case that has taken place that day or on a preceding day. It's read just once and then all the students have to debate it – some are nominated to defend, and others to prosecute.'

'And no one has seen the case before?' Mara thought about this as a teaching method. Her own scholars attended every case that was heard in the Burren and listened to her judgements, but perhaps she could do something like that with cases from earlier years, even the cases that her father had heard.

'The quality of the debate might be better before the meal than after it,' she remarked smiling, but Anthony shook his head. 'Not for me,' he said with a quiet smile. 'I always do well at that because I drink very little. I was brought up by my uncle, Edmond Deane, and when I was a boy he sent me to a school in France. I learned to drink good wine there and . . .'

He stopped, and Mara said with a smile, 'And you learned to appreciate the taste; not to use it just to get drunk.'

'Too much bad Spanish wine here in Galway,' said Anthony. 'Now that . . . well, I can understand a man wanting to swallow enough to drown the taste . . .' He laughed gently and indulgently as one tolerant of his friends' excesses. Mara looked at him with interest. She remembered the knife lodged in the chest of the dead man. It had been inserted expertly, slightly upwards at an angle, avoiding the bones of the ribs and aimed straight at the heart. Certainly, it had not been jabbed recklessly. She wished it had been possible to have a physician of her choice examine the dead body, but even without that, somehow she was strongly of the opinion that the knife had not been wielded by a drunken man.

'Will you come back to Galway to practise law or stay in London?' she asked as her mind ranged over the possible suspects for the murder of Carlos Gomez. The dead man had been rich, had been enterprising, had been judgemental and had been in love. Someone had killed him for one of those four reasons. The last reason would fit Anthony and she waited with interest for his answer to her question.

He had paused, staring straight ahead of him. There was little spare business for a fourth lawyer here in a city of three thousand, she thought. The sensible thing for him to do was to get some sort of position in London.

'Come back to Galway, of course,' he said, and then, almost angrily, 'Have you ever been to London, Brehon? I can tell you it's a terrible place to live, a stinking, violent, unpleasant place.' He laughed slightly, perhaps conscious that his tone had been aggressive. 'When I am in London, I get lonely for the sea, for my sailing boat and for my friends here in Galway. Ah, here we are at the Gate; don't worry, the guard knows me well and we can get through and back again with no trouble.'

'There they are,' said Fachtnan, and Mara was amused to see how the faces of the two young men, one on either side of her, lit up at the sight of the two girls.

Catarina and Fiona were cantering around the ring on The Green and rode straight over when they saw the party arrived. They made a lovely pair: one tall, dark and goddess-like; the other small, blond and vivacious.

'Have you had a nice time?' asked Mara, looking at Fiona's rather bored face.

'Oh yes,' said Fiona. 'But of course, it's not like riding back in the Burren where we can gallop for miles. I was saying to Catarina that she should come and visit us.'

'She would be very welcome; and you, Anthony, if you would like to see a native law school before you return to London,' said Mara, watching him. He had shaken hands politely with Fiona but when he turned to Catarina his whole expression softened and changed. His sharp grey eyes glowed and his resolute mouth trembled in a smile. He had not even heard her invitation and she did not repeat it.

'I think that we should return quickly, Fiona,' she said. 'Our hosts will be waiting for us. I hear that there is to be a curfew tonight, so the sooner we are off the streets, the better.'

She watched Catarina as they returned. The girls walked their horses and the two young men strode beside them, each at the head of his lady's steed. Fachtnan was listening with his gentle smile, looking up at Fiona's animated face as she chattered about Henry Bodkin's horses and about what his stableman had said about the lawyer's ambitions to breed horses that combined the strength and endurance of the Connemara horse with the speed and spirit of the Arabs.

Catarina, on the other hand, had nothing to say to Anthony. Her head was held high and she surveyed the crowds in the streets with a haughty, slightly hostile eye. She was not popular; Mara was saluted more often than she was and several indulgent smiles were aimed at Fiona's pretty face. One young man stopped and seized Fachtnan by the hand and seemed to be claiming undying friendship with him, reminding him of the hour they spent together at the Shrove Festival, while gazing fervently at Fiona.

Anthony, though, acted like an accomplished man of the world, making light conversation and not pressing any unwanted attentions on Catarina.

And why should he rush things, Mara asked herself? He was now left undisputed victor in the field. Carlos was dead and in a few days' time Walter might be hanged – and even if a miracle saved him, it was most unlikely that Catarina would ever look at him again.

Mara's thoughts were interrupted by a sudden exclamation from Catarina.

'There are those brats of Richard Athy and that dreadful untrained dog of theirs,' she yelled in a voice filled with fury. 'Get that unmannerly cur out of here,' she screamed to five small boys, ranging from about three to twelve years old, chasing down the street after an equally muddy dog who was racing ahead, with a large and rather decayed fish hanging from its mouth.

It was the strangest dog that Mara had ever seen – not at all like the tall, lean wolfhounds that she was used to, or like the herding dogs used by the farmers in her kingdom. This dog was massive, with enormous shoulders, a heavy, brutal jaw, a protruding line of bottom teeth and very small, pointed ears. His coat seemed to be brown and white but it was so plastered with mud that this was hard to be sure. It dropped the fish when it came to the butcher's shop and began barking uproariously, big deep barks from his massive chest. The butcher armed himself with a broom, yelling vigorously, women shrieked and the children yelled commands; the dog snarled at the butcher and Catarina's horse squealed in terror.

'Take the horses down Middle Street. Turn their heads quickly. Fachtnan, you go with Fiona. I'll see to the dog.'

Catarina's highly strung Arab horse was rearing up and showing the whites of its eyes, and although she didn't like the girl much, Mara had to admire how quickly her voice changed to a soothing murmur and how courageously she kept a hold of the bridle and coaxed the animal to turn its head away from the ferocious-sounding dog.

'Jake! Jake!' screamed the boys. Passers-by huddled into door-ways and added their shouts to the confusion of noise.

Mara walked immediately into the middle of the road. Pointing a finger at the burly dog, she said peremptorily in a quiet, but carrying, tone of voice, 'Sit!', and suddenly all voices were hushed as everyone stared at this strange visitor to their city.

Jake was equally amazed. He sniffed at the fish and looked around him uncertainly. He did not sit, but possibly had never been trained to know the word. His tail wagged in an apologetic manner and his ears drooped.

'Good dog,' said Mara, walking up to him and taking him by the collar. By now the horses were well out of sight but she kept her hand on the collar and looked down on the boys.

'We seed you,' said the smallest one. 'We seed you at the festival.'

'So you did,' said Mara in a friendly tone of voice. 'Have you a lead for Jake? No, leave it, Jake,' she said sharply as the massive dog bent his nose towards the highly scented fish.

'We losed it,' said the little boy. 'We seed you,' he repeated. 'You called Lady Judge. We was with our dad.'

'And what's your name?' asked Mara. 'Lend me a piece of rope to secure the dog,' she called over to the butcher, and he aban-doned his broom-weapon and plunged back into the shop.

'I'm William,' said the eldest boy, inserting his fingers beside hers into Jake's collar and patting the massive head, 'and these are my brothers: Henry, Stephen, Richard and John.'

'We are all called after the kings of England,' said Stephen with a gap-toothed smile, while Henry scowled and William looked anxious.

Mara kept a firm hold on Jake's collar. She wanted to give the two girls and their horses time to get away, but she also thought this might be a useful conversation. So these were the sons of Richard Athy, importer of horses, and former lord mayor of Galway, and they had been at the festival.

'I suppose you had to go home early to go to bed,' she said sympathetically.

'I were up at midnight,' boasted little John.

'No, you weren't,' said William. 'Father took us home at ten o'clock.'

'He's horrible and cruel and nasty,' said Richard cheerfully. He looked about six, Mara thought. She caught the rope that the butcher had nervously tossed to her and threaded it through Jake's collar, sending a word of thanks across to the man.

'I'll walk back with you to your house,' she said. William, the eldest boy, was an extremely thin, rather nervous-looking boy and did not look strong. It might be just as well to deliver Jake back to his own gate. The dog was still muttering low-pitched growls at the butcher; no doubt he had been beaten off with that broom on other occasions. 'What a shame that you had to go back home early,' she said sympathetically.

'He's old, our father is old; that's what he said. He said that he was sleepy.' Henry sounded scornful.

'And den he goed back by hisself,' said John.

'No, he didn't,' contradicted William. 'At breakfast he told Mother that he went straight to bed and fell asleep almost immediately.'

'Because he was so exhausted looking after such badly behaved brats,' said Stephen cheerfully.

'He tolded a lie,' persisted John. 'I seed him go out again. I seed him from my window. I were up at midnight. He goed creeping out – goed down to the gardens.'

'You're lying,' said William angrily. 'Father doesn't tell lies. Only stupid little boys tell lies.' He looked at Mara apprehensively, and she was shocked to see a look of fear on his face. Had he been warned not to talk about his father? Had he been threatened? Was Richard Athy's son trained to keep his secrets?

She smiled at him. 'Here, hold the rope; you're big and strong and you can manage him now. Take him inside quickly.'

She waited until they were safely inside their gate before walking down towards Lormbard Street and the Bodkin tower house. The gardens were on her right-hand side, just outside the wall and easily reached through Little Gate Tower. If Richard Athy had gone down there at ten o'clock of the evening, then he may well have walked up to The Green.

Did he meet Carlos Gomez there?

And if he did, was he the murderer?

And that, of course, she thought with exasperation, was where it all began to unravel? Could she possibly be responsible for convicting the father of those little boys? She imagined the burden on William's thin shoulders of knowing that his father was a murderer – of passing his tar-smeared body on Gallows' Green every day?

If only she were judging this under Brehon law. Everyone, she thought angrily, should have a chance to repent, a chance to turn over a new leaf and make retribution.

Fifteen

Chronicles of William Harrison (1534-1593): Chaplain to Lord Cobham

The greatest and most grievous punishment used in England for such as offend against the State is drawing from the prison to the place of execution upon an hurdle or sled, where they are hanged till they be half dead, and then taken down, and quartered alive; after that, their members and bowels are cut from their bodies, and thrown into a fire, provided near hand and within their own sight, even for the same purpose. In cases of felony, manslaughter, robbery, murder, rape, piracy, and such capital crimes as are not reputed for treason or hurt of the estate, our sentence pronounced upon the offender is, to hang till he be dead.

All of the scholars had already returned and were waiting, well scrubbed and well combed in Jane's parlour, entertaining her with a recital of the pattern of their days back at the Cahermacnaghten law school.

'But you work so hard!' she exclaimed as Mara came in with Fachtnan and Fiona, whom she had met coming from the Bodkins' stable yard.

'Yes,' agreed Aiden with a saintly look, and then rather spoiled it by adding with a grin, 'That's why we eat so much.'

'Give us two minutes to wash our hands and then we'll be with you, Jane,' said Mara. 'Will Henry be home for the meal?'

'He sent a message to say that he would be closing his office early because of a curfew, so he would manage until then with a slice of pie from one of the shops. He said he thought it would be best if you did not go out again as there may be trouble on the streets. You and your scholars can have this parlour to yourselves this afternoon. This is the day when my housekeeper and I go through the accounts and make up the orders for food. Henry fears that there might even be a riot.'

'A riot!' exclaimed Aidan excitedly. Mara frowned heavily at him to stop the words 'How jolly!'

'I know; it's dreadful, isn't it?' said Jane. 'Henry's man said that there are rumours that the mayor is planning to bring forward the date of execution in order to finish up the matter.' She sighed heavily, and said, 'His poor mother; he was the prettiest baby!'

The scholars, shocked into gravity, stared at her uneasily. Fachtnan had already gone upstairs and Mara made a signal to Fiona.

'Say nothing about your morning until we are by ourselves,' she said to her as they went up the stairs together, and resolved to turn the conversation from these affairs during the meal. At Jane's words, Shane had gone white and Hugh was crimson with a glint of tears in his blue eyes.

Death happened everywhere and no one could be shielded from it, but the death of a boy in their own age group, at the ruling of his own father, was something that they had never come across before. Judicial murder, in fact! Mara tightened her lips, resolving that no one should ever lose a life through her judgements.

And this, of course, was the problem.

'Tell me about the Blake family,' she said to Jane over the meal. 'So far we have met a merchant, a banker, a blacksmith and pie shop owner.' She did not mention the Blakes from Menlough, upriver from the city, though privately she wondered how they made their money – they were farmers and landowners, probably. And how did they get on with their neighbours, the ferocious O'Flahertys, these Gaelic chieftains who were so dreaded by the inhabitants of Galway city, she wondered? Live and let live, perhaps – the Blakes, from what she had seen of them, were a friendly crew.

'Oh,' said Jane in answer to her question. 'That's nothing! The Blakes are everywhere. There are Blakes in every line of business. And, of course, there is hardly a family in the town that they have not married into. You know the funny thing is, though; once a Blake, always a Blake. Our cousin, a horse trainer, he's married to a Blake and had ten children by her and she still talks about "my family" and "us Blakes". And my own grandmother was a Blake; she used to look at me and sigh, saying that I looked so like the Bodkins.' Her lips tightened at the memory.

Her words reminded Mara of Margaret's complaint that her nine daughters were all Lynches, every one of them – somehow as if they were not legitimate offspring of hers, unlike her son who was a Blake through and through. What had become of those nine girls? And what were they thinking of now that their little brother was condemned to die by the hangman?

After the meal was over Jane ushered them into the parlour. Already a large coal fire had been kindled and a small low table was spread with mugs, flagons of wine and beer and platters of small pies stuffed with dried fruits from France and Spain. The scholars, without being prodded, thanked her effusively and Hugh added an invitation to come to see them at the law school the next time her brother came to a horse fair at the Burren.

'It seems a long time since we met him that day,' said Shane, once the door was closed. 'Was he buying or selling?'

'Selling,' said Moylan decidedly. He was someone who always knew what was going on at fairs and marketplaces.

'Catarina says that "Bodkin" as she calls him, gets poor prices in Galway for his horses and that's why he travels into the country, going to places like the Burren. She says that he needs to get some Arab blood into his stock.' Fiona examined her face in the cloudy mirror near to the window.

'How did you get on with Catarina?' asked Mara with interest. 'What was your impression of her?'

'Didn't like her.' Fiona was always decisive in her opinions. 'You won't believe it, but she didn't mention Walter even once and when I said something about pitying him, she just shrugged her shoulders and said that he would have never amounted to much — just as though he were already dead.'

'Did she seem upset about Carlos?' asked Mara. 'I understood from her brother David that they were actually betrothed to be married.'

'It's strange, but she didn't say much about him, either.' Fiona frowned to herself. 'She was quite hard to talk to. I got the impression that she respected him for his business ideas, but she did say something about his weakness of drinking too much. She mentioned, though, also, about David being jealous that she was going to get the entire Gomez fortune and she was rather superior about the fact that she was not angry at the way things turned out now. She seemed to think that she was superior to her brother because of this.'

'What do you mean? "The way things turned out" — what do you mean by that?' asked Aidan.

'I'm coming to that,' said Fiona impatiently. 'Don't interrupt.' She looked around at the others and said, 'Guess what; the Gomez fortune will now be divided between Catarina and her brother David. Her grandfather's new will directed that the fortune was to go first to the son of Fernandez Gomez, that is Carlos's father, on Carlos's twenty-first birthday. And failing any living son from the said Fernandez, it was to be divided equally between the children of Isabelle Gomez Browne – that is Catarina and David. Girls inherit at eighteen and boys at twenty-one, so both of them will get the fortune immediately. And apparently it is quite a fortune! Catarina was very excited. Now what do you think of her for a suspect? And I'll tell you something else,' she went on, 'she's very strong. There was a pole, made from the trunk of a tree, laid across a couple of trestles for a jump and she lifted it with one arm and moved it up to a higher notch.'

'But she would have got the whole if she had married Carlos,' pointed out Moylan.

'Ah, yes,' said Fiona, 'but then she would have to have Carlos as well and that might not have suited her. She would not have liked someone who was keen to rule her and tell her what to do. Carlos was that kind of man and I'd say that she had begun to find that out by the end of the Shrove ceremonies.'

'Yes, but why tell you all about it?' asked Moylan. 'Why put herself under suspicion?'

'You forget,' said Fiona, triumphantly, 'we're not part of the investigation. She would have no reason to think of me as anything other than a girl to gossip with and to boast to. I vote we consider her as a suspect.'

'And what about her brother?' Mara looked around at her scholars.

'The word around the town is that he's an idler,' said Moylan smartly. 'Gets up late, drinks too much, that sort of thing.'

'Hmm,' said Mara, 'nothing too conclusive there.' She looked across at her two youngest scholars who looked as though they were bursting with eagerness to have their turn. 'Did you find anything out at the fish market?' she asked.

'You'll be interested in this, Brehon,' said Hugh. He looked at her hopefully. 'We were thinking, Shane and I, that if only you could tell James Lynch about this that you might persuade him to free Walter.'

'You see, one of the fisherwomen told us that Alfonso Mercandez had stuck his knife in her stall table one day and swore to kill Carlos Gomez as soon as he got him on the high seas again. She showed us the very mark when we were helping her to set her stall up again.'

'Was that what you were talking to Valentine Blake about?' asked Fachtnan, and then added, 'I saw you with him outside Blake's pie shop.'

'No, no,' said Shane impatiently. 'He just bought us a pie.' He coloured a little, but then turned to Mara asking eagerly, 'What do you think about the Spanish captain vowing to kill Carlos, Brehon?'

'That is interesting,' said Mara. 'Did she say why?'

'The fisherwoman said that he vowed that Carlos was trying to take away his good name and that he would be revenged on him.'

'Not much good now, though, is it?' questioned Moylan. 'After all, Alfonso Mercandez has gone back to Spain.'

'On a heavily laden cargo ship,' said Fachtnan quietly. 'Anthony Skerrett was telling me about his sailing boat and how fast it can go. I'm sure that even now a sailing boat could catch up with the Gomez ship.'

'Yes, but,' argued Shane, 'it doesn't really make sense for the captain to kill Carlos Gomez here in Galway. If he wanted to kill him, surely it would make more sense to wait until they were well out to sea, well on their way to Spain and then to push him overboard or something. The sailors would be under Alfonso's command and he could easily make sure that there was no one else on deck at the time. Who's to say that it wasn't an accident?'

'Well argued,' said Mara with an approving nod. Shane had a lawyer's mind, able to see both sides of a case. A minute ago, with Hugh, he had been making a case for the captain of the ship being responsible for the murder and now he had turned the matter on its head and shown that another interpretation was possible.

He looked pleased at her words, and then added, 'By the way, Brehon, we met Setanta. He told us that he was staying another night; one of the fisherwomen had paid him to help her to take her stall down before the curfew bell and to help her to put it up again the following morning. He said to tell you it would be best to stay indoors after dark as he had heard that there was going to be trouble on the streets tonight. He said that there was a rumour—' Shane shot a look at Hugh, and then finished quickly, 'But you know all that, Brehon.'

'That was kind of Setanta to send that message,' said Mara. Setanta had said something else to them; she knew that from the looks that they were exchanging. Something was afoot and Setanta knew about it. As he supplied fish to the Galway market he had picked up quite a bit of English. Had he dropped a hint about something to the boys, something about the trouble that was forecast for tonight? And did Ardal O'Lochlainn know all about this also?

Still, whatever it was, Setanta was reliable and sensible and would not have involved her two young scholars in any dangerous activity, so Mara put the idea from her and began wondering whether James Lynch would compensate the fishermen and women for their losses. After all, if he took rent for the fish market stalls then he should be responsible for the damage. Again, that was not any of her business, so she went back to unravelling the mystery surrounding the death of Carlos Gomez.

'And what about the Athy household?' she asked, looking over at Moylan and Aidan. She would keep her information to herself for the moment and see what the boys had to say.

'Big spender, Richard Athy,' said Moylan succinctly. 'House furnished with the best of everything. Got very splendid stables up near to The Green, too. They make Lawyer Bodkin's stables look like hovels. They are good enough for people to live in. Not too many horses, there, though. He must be waiting for a new consignment from Spain, I reckon – that's if he can afford to import them. We tried to have a chat with the stableman but he wouldn't say anything – seemed in a really bad mood. Perhaps his wages had not been paid. He kept looking over towards the Great Gate as if he expected to see his master coming. But if he was waiting for Richard Athy, then he was disappointed. We walked back that way and didn't see a sign of him.'

'We thought we'd find out if he owed any money in the shops, so we did one of the shop boys in a furniture shop a favour by helping him to mend a window shutter,' said Aidan. 'He had a bruise on his cheekbone and when I asked him about it, he told us that Richard Athy did it to him. It seems that the Athy account was well overdue and the boy had been sent to ask for money. Richard Athy hit him in the face and told him not to be so cheeky.'

'Coward,' said Fiona scornfully. 'Imagine picking on a boy. Why didn't he go around and face up to the shopkeeper, himself?'

'Had no money, I suppose,' said Hugh.

'People get angry sometimes because they are frightened,' said Fachtnan. 'Richard Athy had probably overspent and when he heard that Carlos Gomez, with the Gomez fortune to back him, was going to set up a horse importation business here in Galway city, well, that might have seemed to be the final blow to him.'

'How did you get on with his boys, Brehon?' asked Fachtnan.

'And the dog,' put in Fiona.

'The dog wasn't a problem,' said Mara absent-mindedly as she turned over the problem of taking evidence from small children. She was conscious of an expectant silence and looked up.

'And they said . . .' hinted Shane.

'The older boys seemed to think that their father did not go out again after taking them home, but the little fellow, John – he would be about three years old or so – well, he said he saw his father creeping out at midnight.'

'Probably made it up,' said Aidan.

'Little fellow like that probably doesn't even know when it's midnight,' said Moylan scornfully.

'William probably knows the truth; he's about my age and quite sensible,' said Shane.

Mara said nothing, but she reflected that an older child would be more likely to lie than a younger one. She had not liked that look of apprehension, or even fear in William's eyes.

'We found out something else for you, Brehon,' said Moylan with a satisfied air. He looked around at the assembled law school members. 'No one has mentioned the gates. Well, of course, there are sixteen of them and we didn't get around to all of them, but we visited the Great Gate – the one leading out to The Green – and also the gate at Shoemakers Towers – the two of them are nearest to Lough Atalia – and we were joking with the gatekeepers, and asking them if they were drunk on Shrove and making them prove they weren't by reciting the names of those they remembered.'

'And Anthony Skerret went out and so did the Spanish captain, and he thought he remembered seeing Richard Athy, but he wasn't sure. But he was certain that he saw David Browne. He remembered him because he said he was cold sober and that wasn't like him,' said Aidan triumphantly. 'And it was my idea to do that. We tried various names on them, including yours. They were very positive that you had not sneaked past them,' he added slyly.

'Well done,' said Mara heartily. She had thought of that herself, but wondered whether the record would be reliable. The guards would have had to be prompted she guessed.

'May I sum up, Brehon?' asked Fiona. Mara seated herself at a small side table where Jane had thoughtfully provided ink, parchment and pens. At Mara's nod Fiona rose to her feet and began to enumerate the suspects, ticking them off on her fingers as she went.

'In the matter of the murder of Carlos Gomez on the Shrove Tuesday before the season of Lent I find that the following are under suspicion: Walter Lynch by reason of jealousy; David Browne by reason of greed; Catarina Browne by reason of greed; Alfonso Mercandez by reason of fear; Anthony Skerrett by reason of jealousy; Richard Athy by reason of greed and fear. I gave Richard Athy two motives because he might be greedy but also fearful because of his debts, and because his transactions with the Spanish captain might come to light and disgrace him in the city. And if he is badly in debt he could be frightened of losing his beautiful tower house,' explained Fiona before sitting down.

'But you put in Walter,' said Hugh reproachfully. 'I thought we were on his side.'

'We're not really on anyone's side; we are seekers after the truth,' said Mara soberly. Hugh and Shane exchanged glances, but neither dared say anything. It was obvious that they disagreed but she did not lecture them. Their warm hearts were moved by the plight of a boy whom they knew and liked, and who was now facing a terrible death when the life would be choked out of him on the word of his own father.

In any case, Mara had a problem of her own. Yes, she would

seek the truth with all the power of her brain and her trained intelligence.

But what should she do with that truth once all was uncovered?

A person found guilty of murder in the city state of Galway would be hanged by the neck until dead.

Sixteen

Cecosca Cormaic
(The Teachings of Cormac)

It is said that three things mark a good king:
  1. *A rich harvest.*
  2. *A full cooking pot.*
  3. *Ships putting into port.*

It is a sign of a good king to have ships arriving at the ports of the kingdom because the goods that are carried on these ships bring prosperity to the people. They bring wine from France and from Spain, spices from Turkey, fine cloth from England and horses from Wales and from Spain.

Mara was woken from an uneasy sleep by the sound of a bell clanging imperatively, noisily and warningly. She sat up in bed feeling confused and disorientated. Her head had ached so badly that she had retired to her room and lain on her bed, hoping that a short sleep would restore her to the usual feeling of calmness.

But her sleep had not helped. It had been full of strange nightmares – visions of Ottoman pirates, of English kings, ships laden with cargo and of daggers embossed with silver, something about the Athy tower house and, oddly enough, of Henry Bodkin saying something about the mayor's position which she strove to remember. And when she woke, suddenly all was clear to her. The whole pattern fitted together.

She sat up in bed and looked towards the window. To her surprise it was still daylight. She got up from her bed and listened, hearing now, quite distinctly, the clang of a bell. No, it had not been part of her daytime dream. The curfew bell, harsh and unmelodic, unlike the church bell, tolled its warning and yet the sun had not set. She put on her shoes and then went out on to the landing outside her bedroom. There was a window there and she swivelled open one of the two casements between the central stone mullion and thrust her head out, looking down over Lombard Street.

There were plenty of people still in the street, shopping, visiting their banks, buying from the gold and silver merchants, or even visiting the money lender. They, like she, had been startled by the harsh warning of the curfew bell.

But now the bell had ceased, and yet the people in the streets were still standing, still listening. For a moment Mara wondered, and then she leaned further out, resting her elbows on the stone window ledge. Yes, there was another sound and now she recognized it. The rhythmic thud of soldiers' boots echoed through the stone streets, getting nearer and nearer. The sound seemed to spur the listeners and hurriedly they began to move away, each seeking the refuge of home behind a stout door and well-shuttered windows. Soon only the noise of marching feet could be heard.

The mayor had rung his curfew and called out his army well ahead of sundown.

Quickly, Mara checked her appearance in the convenient mirror beside the window and then went out of her door and down the stairs.

As she reached the top of the flight that led to the door she heard the iron knocker clang and clang again. A servant appeared, but Jane Bodkin was quicker.

'It must be Henry – he's forgotten his key,' she said as she looked quickly up towards Mara. Her face had a worried look and she hastened towards the door, almost tripping over in her speed to get it opened.

But it wasn't Henry. It was Cecily Blake, Valentine's wife, accompanied by a couple of servants. For a moment Mara hardly recognized the pink-and-white, placid, plump face. Cecily looked ravaged with fear and apprehension. In her arms she bore her tiny son, Jonathon, the pride and joy of Valentine Blake. Behind them came a nursery maid and a manservant, both laden down with bags and baskets, but it was obvious that Cecily had not wanted anyone other than herself to carry the precious little boy, heir to Blake's Castle and all its splendours.

'Jane,' she said breathlessly. 'May we stay? Valentine says that all will be safe, but I am worried about my baby. I don't want him at the castle tonight. Not with all those men in and out. Please, please, dear Jane, may we stay with you and Henry? Terrible things are going on.'

'Of course!' Jane was taken aback, Mara could see that, but she was a hospitable woman and she took Cecily by the arm and drew her in, giving a quick look at the maidservant who had just appeared, and mouthing to her, 'The green chamber'.

The manservant who had accompanied Cecily immediately withdrew, almost as soon as his mistress's feet had crossed the doorstep. He shut the door behind him with a determined clang and Mara thought she heard his boots running down the steps outside.

'Is Henry not here, then?' she asked Jane in a low voice as Cecily was being ushered with her baby upstairs.

Jane shook her head. Her small, pinched face was tight with worry. 'No,' she whispered. 'The curfew bell has gone early. I pray that he won't be trapped in his chambers.'

Quite likely, thought Mara. The mayor had taken the city unawares; the curfew bell had been expected at the normal hour of sunset and now it had rung a good half-hour earlier. Still, as long as he stayed indoors he would be safe. Leaving Jane to hasten upstairs after her new guests, she opened the heavy front door herself and stepped outside.

A hush had fallen over the city. The only noise to be heard was the heavily-shod, marching feet of the troops. They would be coming from the barracks beside the Great Gate and were by now making their way towards Gaol Street and the fish market.

Mara went down Quay Street without meeting a single person. At the crossroads, she turned towards the inlet of the sea. The air was fresh and a west wind was blowing. The troops were busy in the streets and the customary guard on these western city walls was missing.

The sun was now sinking down behind the swell of the ocean. The sky above it was still streaked with an angry red, throwing a purple path across the waves. There was cluster of ships out there. Mara narrowed her eyes; she knew these vessels. These were not the traditional fishing boats; these ships were much larger, each sixteen to eighteen feet long, coated in black pitch and they had a distinctive sail formation. It consisted of a single mast with a main sail and two foresails, all of them a dark red-brown.

O'Malley of the Ships, thought Mara. What was the O'Malley clan doing so near to the city of Galway on this night out of all other nights? What was going to happen?

Immediately, she thought of the two people from the Burren. Setanta and Ardal O'Lochlainn. Traditionally there was great enmity between the merchant families of Galway and the Gaelic clansmen. Her mind went back to Setanta. That may have been the news that he had whispered to the boys, had told them to keep secret, perhaps. Setanta, as a fisherman, would have often encountered the O'Malleys.

Nothing to do with me, she told herself firmly and yet she found it very hard not to worry about the situation. There was little doubt in her mind that Valentine Blake had organized the night's events. He was determined to put the utmost pressure on his brother-in-law to free Walter.

And if he did not succeed? What then?

It was easier to unleash war dogs, like O'Malley of the Ships, than it was to rein them back in again.

The clouds had gathered, blotting out the last vestiges of the sunset. The sky was inky black. Nightfall was coming early. There would be no frost tonight and the stars were quenched. Only the pitch torches stuck into iron holders at every corner of this well-run city gave light to the streets.

There were no lights from Blake's Castle, though, and this struck her as ominous. Where was everybody? And, in particular, where was Margaret? Cecily had spoken of all those men, but had not mentioned her sister-in-law.

And then she heard something. It was the turning of a large key in a lock. She distinctly heard the click and saw the gatekeeper at the western entrance to the city, The Bridge Gate, as it was known. He locked it and then he walked briskly away towards the city centre. The mayor had organized this day like a battle. The bell was to be rung early; the gates were to be locked early. This martial rule of the city would probably go on until the unfortunate boy, Walter, was hanged.

But not all observed the curfew. From out of the shadows stepped some men. Mara turned her face towards the sea, thankful that her cloak was dark. The silence now was complete; only the stirring of the waters of the incoming tide broke it, but somehow Mara felt that there were people all around her. She could not analyse why – it was just a series of tiny noises, nothing in themselves, but together they seemed to add up to a presence.

And then there was a sneeze and a sudden chuckle. It was

hushed immediately but she had an impression of movement, of whispers and then nothing. The torch on the top of Bridge Street Gate was suddenly quenched. A stone fell with a dull sound and rolled on the hard ground. A suppressed whisper sounded from the other side of the street and abruptly a large, waterside rat ran across from there, just missing her feet by an inch, and from the metal gate that led to the bridge crossing over the Corrib River there came the sound of a sudden, hard blow and then a creaking of hinges. The gate to the west had been thrown open.

It was beginning to get pitch dark now and she was conscious that she was alone in an alien city. She began to walk briskly back towards Lombard Street. Mara had often walked by night on the Burren. She had found that she slept well after taking a walk before going to bed, but the Burren was different. It was her own kingdom, and none, she thought, would harm her there. Here was different. If only she had her wolfhound Bran with her, she would have been more confident. But she didn't and the sensible thing now was to get indoors before any harm befell her. In a few moments she had reached the top of Bridge Street, passing the dark, shuttered premises of Blake's pie shop, and looked thankfully at the pitch torch flaring on the corner of Lombard Street. The Bodkin tower house was well lit and inviting, with candlelight shining from every window. Mara wondered whether Henry had managed to return in her absence. The scholars, she thought, were on the roof looking down; at least she could see four heads appearing between the merlons of the battlements.

The bell from St Nicholas's Church chimed the hour of four o'clock, but the church itself was only dimly lit with the light of one candle coming from a single window. No evening service was planned. A sound came from behind her – not a rat, but perhaps more dangerous: it was the sound of a footstep and of another quickly suppressed whisper. She glanced over her shoulder up towards the junction to Gaol Street and saw a detachment of soldiers, with torchlight glinting on drawn swords, standing guard.

And yet that was not what she had heard. The soldiers had no reason to be quiet, no need to suppress a whisper. They were making as much noise as possible, shouting orders, drilling with their swords; the clash of iron against shield would frighten the townspeople to obedience was the reasoning behind all of the noise, she supposed. No, that had not been the soldiers that she had heard. In fact, there had been something familiar about the whisper and then she realized that the half-heard words were in Gaelic.

Mara took a few decided steps towards the Bodkin tower house and then whirled around. She was right! Two small, slender figures darted out from a doorway and began to run down towards Gaol Street. They were careful, keeping well into the shadows of the houses and shops, but one shopkeeper had a flaming pitch torch stuck into the bracket outside his door and the light showed two heads, one was jet black but the other had curls of red-gold.

Hugh and Shane were out in the Galway streets and they were running straight towards where the soldiers had lined up ready for battle.

Mara gasped and immediately began to run after them. Her shoes were of soft leather so made little sound and neither boy looked behind. When they approached Cross Street, they did not continue, but swerved into one of the small alleyways that led off to the left. Unhesitatingly, Mara followed, furious with herself that she had not picked up on the reason for their conversation with Valentine Blake this morning. How smoothly young Shane had turned the conversation back to Carlos Gomez and the Spanish captain, she thought, feeling exasperated that she had not pursued the matter.

Of course, she thought, Valentine Blake needed someone who spoke both English and Gaelic so that communications could be passed between the Blakes and the O'Malleys. Shane and Hugh, adventurous young boys, were ideal for his purpose.

The alleyway, with its tall houses on either side, was very dark. She could no longer see either boy, but from time to time heard a mutter or a stone kicked by a boot. Now they would be going parallel to the gaol. The buildings opposite all housed shops, Mara remembered, and they were empty and dark. She had to feel her way, now, keeping one hand on a side wall. She dare not call the boys. None of them had the right to be abroad after the curfew bell had sounded. The penalty for all three would be prison, or worse.

And then her groping hand found only space in front of it. She took a few more steps and stopped abruptly. There were lights ahead of her and she realized that she had reached another of those small narrow alleyways that formed a network of passages between the main streets of the town. She waited for a moment, hesitating and listening intently, but there were no sounds from further up so her instinct led her towards the light. If Shane and Hugh, normally very well-behaved boys, had stolen out at night, it would have been something to do with Walter, she thought. Slowly and carefully she turned up the alleyway and crept onwards until she stood in a dark doorway, just opposite the entrance to the gaol.

The door to the prison was shut firmly and in front of its blackened, studded surface stood the figure of James Lynch, flanked by a soldier on either side. The torches flaring from iron holders on both sides of the door illuminated his face. Mara studied him carefully. His expression was stern, remote and determined; the mouth set firmly. His eyes, though, were disconcerting. From where she stood, she could see that, unlike the soldiers whose eyes darted here and there, his eyes were staring fixedly at the sky, just as though he were communicating with his God – the God of anger – above.

And then suddenly there was a shrill whistle from her left – coming from the fish market – a seaman's whistle, thought Mara with a slight thrill of excitement. The boats that fished and plied their trade between Doolin and the Aran Islands all used whistles like that in order to summon aid. She had heard it said that the sound from one of these could travel five miles across seawater and here, in the small, enclosed streets of the city, it rose up loud and shrill with an almost frightening intensity.

And then it was answered by another that came from the area around Bridge Street Gate, with its warning notice about the ferocious O'Flahertys, and yet another from the eastern side towards The Green. It seemed as if the city was surrounded by a wall of sound from the west and the north. O'Malley of the Ships and his men had encircled the town. How her kingly husband, Turlough, would have liked to be here with his old comrade-in-arms, O'Malley from Sligo, he of the ships, who patrolled the Atlantic coast and cared nothing for the English and their pretensions towards the civilized rule of law.

And now she began to understand. O'Malley and his clansmen probably spoke only Gaelic, with perhaps enough seaman's Latin to make their way in the Mediterranean countries, but were unlikely to speak English. Hugh and Shane were there to let them in through the gate and to direct them towards the gaol and, then, boy-like, had crept along to see the attack.

And the battle had started. From both sides of Gaol Street came the clash of swords, and this was no drill. The soldiers shouted and warlike howls responded. Mara edged a little further out.

'The Cat! The Cat! The Cat!' chanted the attackers and she recognized the war cry of the Blakes. She thought she glimpsed the tall figure of Valentine Blake using his sword to beat his way through the massed ranks of the soldiers, rather like her house-keeper, Brigid, used a broom to go through a flock of cackling geese. Valentine would not want to be responsible for any deaths; he was, after all, bailiff in this city, and the protection of the troops would be important for the citizens.

Now another attack began at the other end of Gaol Street, just where it abutted on to Cross Street. Mara could hear the shouts and the clash of steel. And from there, too, rose up the war cry of 'The Cat! The Cat! The Cat!' The Blakes had divided their forces and were progressing towards the prison in a pincer movement, one approaching from the north side of the town, from where Gaol Street joined to the corn market, and the second from the southerly junction with Cross Street. Mara held her breath. Could they possibly rescue Walter from his cell? And if they did, she determined, she would make sure that poor old Sheedy was rescued, also. Despite the danger, she would stay here until all was over.

The Blakes were large in numbers; by the light of the torches, Mara could see how they thronged together and faced into a smaller amount of soldiers. But piemen, bankers, innkeepers and merchants were no match for a detachment of trained and well-armed soldiers and gradually they were being driven back into the corn market. For the moment the battle on the southerly side, on the Cross Street side, was still going on – she thought she saw the huge form of the blacksmith leading this detachment – but the soldiers had certainly begun to prevail at the northerly end, at the crossroads where Valentine Blake commanded. The troops made a forward rush; the Blakes retreated out of sight. A man screamed and a volley of curses broke out.

But the only words she heard from both sides of the battles were English words. So where were the O'Malleys? Perhaps she had been wrong. She heard Valentine Blake's voice roaring orders and his men rallied and made another surge. There was a brief clash; for a moment the white uniforms of the soldiers were mingled with the colourful doublets of the Blakes. But it was all over soon. With dismay she saw that Valentine Blake's cohort was once more being driven back. They had retreated back into the corn market and the soldiers were lining up, with drawn swords, forming a wall of steel to keep them from coming back into Gaol Street.

And then, from just opposite to where she stood, a stone slate came crashing down and landed almost at the foot of where the mayor stood, surrounded by his bodyguard of soldiers. One of the bodyguards ran forward, torch in hand, and looked upwards towards the sky. For a second his light illuminated the scene, before he was cut down by a well-aimed throwing knife.

On top of the roof of the gaol were the figures of men, men to whom climbing ships' masts on violently turbulent seas was an everyday affair. Even as Mara looked up, a hail of stone slates came raining down on to the street. O'Malley and his men had made their way by the rooftops and had reached the gaol without anyone being aware of their presence.

'They've stripped the roof,' shouted some soldiers, running down Gaol Street from its junction with Cross Street.

'The Cat! The Cat! The Cat!' came the cry from the Blakes and from above their heads it was answered by roars of 'O'Malley *Abú*'. Everything seemed to be happening at once. At roof level the slates were being torn and cast down as missiles; at this rate it would not be long before the O'Malley and his sailors would be into the top storey of the gaol.

From Cross Street the southerly detachment of Blakes, under the leadership of the blacksmith, had begun to force the soldiers to retreat down Gaol Street. Step by step, with swords, crowbars, cudgels, hammers, daggers and kitchen knives held in front of them, they were making progress towards the gaol, driving the soldiers in front of them.

When it was that James Lynch had disappeared, Mara could not tell. The Cross Street detachment of soldiers had been steadily driven back by the blacksmith and his men and was now between her and the door to the gaol. The chant of 'The Cat! The Cat! The Cat!' had doubled; Valentine Blake's men must have gone back down Corn Market Street to the Cross Street junction and joined their kinsmen from the back. The roars of 'O'Malley *Abú*' were muffled, but the Sligo clansmen were now within the building.

And it was at that moment that James Lynch must have reappeared. His voice rose up, high and fanatical, 'Make way! Make way! Make way to Gallows' Green!' The solid block of soldiers moved slightly, those at the back presenting a line of drawn swords to the Blakes coming up from the south side of the town, those at the front forming a guard for the mayor who was going north.

'He's got Walter!' The shrill scream of Hugh's voice came from the top of the roof, and by the light of the torch Mara could see the head of copper curls, so admired by Jane Bodkin, leaning over the drip ledge of the parapet on top of the gaol. Beside him was Shane's dark head. Mara's heart stopped at the peril that her boys were in. She came forward from her place of concealment and stepped out into the street, only to shrink back as the soldiers, fighting hand-to-hand with the Blakes, passed her so closely that she could only save herself by returning quickly into the alleyway.

And then Mara saw what they had seen.

James Lynch was dragging his son up Gaol Street, up towards Middle Street and from there through the Great Gate and out on to Gallows' Green.

And Walter Lynch, manacled and shackled with heavy iron chains, had a noose around his neck and was been led by his own father like a beast to the slaughterhouse.

Mara acted quickly. There was, she reasoned, nothing that she could do for Hugh and Shane just now. They were with the O'Malley in the gaol and the gaol was now no longer the focus of the battle. Somehow, she felt confident that the clansmen would look after her two boys.

But Walter Lynch, no more than a boy himself, would be hanged by the neck, hanged until he was dead, within the hour unless someone rescued him.

Was it possible that, even now, she could make James Lynch hesitate? That what she had to tell him would ring true and that he would spare his son until a just trial could be held?

Gallows' Green, she thought. The fanatical father was going to drag his son there. How could she get there before them?

Mara knew Galway quite well by now and quickly she pictured

her route. A moment later she had gone back down the alleyway, had crossed Market Street, gone through the gate into the grave-yard of St Nicholas's Church and out of the back gate and into Lombard Street.

Lombard Street was no longer empty. Lights were on in all the shops, tower houses and dwellings. People were coming out through opened doors, or thronging up from Quay Street. She saw David Browne, with his sister Catarina, hurrying forward, but she did not wait to greet them. There was a murmur of conversation and then a swell of voices. The words 'Gallows' Green' were on all lips. Mara pushed her way through them and went rapidly up North Street, noticing Richard Athy, standing with a perturbed face, at the gate of his splendid mansion.

And then she became aware that she had a companion. By her side was Anthony Skerrett with a drawn sword in his hand. He saw her look at it and smiled.

'Got used to carrying this around the streets of London at night,' he said casually, and kept his place at her elbow as she turned down Little Gate Street, praying that she would get to its junction with Middle Street before James Lynch. She went faster now – Anthony and his sword ensured that a path opened out in front of her.

And she was just in time. The soldiers had to fight every inch of the way with their pursuers, and the boy Walter, dragged by the noose, was in chains and could not make good progress. Despite her circuitous route she had arrived at the junction before the father and son and was ready to say what had to be said. This life had to be saved. That other life would have to take a chance. At least the warning would be public and would give a chance of escape. But she had no choice. She would have to tell this madman, James Lynch, what she believed had happened on that fatal Shrove and she would have to tell him before he reached Gallows' Green.

Seventeen

Crích Gablach
(Ranks in Society)

A king or his representative, a Brehon, can issue an ordinance in times when law and order begins to break down and where the orders are necessary for the preservation of life. It follows then that a Brehon must be skilled in talking to incensed multitudes and negotiating their consent to a new order or law.

Triad 49
There are three things that are the sign of a well-run kingdom:
1. *Suppressing robbers.*
2. *Crushing criminals.*
3. *Preventing lawlessness.*

Just as Mara and Anthony Skerrett emerged into the crossroads, she realized that James Lynch could go no further. The street between him and the way to Gallows' Green was completely blocked with people. Men came running down towards him from the Great Gate, but these men were not sailors; these were men with bare legs and huge moustaches, wearing woollen cloaks or short jackets over their Gaelic *léinte*. They were armed with short swords and small, light, slender throwing knives, and they yelled their battle cry of 'O'Flaherty *Abú*' as they came.

The ferocious O'Flahertys, hated and feared by the people of Galway, had arrived.

Mara could picture how they had arrived at this spot and admired the quick wits of whosoever had directed them. The message would have been passed to them, probably by Hugh and Shane as soon as they had come in by the open gate to the west. They would have circled the town on the side of the sea and then cut across its eastern side, keeping always inside the walls of the city and finding nothing but empty streets and scared citizens hiding within their houses.

But were they in time?

James Lynch, dragging his son by the noose, and accompanied by the ranks of soldiers, had reached the junction of the four crossroads where Little Gate Street and Great Gate Street joined on to Skinner's Street and High Middle Street – by coincidence just beside his own house. Ahead of them was the short length of Great Gate Street and then, on the other side of the gate, was Gallows' Green. The entire regiment of soldiers was with him, forming a human shield to his back, and on both sides.

But the O'Flahertys had been too quick for them. They had wedged themselves into a solid fighting mass, blocking the way forward. The soldiers hesitated and then stopped, their swords in their hands and their eyes on the ferocious clansmen ahead of them. And behind the soldiers came the cohorts of the Blake family reinforced with the clansmen of O'Malley of the Ships.

'Walter, Walter,' screamed Margaret, and she burst through the crowd of soldiers, desperately clawing her way towards her son. Her hair streamed down her back and her face was blotched with tears. At the last moment a soldier seized her by an arm and she clawed at him as if she had been the cat depicted on the Burke shield over her brother's castle.

'Let me go, let me have my son,' she wept, and her nails raked the man's face until he managed to seize both of her hands. Another soldier put a hand over her mouth and she was dragged back.

The boy was almost unconscious, Mara could see. The noose was pulled so tightly that his face was purple and his eyes were staring. His head slumped down over his chest and when a sudden silence fell after Margaret's shrieks were suppressed, Mara could hear him retching desperately, his chained hands trying to rise high enough to be able to grab the rope from his neck.

A second later, James acted. The noose, shortened to a dangerous extent, was in one of his hands, but with the other he seized the boy by a fistful of curls and hauled him over towards the studded oak front door of his own tower house. Somehow he must have got the key into his hand, because a few seconds later he had jerked his son over the threshold and had slammed the heavy door behind them.

'My son, my son,' screamed Margaret again as her captors released her.

And then a great roar broke out — a roar of anger, but of triumph, too. No door in the world was strong enough to stand against the combined might of the Blakes, the O'Malleys and the O'Flahertys!

'Let go my arm,' said Mara irritably to Anthony Skerrett. 'Let me go. I must talk to him. He might listen to me. He is making a terrible mistake. I must get in there. I must get into his house and go after him.'

'Let her go,' said Henry Bodkin, who had fought his way to her other side.

But it seemed as though it was too late. No one took any notice of her. The stone buildings of the city resonated to the cry of 'Kill, kill, kill', and the timbers of the door began to splinter. The well-trained soldiers' iron discipline had collapsed in the face of the mob's fury and now they fought for their own lives, desperately trying to escape the trap in which they were placed with enemies on both sides of them. There was nothing Mara could do. The noise was too great. Even Margaret's shrieks could no longer be heard as she stood with her hair streaming loosely down her back and her mouth widely opened in anguish.

Blake, the blacksmith, was to the fore now and he had an enormous hammer in his hands. He shed his tunic and swung the hammer a few times, as if testing his muscles as well as its weight. The O'Malley called to his men and they began to scale the wall of the tower house, using slightly protruding stones as if they were steps on a staircase and swinging themselves upwards by the protruding drip ledges above the windows.

Then the blacksmith hit the door. The hammer bounced off the iron studs and he frowned calling for another. A smaller hammer was put into his hand and with that he split a board. A gaping hole, the size of a man's head, appeared in the door. Other men with hammers and cudgels fell upon door, blows rained on it and it began to crumble. A cheer went up, but then it was followed by a sudden silence and a terrible scream, a scream like that from a banshee, and it came from Margaret.

'Oh, my God, look! He's going to hang my son himself.'

There was a dead silence. The noise of blows ceased; no one spoke; every eye went upwards. A gasp ran through the immense throng and then silence again.

A candle had been lit in a window at the top of the tower

house. One of the two casements had been pushed open and the rope knotted to the stone mullion between the windows. With almost supernatural strength James Lynch lifted the body of his son on to the windowsill.

'You're wrong, Mayor Lynch,' called Mara into the silence. Her voice had been trained by her father from a very early age, trained to be heard in an outdoor court where hundreds of people stood in a five-acre field. Project your voice towards the stone cliff at the back, he used to advise. She spoke now without strain and without emotion, and the cool, calm tone took the man's attention. He stopped and leaned out of the window. Walter's legs were still inside the room. It was impossible to know whether he was dead or just unconscious, but the body slumped helpless on the stone sill of the mullioned window.

Mara continued. A life hung by a hair; she knew that.

'The murder of Carlos Gomez of Spain was not committed by your son, Walter Lynch,' she went on. Her voice was pitched at the roof of the tower house and she knew by long experience that the stone there would act as a sounding board and would bounce the sound back to the crowds that thronged the crossroads. Let the guilty take warning; the innocent had to be saved.

'On that night, the night of Shrove Tuesday,' she continued, just as if she were giving judgement at Poulnabrone in the Burren, 'many young men went outside the city gates. The mayor kept strict order within the town and no drunkenness or fighting was tolerated there. Outside the city gates was a different matter,' said Mara, her tone crisp and assured, her eyes on the roof of the tower house.

'Carlos Gomez,' she went on, 'was one of those who went outside the gates.'

'Enough of this,' screamed James Lynch. 'You've claimed to know the truth in this matter. Give me the name of the murderer, or hold your peace while I make sure that justice is carried out.'

There was a faint sound of splintering wood and Mara made a slight gesture of her hand to silence it and spoke quickly and firmly.

'Carlos Gomez,' she said, 'was murdered, but not murdered in the place where the body was found, on the hill overlooking Lough Atalia, on the grass beside the windmill. He was murdered just beside The Green, not far from the Great Gate itself.'

There was a slight stir, a murmur from the crowd and she waited courteously until it had subsided. James Lynch had turned away and she had to get his attention back on to her. When she spoke again, her slightly raised voice was severe.

'James Lynch, you are a judge without judgement. You claim to represent the law, to act as a lawyer, but you have not studied the law. You carried out a trial without ascertaining the merest facts. If you had examined the body of Carlos Gomez you would have found abrasions on the back of the head, a quantity of fine limestone gravel in the hair around the abrasions and a bruise under the chin. Carlos Gomez was probably knocked to the ground by a blow to the chin, knifed as he lay there and then either dragged or carried to the windmill and his body deposited in that place just beside the windmill where an innocent boy slept.'

She had got his attention now, Mara noticed, feeling a slight thrill. Mad as the man was – and by now she had little doubt that he was insane – he was as he was said to be; a man of integrity, a man who upheld the law as he understood it. That image was central to his belief in himself and perhaps she had momentarily shaken it. She pursued her advantage.

'And when Carlos Gomez was killed, Walter Lynch was already insensible from the effects of the strong drink that he had consumed.'

Mara held her breath, her eyes raised. Was it going to work? Could anyone accomplish this impossible deed?

James Lynch gave a groan that echoed around the street.

'Mad woman; you are mad and bad!' he exclaimed. 'It was Walter Lynch's dagger that killed the Spaniard. A life for a life! Never let it be said that a murderer's unhappy father allowed him to escape from the gallows.'

Reaching down he hoisted his son into an upright position. Now everyone could see from the violent trembling of the boy's limbs that he was still alive. He stood there for a second looking downwards, the noose around his neck, and it seemed to Mara that his eyes found the face of his mother.

'Now may the Lord have mercy on your soul,' called James Lynch, and looked up towards the heavens above as he pushed the boy over.

But he was too late. If he had looked a minute earlier, he

might have still carried out the execution, but now he did not have time.

O'Malley's son, Donal of the Pipes, his ankles held securely by two men on the roof, had leaned over between the parapets and had grabbed Walter by the cluster of curls on top of his head and dragged him up. With one quick movement another of the O'Malleys sliced through the rope of the noose with a sharp dagger.

And at that moment a throwing spear, aimed with deadly accuracy from the crowd, found its mark in James Lynch's breast. He toppled over and fell dead on to the street below.

Eighteen

Bretha Crólige
(Judgements of Bloodletting)

A killing is described as dúinetháide if the body is left in a remote place and the killer does not acknowledge the crime. The penalty for this is double the penalty for an acknowledged murder. The murderer, or his clan, must pay to the family of the dead person the following recompense:

1. *The honour price of the victim – ranging from one sét for a servant to forty-two séts for a king of three kingdoms.*
2. *Double the fixed penalty for murder – forty-two séts or twenty-one ounces of silver or twenty-one cows.*

'I called to say goodbye.' Mara looked at the figure in front of her wearing his striped robe, coif and cap of office. She had deliberately not gone to his home, but to the guildhall; this was a business matter.

He gave her his good wishes for her return journey, for her continuing health and happiness, issued an invitation for whenever she was next in Galway, but there was a slight air of uneasiness about him. After a few minutes, she decided to come to the point.

'I wanted to tie up all loose ends,' she said, accepting with a smile his offer of some wine.

'Loose ends,' he echoed, glancing at her rather nervously.

'Loose ends,' she repeated. 'As you might guess, this case of the murder of Carlos Gomez presented me with a dilemma,' she said, sipping the choice wine that he had provided.

He looked at her and said nothing.

'I would have spoken out to save the boy's life,' she said, 'but even so, I would not have wanted it to be at the expense of your life. The laws of England make the investigation of crime to be a very difficult one. Only God himself knows all the truth. Man can always be mistaken.'

He smiled a little at that. 'But not woman,' he said with a vestige of his old teasing manner.

Mara did not smile back. The matter was too serious. A young man had lost his life.

His face changed. He was good at reading feelings, interpreting emotions. He looked an appeal at her.

'This crime is different to any other crime that I have ever uncovered, and it is different because of the savagery of those laws,' she said soberly. 'I am as sure of the facts as I can be, but I cannot find it within myself to condemn you to death by hanging. It has never been part of my brief to take lives; rather it has been my aim to mend them.'

He looked more cheerful at that, his expressive face lighting up and a slight flush darkening the colour in his cheeks.

'Nevertheless,' she said emphatically, 'I don't want to slide over this deed as if it were a matter of no account.' And when he did not reply, she continued, 'I want to handle this as if it were a crime committed in my own jurisdiction. I want you to make full confession and I want to impose a penalty. And I swear to you that if you agree, no word of this will ever be spoken by me after I leave this place.'

He nodded reluctantly, listening to her opening preamble.

'How did you guess?' he asked eventually.

'I reasoned,' she contradicted him.

'I don't see how,' he said reflectively. 'What on earth connects me to the murder of Carlos? I was not jealous of him; he had not robbed me of a girl. His plans to import horses did not trouble me; I was in a different way of business, entirely. I had committed no fault that would allow him to blackmail me or to put me in jeopardy. I was no relation to the Gomez family; I could gain no Spanish gold by his death. There was nothing whatsoever to connect me to this killing and yet you say that you deduced my name by reasoning.'

'Ah, but you see the killing of Carlos Gomez was not the real object of this murder,' said Mara quickly. 'The real object was to destroy James Lynch.'

That alarmed him. He stared at her with an amazed expression.

'You wonder how I deduced that,' said Mara. 'Well, I suppose that the answer is partly that the corpse told me. I was, of course, only able to make a very covert and cursory examination of the body, but it was enough to see the gravel and blood at the back of the head as well as on the breast, and also the thick mud on the back of the clothing. Why should it have been moved from the place where the murder occurred?'

'Nobody but James would have laid out the corpse for all to see without even washing it,' he muttered between his teeth.

'It was a help,' said Mara evenly. 'When I saw that gravel, then I guessed that the man was knocked to the ground, on to that limestone gravel path, not far from the gate and then stabbed. The only puzzle was how Walter's dagger came to be in the wound, because Walter, I reckoned, was nowhere near that spot, but had probably – and this is guesswork – passed out in the room on the ground floor of the windmill sometime earlier.'

'So how did his dagger end up in the dead man's chest?'

'We'll come back to that later,' said Mara. 'You asked me why you should kill Carlos Gomez, and I suppose you are surprised at my knowing the reason for the murder. But, you see, you and your sister told me the answers to that question. You told me when you displayed your son and showed your huge love for him – you would want the best for this late-born son of yours – but could you even afford to keep that magnificent castle that you had built? Your sister had told me that your fortune was founded in salt. But the Barbary pirates from the Ottoman Empire had stopped your trade of salt importation, and your future now looked bleak. I guessed that unless something was changed that your son might not have a prosperous future. But there was some hope. You were a bailiff and the other bailiff was an old man, unlikely to be elected to the office of lord mayor, so when James Lynch finished his term, then it was almost certain that you would be the new sovereign if he were not re-elected once again. The example of other mayors had shown that vast sums of money could be quickly accumulated for the post holder. But James Lynch was popular with the townspeople, who recognized his integrity and trusted him to do his best for the city. But if only James Lynch could be voted out of office, if only he committed a deed that would make the people of Galway think that he was as corrupt as other mayors whom they had rejected, if only these things could be brought about, then your future could be bright.'

Valentine Blake was watching her now with narrowed eyes,

but she did not allow herself to fear. Terror, she knew, weakens those who experience it. She had to remain strong, remain in the dominant position.

'You are a man of strong affections, all of the Blake family are, I think,' she said. 'Family feeling is very strong in the Blakes. I have heard it said that even the women who marry into other families still consider themselves to be Blakes. Once a Blake, always a Blake! And you Blakes find it hard to understand those whose head rules, not their heart. I do believe that you had not the slightest notion that James Lynch would condemn his own son to death. You judged him by what you would do in similar circumstances. You probably imagined that the trial would be postponed for a month or so, long enough for feelings to die down and for a few pieces of evidence to accumulate that would give an excuse for an open verdict to be given. The most the young man would suffer would be a few weeks' stay in the gaol before his father found that there was not enough evidence to hang him. The abrupt notice of the trial took you aback and you did your best to stop that.'

'And then he found him guilty – guilty with hardly enough evidence to hang a dog!' said Valentine bitterly.

'You forget the dagger owned by Walter was found in the dead man's chest,' reminded Mara. 'And now we come back to the dagger. I had a number of possible suspects in my mind, people who would have benefited from the death of Carlos Gomez, but the dagger puzzled me. You see, every man, and possibly many women, who were present at the Shrove Tuesday festivities, would have had their own dagger in their belt. It would have been easy, on that night of chaos and drunkenness, for anyone who desired the death of Carlos Gomez to have stabbed the Spaniard some-where outside the city walls, to have cast his body into Lough Atalia, where the ebbing tide would have dragged it quickly out to sea. It may not have been ever found, but even if it turned up, then it would have been hard for any judge to say what had happened after the body had spent a few days being dragged by the tides and eaten by fishes.'

Valentine Blake groaned; his head in his hands. He seemed utterly defeated, but Mara kept alert and watched him carefully.

'You see,' she continued, 'once I had decided that Walter himself had nothing to do with the killing, I saw the use of Walter's dagger to be of huge importance. The only reason for the use of it that I could come up with was that someone wanted to injure Walter, wanted him to suffer. But who could that be? The boy was well liked, affable, a threat to no one; Catarina's attitude to him was of indifference – nobody but his adoring mother could have thought that she was in earnest about him. People like Carlos Gomez, or even Anthony Skerrett would have seen at a glance that he was not a serious rival.'

She stopped for a moment. The picture of that boy full of life and energy, polished like a new chestnut and gleaming like copper, came before her and she had to pause for a moment. However, it was now her duty to set the record straight as far as she was able and ensure that the crime was accounted for, so she turned a stony gaze on him and resumed.

'And then,' said Mara, 'I suddenly realized everything. I realized that it was not Carlos Gomez, not even Walter who was the intended victim. It was Mayor Lynch himself. This crime was intended to destroy him. If he pardoned or exonerated his son then he would have to resign. If he went ahead, then your popularity with the numerous members of the Blake family would have been enough to cause a riot in the streets and you would have rescued the boy, perhaps shipped him off to Spain for a few years, but probably his position would have been untenable and he would have resigned also. I think you salved your conscience with thoughts like that.'

'I would not have seen Walter suffer,' muttered Valentine.

'You almost did,' retorted Mara. 'Without the courage, agility and sheer nerve of the O'Malley's son, young Donal of the Pipes, then Walter would have been hanged by his father from the window of his own tower house.'

She gave him a moment to think of that and then resumed.

'So the dagger was a puzzle. If Gomez was killed by the gate, then why was Walter four or five hundred yards away from the place where his dagger was used? And then, I suddenly saw the solution. You were Walter's uncle. You were concerned about him. He was obviously very drunk. You didn't take him to his home because you were afraid that his father would find the boy there and would be angry. But you did what a concerned uncle or father would do. You followed him outside the gate, then you found that he gone into the mill to sleep off his drunkenness.

You probably thought that he was safe there, but you took his dagger from him so that he could do no harm . . .'

'To himself,' interrupted Valentine. 'Walter was a gentle lad, but he was sodden with despair over Catarina and had been talking wildly about cutting his throat. I was relieved to find him and reckoned that he would sleep the night through. The mill was warm – the miller had been grinding corn earlier in the evening – and Walter had enough sense left to have made himself a bed in the sacks. So I took the dagger from him and I let him sleep on.'

'And then decided to frame him for a murder,' said Mara harshly, and he groaned, dropping his head into his hands and then lifting it again. His eyes were moist and his colour high.

'It wasn't the way that you said, not quite, anyway.' He groaned loudly again. 'You've seen into my thoughts, gone to places in my mind where I am ashamed to go myself, but I'm not quite as bad, or as calculating, as you have made out.'

Mara nodded. 'You had Walter's dagger there in your belt and you stabbed young Gomez with it. And then you thought of how you could make this work to your advantage.'

'I stabbed him on an impulse,' he said hurriedly. 'I had no notion of it when I left Walter. I decided that it was the best plan to let him sleep the night out there and then to come home next morning when his father had already gone out. I swear to you, that's all that I had in my mind. And then, just near the gate, I met Gomez. He had been guilty of gross conduct towards Catarina, a girl I have known since she was a baby. I didn't want him to find Walter so I picked a fight, shouted at him – I suppose I was drunk, too, and I had a row with him. He was insolent, foul-mouthed . . .'

But the young man did not pull out his dagger, thought Mara, remembering the unblemished dagger in Carlos Gomez's belt.

'I lost my temper,' admitted Valentine. 'I had stabbed him before I realized what I was doing.'

The murder of Carlos Gomez was easier for him to talk about than his plan to transfer his guilt on to the shoulders of his innocent and immature nephew. He explained to her very carefully the insults that had been given to Catarina, the gross and crude attempts to bed with her, the fury of the girl, and described his own loss of control.

He has the soul of a criminal, thought Mara. He is just good at hiding that soul from himself. What will he turn out like? How will he use the power that has now been granted to him since the death of his brother-in-law? Am I doing the right thing?

'So you dragged the body – I saw the mud caked on the back – and you placed him beside the mill where Walter lay, knowing full well that the connection would be made between the two young men once morning came. Now tell me about the part that the cloak played?'

He was taken aback at that. 'How did you know?' he asked almost angrily.

She ignored that question. It was for her to question, for him to accept the punishment. That was the essence of Brehon law – the scales of retribution had to be balanced. She could see how it had happened. This man was needy – was greedy – and he had succumbed to temptation and involved his nephew and his sister in a terrible ordeal that almost ended in a terrible tragedy for both. Mara thought back to Hugh's innocent words about Lucius Junius Brutus, who agreed to the execution for conspiracy against the Republic of his own two sons, and hoped that had not been in Valentine Blake's mind on that night of Shrove Tuesday. She preferred to think that he had truly believed that James Lynch would pardon his son.

Mara was sensible enough to know that Margaret Lynch, born a Burke, would not mourn her strange, hard-hearted, upright, and honest husband too much, but at the same time she had been deprived of a husband, left without means to support her son and herself in the lifestyle that both had been accustomed to. I will clear up the last detail, impose the penalty and then be on my way, thought Mara. She was hungry for the sight of her little son, and for the clean, pure air of the Burren.

'The cloak,' she reminded him.

'I dragged the body for a while, but then I came across a cloak lying on the ground and recognized it as Walter's. I wrapped Carlos in it so that I wouldn't get his blood on my clothes. That was all that was in my mind at that time,' he said pleadingly. 'I was going to throw the body into Lough Atalia.'

And yet, thought Mara, Valentine had been dressed in black velvet that night. Any smears of blood would not have shown on his clothes. She suspected him of not telling the entire truth.

She suspected him of having drafted the whole plan in his mind, either just before he had used Walter's dagger to kill the man, or perhaps immediately afterwards.

'And when you reached the mill, you thought of Walter lying drunk inside it, you left the body near to the doorway, took the cloak, now soaked in blood, and arranged it on top of your nephew so that his white shirt should be stained, so that there should be no doubt as to his guilt. Then you went home and waited for the news to break.' Mara paused, then said solemnly, 'Valentine Blake, I find you guilty of the murder of Carlos Gomez, how say you, guilty or not guilty?'

'Guilty,' he mumbled with a look at her that said, '*Yes, but . . .*' She silenced him with an authoritative gesture.

Mara pondered for a moment. It was pointless taking money from this man who was in financial difficulties and sending it to the enormously rich Gomez family, who would not understand its significance and who would be content only with the life of the murderer. No, the money should be to compensate Walter and his mother for the loss of a father and of a husband. James Lynch, after all, had been the intended victim. There was another victim: poor Sheedy had died in his cell on the night of the riot – perhaps of terror – to the great distress of Hugh and Shane, who had looked forward to releasing him when their part in the night's drama had been played through. However, Sheedy had no near relations; and who knows, she thought, death may have come as a merciful release to his troubled soul.

'I sentence you to a fine of forty-two cows or forty-two ounces of silver for the secret and unlawful killing, and added to that is . . .' She stopped for a moment. What was Walter's honour price? A merchant had no status under Brehon law, so she decided to use the honour price of a craftsman, and continued rapidly, 'Added to that is fourteen cows or fourteen ounces of silver, making a total of fifty-six ounces of silver. This money is to be used for the benefit of Walter and Margaret, perhaps some of it could be initially used to apprentice the boy to some trade where he would be happy.'

'I shall apprentice him to a potter!' Suddenly Valentine was blazing with excitement. 'I've just thought of a wonderful idea. I shall import pottery from France. It is very elegant stuff. The merchants of Galway will buy it up and I may even find some salt mines in France to supply me. I'll take Walter with me. I swear to you that I will use him like a son and that he and Margaret will have a home with me for as long as they want it.'

'See that you do,' Mara said coldly. He was getting off too easily for her liking, but she could see no alternative. She did not wish to see his body swing on the gallows, to be mourned by the sister and the nephew who loved him, by the wife who would be left a widow and by the baby son when he grew up fatherless. She got to her feet. It was time for her to leave this city of alien laws and alien practices, but she had one more thing to say and she said it looking intently at him.

'Valentine Blake, you are now Mayor of Galway,' she said. 'See that you remember the mercy that was extended to you and when you judge other fellow men, judge them with mercy in accordance with the law that has spared you to your wife and to your son.'

Author's Note

In the fifteenth and early sixteenth century the medieval city of Galway, situated beside the Atlantic Ocean, was a tiny island of English law, English language and English dress within the Gaelic land to the north, east, and south of it. Galway, then, was a fine city of stone as can be seen from the three pictorial maps drawn about that time and from its description by a traveller who described it as '. . . fenced with such a huge strong wall that travellers affirm that they have not seen the like in Europe . . . built from one gate to the other in the one form, looking like the colleges of Oxford, so magnificent that at my first entrance it did amaze me'.

Nowadays it is fascinating to wander around the ancient part of the city and to see Lynch's Castle almost as it looked in the early sixteenth century, to see the remains of Blake's Castle and throughout the streets to be able to glimpse late medieval drip ledges, gothic windows, stone mullions, ancient doors here and there among the shop fronts and restaurants of the last few centuries. Many of the places mentioned in my story still exist: King's Head Inn is still there and its medieval past is shown in the magnificent fireplace.

The tale of early sixteenth century James Lynch and the murder trial is one that is embedded in the history of Galway. Since it seems to have been first told some considerable time after the events, and since there has been doubt thrown on the nineteenth century retelling by James Hardiman, first librarian of the university at Galway, I have felt at liberty to change some details and to incorporate it into one of my stories about Mara the Brehon, who was the notorious mayor's contemporary.